THE CHRONICLES OF STELLA RICE

Adrienne Kama

Erotic Romance

New Concepts   Georgia

Be sure to check out our website for the very best in fiction at fantastic prices!

When you visit our webpage, you can:
* Read excerpts of currently available books
* View cover art of upcoming books and current releases
* Find out more about the talented artists who capture the magic of the writer's imagination on the covers
* Order books from our backlist
* Find out the latest NCP and author news--including any upcoming book signings by your favorite NCP author
* Read author bios and reviews of our books
* Get NCP submission guidelines
* And so much more!

We offer a 20% discount on all new Trade Paperback releases ordered from our website!

Be sure to visit our webpage to find the best deals in e-books and paperbacks! To find out about our new releases as soon as they are available, please be sure to sign up for our newsletter (http://www.newconceptspublishing.com/newsletter.htm) or join our reader group (http://groups.yahoo.com/group/new_concepts_pub/join)!

The newsletter is available by double opt in only and our customer information is *never* shared!

Visit our webpage at:
www.newconceptspublishing.com

The Chronicles of Stella Rice is a publication of NCP. This work has never before appeared in book form. This work is a novel. Any similarity to actual persons or events is purely coincidental.

New Concepts Publishing, Inc.
5202 Humphreys Rd.
Lake Park, GA 31636

ISBN 1-58608-742-8
2006 © Adrienne Kama
Cover art (c) copyright 2006 Kat Richards

All rights reserved, which includes the right to reproduce this book or portions thereof in any form whatsoever except as provided by the U.S. Copyright Law.

If you purchased this book without a cover you should be aware this book is stolen property.

NCP books are available at special quantity discounts for bulk purchases for sales promotions, premiums, fund raising, or educational use. For details, write, email, or phone New Concepts Publishing, Inc., 5202 Humphreys Rd., Lake Park, GA 31636; Ph. 229-257-0367, Fax 229-219-1097; orders@newconceptspublishing.com.

First NCP Trade Paperback Printing: March 2006

For my friend, Marianne LaCroix, who believed my idea to write a book about an eccentric thirty-something's life was a good one. Thank you for being Stella's first fan.

CHAPTER ONE

Journal entry 1/10/05, 6:14 a.m.
Men suck!
It's 2005, I'm gonna be thirty-one in a few months, and my biological clock is bugging the hell out of me.

Where are all the good men? I don't believe for a minute that they're all either married or gay. I think that's an urban myth propagated by married men as a way of taunting unmarried women. It's the verbal equivalent of sticking their tongues out and wagging them at us. It's their way of saying, "Bet you wish you'd paid more attention to me in high school."

Well, I don't--wish I'd paid more attention to them in high school, that is. These men operate under the erroneous premise that as a single woman gets older and sees her chances at happily-ever-after fade, the qualities she looks for in a man dwindle in correlation with the passing years. That's not true. The sad truth is that with every passing year, my standards don't lessen, they get higher. I figure I've waited this long for a man so why the hell should I settle now? At the rate I'm going, by the time I'm forty, not even the President of the United States will be good enough for me.

When I was twenty-one I could have easily fallen in love with an *artist,* i.e., a man without a job. You know the types. Guys who are sexy as sin, wax poetic on subjects ranging from fashion to politics, yet they fritter away their days in some dingy one room apartment in the city struggling for their craft--usually music or art. I would never even contemplate dating a man like that these days.

Today, any man I would consider dating has to have a job, making at least the same amount of money as me or more, a nice car, a 401K plan, a few well-chosen stocks, health insurance, a nice home, and good teeth. Oh, and no children. Children are non-negotiable. Children mean there's an ex-spouse in his past. I for one have no desire to share my man with his ex.

This shouldn't be so hard! I'm not asking for too much, am I?

Case in point–Paul the Prick.

Paul the Prick, as he's come to be known in my circle of friends, is the latest addition to my ever-increasing list of ex-boyfriends. Paul the Prick is, quite simply, a prick!

We dated for approximately two months. Those were two of the longest months I've ever had the misfortune of wasting. You tell me who's wrong.

I met the Prick at the bank when I was making a deposit. At the time he was the new branch manager. Dressed in a well-fitting black suit and looking good enough to eat, I didn't bat a lash when he asked me for my number or when he showed up for our date wearing Versace and driving a white on white Beamer.

I enjoyed seeing *Phantom of the Opera* at the Hippodrome and our dinner in Little Italy.

What I didn't enjoy were those last moments of our date when he stretched over the passenger seat, mouth open, tongue extended, and proceeded to douse my face in saliva. I can only suppose what I was experiencing was a kiss. This was unlike anything I'd ever experienced in my life. It felt like someone rubbing a wet toad all over my face. A smelly, wet toad. Even the memory of it makes me cringe.

I probably should have ended things right there and then, but I didn't. I made the same mistake women throughout the centuries have been making. I gave him the benefit of the doubt. Maybe he was nervous, or maybe he needed someone to teach him how to kiss properly, I reasoned to myself.

All illusions were quickly dismissed, however, when he showed no interest in improving his methods. Quite the contrary, all I got from him was the question, "Stella, when are we gonna have sex? Stella, when are we gonna have sex?"

How's about the tenth of never!

Well, I finally had enough. I broke up with him last night.

No more tongue dousing for me. In fact, I decided no more men for me. They all seemed to have something wrong with them. Either they're too short, spineless, clueless when it comes to sex, or they don't have a job. I could go on. The list is endless.

So, it's January tenth and I'm determined to start this year right. Number one on my list of life changing decisions: *I'm on a vacation from men.*

I want a real man in my bed. What woman wants to sleep with a man who whines about how horny he is yet couldn't arouse a wanton desire in a hooker?

Not this woman. If you're horny, show me. Don't beg me for sex, persuade me.

* * * *

About me.

My name is Stella Rice. I'm a single, black, female living in Baltimore, Maryland. I own a condo in Mount Vernon, Baltimore's art district, and I own my own business. The latter affords me the convenience of working out of my home. My company's name is AIR, which stands for Accurate Individualized Resources. AIR provides business support services for corporations and small businesses, as well as offering resume services. AIR covers everything from typing up proposals to organizing multi-media presentations. AIR, *helping you with your business and career goals.*

Damn! There's the phone.

It can't be my mother calling this early ... but who else would call me at this hour? Maybe I shouldn't answer it. Maybe I should ignore it and pretend I'm still sleeping.

Argh! Stop being a wimp Stella. Grown women; sexy, professional women who attract sexy, professional men who know how to kiss don't cower away from their phone, even if it is their mother on the other end. They answer it.

Gotta go.

* * * *

6:37 a.m.

Argh! I don't know why I ever agreed to join a gym. I must have been experiencing a moment of masochism. I hate exercising. I hate the gym. And I hate Katarina for talking me into joining one.

Oh well. I'm off to be tortured.

Be back soon ... I hope.

* * * *

8:24 a.m.

I've come to the conclusion that I am not only a masochist, but so is Katarina. Apparently, Baltimore is full of masochists and every one of them was at the gym this morning. They stood in military formation, waiting their turn to have the crap beat out of them by Jake, kickboxing instructor extraordinaire and owner of Fit For Life gym. What on earth possesses normal, well-adjusted people to pay good money to be pummeled, assaulted, and verbally attacked? We all need our heads checked.

I met up with Katarina in the ladies locker room. By the time I got there, a little after seven, she'd already swept her blonde hair into a pony-tail, pulled on matching designer leggings and tank top, and was delicately applying a thin layer of lip-gloss. The trick was to get the lip-gloss on in a way that made your lips look moist and kissable, while not making them look like you had actually put lip-gloss on at all. It was an art, and Katarina was a master.

"You're late again," she said, glaring at me in the mirror as she blotted her lips with a tissue.

I shrugged. "I forgot." Really I'd been hoping she had forgotten.

"You forgot three times last week, too. This gym costs fifty bucks a month. How can you forget something you're spending fifty bucks a month for?"

I pulled off my jeans and T-shirt and shoved my legs into black, spandex shorts--another purchase I could blame on Katarina. I've no idea what I was thinking when I brought them. It was what every thirty-something woman wanted a room full of eligible men to see her in, skin-tight spandex.

"I'll remember tomorrow."

I know you will 'cause I'm picking you up tomorrow morning."

I pulled my matching spandex tank top over my head, wrestled with it until I'd managed to pull it over my breasts, then straightened it out. I let out a yelp of surprise when I felt my hair being lifted off my back and tugged into an elastic band.

"Jake isn't gonna be pleased," Katarina continued as she pulled my hair into a ponytail. "You heard what he said yesterday when we were late."

At the mention of Jake a shudder of fear swept through me. I suddenly felt like I was ten and being sent to the principal's office. I remembered well what Jake had said. 'You better be on time tomorrow ...' or what, I had wanted to ask, but before I could, Katarina gave me a jab to the ribs. "Maybe we should think about taking a different class this morning," I said, hopefully. "There's a step class down the hall, a cycling class that I hear is real popular, then there's--"

Katarina, who apparently had scared herself with the mention of Jake, hurried to the locker where I had stored my purse. She rummaged in it for a few seconds, then came up holding one of my bottles of lip-gloss in her hand. It was the brown shade I wore whenever I wanted to appear as if I wasn't wearing make-up.

She crouched in front of me, told me to pucker, and applied it to my lips.

"I don't want to take another class," she said as she worked. Her hand was moving so fast that I feared I'd come out looking more like Ronald McDonald than the sexy, kickboxing siren I hoped for. "We waited six months to get into this class," she went on, "Adam Green even did a story on Jake for the *Sun*. This is the hottest kickboxing class in town. You know how many single men go to this class. We've already discussed this, Stella. This is an investment for the future. Our future. We can't quit. We'll just have to start getting here on time."

The idea of meeting a husband at kickboxing class seemed like a good idea on paper. It was one of those, kill two birds with one stone kind of plans. Get in a good work out while meeting Mr. Right. When Katarina laid the scheme before me back in July--before I'd decided on my little vacation from men--I readily agreed.

Unfortunately, neither of us had factored in Jake, the kickboxing nazi, who took his work way too seriously. How on earth could we focus on meeting men when Jake was hogging up every spare second with exercise? After the first class I knew our strategy was doomed. Katarina, on the other hand, simply re-worked the plan and plowed on.

Knowing well when I'm beat, I sighed. "I'll be on time tomorrow, I promise."

She got to her feet. "Hurry up. Get your sneakers on."

Katarina led me out of the locker room after I was appropriately garbed. I don't mind admitting that I was hesitant about walking into Jake's class eleven minutes late. No doubt he'd take such an infraction as a direct insult and make us submit to a whole host of unpleasant, humiliating, and physically impossible exercises. Briefly I wondered what he'd do if I simply refused. I quickly discarded the idea though, since at heart I'm a wimp and would be too petrified to challenge him.

In the similar way that many short men suffer from the Napoleon Complex, Jake suffers from the Pretty Boy Complex. Our poor kickboxing nazi instructor had the misfortune of being born with a face Caravaggio would have longed to paint. He looked Native American, but he could have been Mediterranean, Portuguese, Hispanic, or even bi-racial, who knew. Nobody was brave enough to ask.

Jake had exotic good looks. His emerald eyes were so achingly beautiful as to be obscene. His hair was long, jet-black, and lush with thick waves. On one rare occasion he paused to smile at me and I saw the perfection even held true with his teeth. Jake was pretty. And all pretty boys find out early in life that, unlike normal people, they only have five paths open to them.

The Hollywood heartthrob path.

The gorgeous Rock Star path.

The sexy struggling artist path.

The path of least resistance, i.e., you accept the fact that no man or woman will ever take you seriously.

The Pretty Boy Complex path, i.e., over compensation, i.e., you learn various ways to maim, torture and physically dominate anyone stupid enough to question your manhood.

Jake was constantly berating the class, ordering us to work harder, standing over us with his hands on his hips and demanding we do 'one more' knowing good and well he planned to make us do at least another five or six more. What was worse, I was paying this sadistic Adonis my hard-earned money to do this to me.

We reached the end of the corridor and stood before Jake's classroom. Even though his door was shut I could hear him barking orders, sounding more like a general preparing his troops for battle instead of a kickboxing instructor.

Dread washed over me and I took a tentative step back.

"Come on," Katarina said, still holding tight to my hand. At the same time she clasped the doorknob with her free hand, twisted, and pushed the door open.

Cool air whooshed out of the open doorway and chilled my face. Goose flesh popped out along my arms and I bit my lip. The only thing that kept me from running headlong back the way I'd come was knowing that to do so would mean dragging Katarina along with me. It was bad enough that we were arriving late. We didn't need to compound our problems by engaging in a ridiculous tug of war at the door. Instead of retreating I stepped into the room and gently closed the door behind me.

To my surprise our arrival on the scene was barely noticed. It was a bit of a blow to my ego.

Katarina and I found a spot on the floor, settled down on mats, and began stretching.

"Stretch properly," Jake directed the room in general. "Stretching properly will lessen your chances of hurting yourself."

As newbies to the class, Katarina and I weren't as adept at stretching as were the veterans. Still, I spread my legs wide, took a deep breath, and attempted to touch my head to the floor.

I didn't make it very far.

Jake, who could do a perfect Jean-Claude-Van-Damme Chinese split, demonstrated the stretch I struggled to emulate. In the first row, directly in front of him, Julianne Saunders was the perfect mirror of him. Head placed delicately on the floor between her knees, hands clasping her ankles, and a body so tight you could bounce a quarter off her butt.

I let out a groan of disgust.

"She's such a show-off," Sadie, another regular, said from beside me.

I glanced at Sadie and saw her eyes were trained on Julianne. I nodded in agreement.

"Teacher's pet," Katarina added.

"Oh, I think she'd like to be more than that," Jim said from the row in front of us.

I had to bite my inner cheek to keep from laughing. I couldn't disagree. Julianne was always at class on time, always took up a position in front of Jake, and was always staring adoringly at him. It got annoying after a while.

"If I were you, Stella," a male voice barked, "I'd be

focusing more on stretching and less on telling jokes."

I froze, mid-stretch, and looked up.

Jake loomed in the front of the room. His emerald eyes glimmered with malevolence. Hands on hips and legs spread wide, he raised an eyebrow daring me to say something.

Though my face was burning with embarrassment, I gave him my most winning smile and squeaked, "Sorry."

When he returned to the mat and I knew his focus was elsewhere, I glared at Katarina.

She grinned.

"I didn't say a word," I mouthed, terrified I'd attract his attention if I did more than breathe and stretch.

She shrugged.

I spent the next few minutes trying to make my body to do things nature hadn't intended. Already my legs were beginning to ache and we were only warming up.

When Jake sprang to his feet, I knew my real pain was about to begin.

"On your feet," he ordered.

Rather than conducting the punishment himself, though, he nodded to one of his assistants who moved to the front of the room and took up Jake's position. Jake, it seemed, had more pressing matters to attend to.

Damn! Damn! Damn! I should have known our late arrival hadn't gone completely unnoticed.

I watched, horror, fear, and dread freezing me to the spot, as Jake walked toward me. Katarina took a step to her right, putting just enough distance between us to make it look like she didn't know me.

Jim glanced at me over his shoulder. "Looks like someone pissed off the teacher."

I glared at Jim, then figured if I looked like I was doing something maybe Jake would pass me by. I jabbed the air with my right fist, following quickly with my left and repeated.

Jake breezed by me, pausing long enough to say, "Come with me, Stella."

I looked at Katarina who was exercising with a fervor I've never seen, and doing her best to pretend I didn't exist. Jim and Sadie seemed suddenly occupied as well.

Well damn the lot of them. I'm a grown woman. I'm a

business owner and a professional. What do I have to be afraid of?

Making a point to hold my chin high, I turned and followed Jake to the back of the room.

He stood against the far wall, arms crossed imperiously over his chest, as he marked my progress. He'd plaited his hair today and a long, black braid hung over his chest looking disturbingly like a whip.

When I was a few feet from him he pushed away from the wall and walked to the antechamber off the back of the classroom where equipment was stored. I entered the room behind him and he motioned for me to continue in.

I did, and then turned to look at him. He leaned against the doorframe and stared at me.

"You were late," he said by way of opening the conversation.

I smiled. "I'm sorry. It won't happen again."

"You said that yesterday."

He had a point there.

Instead of arguing with him, which would have been an exercise in futility, I upped the wattage on my smile.

"There's a waiting list for this class, Stella. People who actually *want* to be here. If you're not going to take this seriously, tell me now and I'll replace you. Full refund of course, since you've only been here one week."

Was he offering me an out? A chance to erase this particularly unpleasant episode of my life? It was tempting, and I wanted to accept. However, I knew if I let myself get kicked out of class, Katarina would quit and blame me for ruining her chances at meeting Mr. Right. "No," I said quickly, staring at Katarina over his shoulder. "I promise, I'll be here tomorrow on time. No excuses."

He studied me for a moment, twisted around, glancing at Katarina, then returned his gaze to me. Then he did something that completely unnerved me. He shook his head and grinned.

Still grinning, he stepped further into the equipment room and closed the door behind him, effectively cutting us off from the rest of the class. "You can't leave the class can you?"

"I can do anything I want."

He nodded. "True. But you won't. Not as long as Katarina

wants to be here." He smiled then, and heat rose to my face. Slowly, his eyes scanned the length of my body.

Unbidden, my flesh began to tingle. I could feel my heart thrashing around in my chest as he eyed my breasts. My stomach clenched when his eyes dipped lower, and a tickle of awareness between my thighs grew as my neglected quim came alive.

"You and Katarina are very beautiful women," he said so softly I had to strain to hear him. "Your faces are always perfectly made up, never a hair out of place, and you seem to have bought your workout clothes from Bloomingdales. I hope you didn't take my class as a means to meet a man. It wouldn't be the first time a woman made that mistake."

Crap! We'd been busted.

"The only action you'll be getting here, Ms. Rice, will be of the kickboxing variety. Got me?"

Knew I should have worn the clear lip-gloss. "I'm not interested in men." *That's it Stella, make him think you're a lesbian.* "I mean to say that I am interested in men, but not here. And I'd never try to meet a man during one of your classes."

"So you didn't join my class hoping to meet Mr. Right. Good." He tilted his head to the side and arched a brow. "But understand one thing."

I stare dumbly at him while my insides turned to mush. Dear God, Jake was gorgeous. I'd never been this close to him before, and being so close was intoxicating, even if he was an exercise fanatic. "What's that?"

"I own you, Stella."

"Own?"

He pushed off of the door and closed the distance between us. He was careful not to actually touch me, but he didn't have to. I could feel the force of him envelope me. I was eye to chest with him. I couldn't move or utter a word.

"Own," he confirmed. "For the next forty-five minutes I own everyone in my class. That's one of the perks of being the instructor."

I stared at his chest and tried to think clearly. It was proving difficult with his enticing scent filling my nostrils. He was sticky with sweat and smelled of primal man. The musky aroma left me dazed.

"Understand?"

"I don't know about this whole *own* thing, but I suppose I can see the point you're making." I was prepared to elaborate on my understanding of his speech when the door to the equipment room opened and a man I'd never seen before sauntered inside, long black trench coat fluttering in his wake. He was tall and lithe, with a mane of shaggy shoulder length hair the color of honey. His pale skin was flawless under the fluorescent glow of the lights, and his brown eyes scanned the room then fixed, unwaveringly, on me.

I emitted a tiny mew of pure, unadulterated lust and stared shamelessly at his glossy leather pants, marveling at how well he filled them.

Looking mildly annoyed, Jake turned to face this very enticing stranger. "Oh, it's you. What are you doing here?"

The man shifted his focus from me to Jake and shrugged. "Need the keys."

Crap! Even his voice was sexy. It was husky and had a slight British lilt.

"What'd you do with yours?" Jake asked.

"They're at home."

"I should make you wait till I finish this class." He exhaled. "Mine are up in the office. Give me a minute, I'll run up and get them." Jake turned back to me. "Stella, this is Dev. Dev, Stella."

I was going to hyperventilate, or faint, or drop dead on the spot. Being in a tiny little room alone with Jake and maintaining a cool, detached façade was difficult enough without adding his gorgeous friend, Dev, to the mix. I didn't know where to put my hands, how to stand, or where to look. Having spent my last thirty years around decidedly average, ordinary looking men, I was completely out of my element.

"This couldn't possibly be the Stella you told me about, Jake?"

Jake glided past Dev, nodding in the affirmative as he went. "That's her." He paused at the door and turned briefly to face me. "I'll be right back, Stella. Will you wait for me before rejoining the class?"

Wait there, with Dev? "Sure."

Then, with a click of the door behind him, Jake was gone. And I was alone with Dev. And my throat was suddenly very dry. What had Dev meant by asking if I was the one Jake had told him about? What had Jake meant by saying yes? Jake talked about me to his friends? What did he say? Why did he say it? Was it good talk or bad talk? Should I ask Dev what Jake said or would that seem desperate? Better not to ask, better to feign indifference.

I jumped about a hundred feet into the air when Dev stepped forward. His leather coat whipped around his ankles. He was wearing black leather biker boots that ended just under his knees. Very, very nice.

"You don't seem the type to be in one of Jake's classes."

"Huh?"

"You don't seem the type to be in one of Jake's classes."

"I don't?"

He closed the distance between us, moving forward until I again found myself face to chest with a man. "No, you don't. You seem rather..." He frowned for a moment and stared at the back wall, "...innocent."

"Innocent?"

"You don't have that harsh look about you, that hard-eyed, determined look I see on the others. Most of the women who come to this class come for one reason."

"Yeah, yeah, I know. They come for Mr. Right."

Dev brushed an errant brown curl from his eyes and grinned. "Yeah, and for them Mr. Right's name is Jake Santos."

Was that what Jake had been getting at with his little speech? Did he think Katarina and I had joined this class in hopes that one of us could land him?

"But like I said, you don't seem the type. You're not the sort of woman who'd need to spend fifty dollars a month to meet a man."

Ha! If he only knew. "Thank you."

"You're very welcome."

"Are you British?" I blurted, surprising myself with my tactlessness. "It's just, I notice you have a slight accent."

"Irish, but I've lived in the states so long the Irish has been diluted out of me. I moved to Virginia with my family when I was twelve."

"Have you been back home...to Ireland I mean?"

He nodded, sending his lush waves bouncing around his head. "A few times. How about you? Where are you from?"

"I'm boring. I'm from Maryland."

"Never lived anyplace else?"

"Nope."

He shoved his hands in the pockets of his coat and smiled. "So tell me the truth. Do you enjoy Jake's class? I took it once a few years back and absolutely abhorred it."

I couldn't help but smile back at him. "It's all right. He's very thorough."

"Thorough isn't the word. Wanna see what I could do by the time I left his class?"

Eager to find out, I nodded.

"All right then, watch this." He slid out of his coat and handed it to me. "It's the most useless thing in the world, except, of course, when I'm trying to impress a beautiful woman."

I giggled, rather stupidly, and hugged his coat to my chest. The leather was supple under my hands and smelled of cologne and soap. I watched him grab a metal chair from a corner of the room and set it a few feet in front of me. When he got on all fours, facing away from the chair, I was tempted to ask what he was doing, but I figured it out when he propped the tips of his boots on the metal seat and set his weight on his arms.

"You watching?"

"I'm riveted."

Lifting one hand off the ground so all of his body weight was resting on his left arm, he proceeded to do twenty-one arm push-ups, ten on each arm. He did them quickly and without seeming to exert much effort. His movements were smooth and efficient, much as Jake's would have been if he'd been doing the push-ups.

"Liked that did you?" He rose to his full height and grinned. "I can tell you're impressed. I can see it in your eyes."

"In my wildest dreams I couldn't do that."

"I can do twenty-five on each arm ... of course Jake can do fifty. He's annoying that way."

But I could tell by the glint in Dev's eyes he wasn't annoyed by Jake. The way he spoke of my sadistic instructor made me think Dev was actually very fond of him. "I can do twenty push-ups, but only if I use my knees."

"Is that right?"
I nodded. "Yep."
"Can I see?"
"See what?"
"You do twenty push-ups."
I opened my mouth, then shut it with a snap. "Are you serious?"
"I showed you mine…you know what comes next."
How on earth could this sweet, down to earth guy be a friend of Jake's? "All right, I'll show you. But you have to promise not to laugh. I'm not very good."
He covered his heart with a palm and nodded. "You've got my word. I won't crack a smile."
Feeling idiotic, I handed his coat to him then lowered to my knees.
His thighs were splayed before me, and his booted stance was wide. As I knelt there, an unexpected surge of desire had me struggling to catch my breath. More embarrassing, when I chanced a look up at his face I saw the edge of his lip quirk up into a, half smile. "You sure you can do twenty, Stella?"
I sat back on my heels. "Did I say--?"
Dev nodded. "Twenty."
"All right. Here goes." I knelt forward and began.
Eight push-ups in, I knew I was in trouble. There was no way I could possibly do twelve more of those things, half my weight resting on my knees or not.
Dev seemed to be coming to the same conclusion.
He crouched, setting one knee on the floor in front of me and resting his elbow on his other knee. "Why don't you stop at ten?"
I grunted out two more push-ups, shaking my head in the negative. "I-can-do it."
"Rest for thirty seconds, then do the last ten."
I collapsed on the floor, gasping for air. It was pretty safe to assume I wasn't at my most alluring.
Unexpectedly, the equipment room door shut--I hadn't realized it was open--and I knew by the sound of the heavy footfalls coming toward us that Jake was back. "Your upper body strength is non-existent." Jake advanced, jangling a key chain from one hand and surveying me with obvious displeasure. "And your lower body strength isn't much

better."

He crouched beside Dev, then spent the next twenty seconds ticking off a list of my weaknesses, expressing his shock that a grown woman could take such poor care of herself, and making a whole host of suggestions on what I'd need to do to improve my body. They all sounded unpleasant and painful.

"You're weak Stella," he continued, bringing his lecture to a close. "You should consider acquiring a personal trainer. Only with extensive work on your part, and the personal attention a trainer can give you, do I see any real hope for you. I have five personal trainers here, and on occasion, depending on the client, I also give personal attention to my clients."

Dev elbowed Jake in the side, something I would have loved to do myself. "What a horrible thing to say to a woman."

Rubbing his side gingerly with two fingers, Jake faced Dev, wide-eyed and surprised. "I'm her instructor; it's my job."

The two stared at each other, and I could see some silent exchange passing between them. A moment later, the corner of Jake's lip nearly curled into a smile. When I looked at Dev, he was smirking.

What was that all about?

"If that's how you do your job," Dev began again, "I'm surprised your students haven't banded together and beat the shit out of you." I felt his eyes glide in my direction. "His problem, Stella, is that he's forgotten how a woman's supposed to look. You're perfect the way you are, don't listen to him."

I would have smiled at Dev, but I was too busy trying to figure out what just happened. "I've got ten more to do. You have anything else to say Jake, or can I finish?"

Jake nodded for me to continue.

As I struggled to do my nineteenth push-up I glanced at him again. I hadn't meant to look at his crotch, but I couldn't help it. Positioned as we were with my stomach down and Jake crouching, knees spread wide, in front of me, I couldn't help but look.

My quivering arms gave out at once, I landed hard on the floor, and an intoxicating blend of erotic need and carnal desire had me gasping for air. I looked at him again--looked at *it* again--just to be sure my eyes weren't playing tricks on me.

They weren't.

He got to his feet. "So we're agreed that you're going to be on time to class from now on, right Stella?"

I was too stunned to look at him, to look at either of them so I mumbled "yes" into the side of my arm.

"Good. Catch your breath then rejoin class."

"It was nice to meet you Stella." Dev gave my shoulder a squeeze, then got to his feet as well.

I nodded. "Yeah. You too."

Then both men left.

* * * *

9:07 a.m.

"He had what?"

I darted a quick look at the car windows to make sure they were closed. The closest people were a family standing across the street and staring up at the traffic lights. Nevertheless, I told Katarina, "Hush!"

"Was it big?"

"From what I could see, it was nice sized."

"So what did you do to him?"

"I didn't do anything."

She turned left at the light then glanced at me from the corner of her eye. "If he had a hard on, you had to have been doing something."

"I already told you what happened. It was me, Jake, and his friend Dev…and I think his friend was flirting with me." I prayed his friend was flirting with me. "Maybe Jake got off on watching me do push-ups or something. I don't know."

Katarina grimaced. "Who knew Jake was such a sadistic weirdo? Don't worry. If he calls you into the equipment room again, I'll go with you."

I looked at Katarina, her blonde hair plastered to her face with sweat, her manicured fingers gripping the steering wheel. While she wasn't my first choice as bodyguard, I knew, despite her delicate good looks, she would be the fiercest.

In truth, I wasn't sure if I even wanted any protection. While it was true, Jake was a bit of a sadist, he was also sexy as hell. And if I left his class I might never see Dev again. Granted, Dev most likely wasn't coming on to me, but I'd never know for sure if I left class. As for Jake's hard on, that could have been due to any source. Who knew, even though I was with him, he could've been thinking about someone else. Say for instance, Julianne, and her rock hard buns.

"You getting out or what?"

When I looked up I realized Katarina was idling in front of my brownstone.

"If I can walk," I deadpanned, rubbing at my aching shoulder as I shoved the car door open.

* * * *

8:58 p.m.
"He had what?"

I rolled my eyes as Katarina lowered herself onto the cushion beside me, an Apple Martini carefully balanced in both hands. I contemplated giving her a shove hard enough to send her sprawling, but decided against it. Even though the light green liquid in her glass wouldn't show on the red velvet of the sofa, I knew such an action would be adolescent on my part. It was a shame too because we hadn't been at The Oak Room five minutes before Katarina relayed all I told her about Jake and his hard on to Meagan and Ann, who both had listened with rapt interest.

Meagan eased forward, discarded the menu she'd been looking at, and stared at me over the table. With the flickering candlelight and roaring fire in the hearth, her grinning countenance seemed for a moment, grotesque. "What the hell were you wearing, Stella?"

Beside Meagan, Ann studied me. "How big was it? Was it thick or thin? Girth makes a big difference."

"I bet he's hot," Meagan said. "He sounds hot. Long black hair, built like a truck. I say go for it."

"I think it's disgusting," Katarina interrupted. "Shouldn't he be wearing a cup or something?"

"Katarina, a hot guy with a hard on is never disgusting."

"He's a treat," Ann agreed, running her fingers through her short, chestnut waves. She grinned, and asked, "So what're you gonna do about it?"

I opened my mouth to respond but Katarina beat me to it. "Nothing," she declared. "He's our instructor. It would make things too icky if she did anything with him … or his friend."

"Jake owns the gym too, right?" Meagan asked.

"Yeah," I said, finally able to get a word in.

"Well, he sounds like prime husband material. A sexy business owner with all his *equipment* in perfect working order."

"Well he's not a candidate, prime or otherwise," Katarina insisted.

"I think Stella can decide that on her own." Meagan twisted one of her honey-blonde corkscrew curls around a finger and studied me. Her smooth, café au lait skin crinkled slightly at her forehead as she raised her brows.

About Meagan: Meagan is gorgeous. Half-white and half black--Oh, that wasn't politically correct, was it? Half Irish American and half African American, Meagan had the kind of exotic beauty that's made her the envy of females all her life. For Meagan, deciding to have an affair with a man is as simple as saying, "I want to sleep with you." The men never protested, never put up a fight, and were always willing. She never had to worry about such mundane things as rejection and humiliation. There wasn't an unattached man on the planet who would reject Meagan if she voiced an interest in him.

Seeing as Meagan is so gorgeous, it's understandable that she assumed relationships were as easy for everyone else as they were for her. For her it was a simple act of deciding whether she wanted a particular man or not, then informing said man of her decision.

"I don't think either guy is interested in me," I said. "Jake was probably thinking about someone else when he got that hard on."

Ann sighed and Meagan shook her head. "Who else could he have been thinking about," Meagan wanted to know. "You were the only one in the room."

I shrugged. "Me and Dev."

"All right, so you were the only woman in the room, same difference."

"Who cares who Jake was thinking about," Katarina insisted. "It's a non-issue."

Our waitress approached the table to deposit more drinks and take our orders.

I took a long swallow of my Dogfish Head beer. I was disheartened to see so much focus was on my encounter with Jake.

"I thought you two took that class so you could meet a man." Ann said.

"Men," Katarina agreed. "Jake isn't a man, he's our instructor. What if Stella went out with him and things didn't work out? Then we'd have to drop the class. We waited six months to get in."

I studied the label on my beer and casually offered. "Jake's friend was really cute."

This statement was unanimously shouted down. Ann's booming voice rang out above the rest. "A grown man running around the city at eight in the morning dressed in leather, what's wrong with that picture?"

Meagan threw an arm into the air. "How about this, the man doesn't have a job."

"You don't know that," I tried, and was shouted down again.

"And what do we think about men without jobs?" Ann was asking the table at large.

"Loser!" my lovely friends announced in unison, then clicked their glasses together like the drunks they were.

"And we don't date losers," Meagan finished.

"Well I'm not dating Dev or Jake, so let's change the subject."

Ann shoved aside the frosted mug the waitress had placed in front of her, opting to take a swig straight from her bottle. Her throat worked as she took three deep swallows. Closing her eyes momentarily, she sighed. "After dealing with crotchety old, Harlow Jackson, I needed that."

Harlow Jackson is neither old nor crotchety, and I'd said as much. "He just wants things his way."

"Fuck his way."

Katarina glanced around the lounge to see if anyone had heard. "Don't swear," she whispered, as though everyone in the room was listening to our conversation with bated breath.

"There's nothing wrong with a client being precise about what he wants," I said. "Our entire business is about giving our clients what they want."

"Hell," Meagan added, "it's your motto."

Ann rolled her eyes and took another swig from her bottle. "If he knows so damn much about PowerPoint, he can do the presentation himself. Why the hell did he hire us anyway?"

"Because he wants it done right," I offered.

I'd grown up with Katarina and Meagan, Ann was a relatively new addition to our little family. She'd moved to Baltimore three years ago. We met two years ago when the demands of AIR became too much for me to handle alone. I placed an online ad, interviewed seven possible candidates, and eventually hired Ann.

At first Ann and Katarina, polar opposites, meshed as well as oil and vinegar. Katarina wasn't fond of Ann's "Virginia drawl," and Ann thought Katarina needed to "... get that stick out her ass." Eventually though the two had found common ground.

"I got a date today," Katarina announced, happily.

I turned to look at Katarina. "You didn't tell me that. Who?"

"Jim."

"Jim? Gym Jim?"

"Yeah, Gym Jim. What other Jim do we know?"

"Okay," Ann said, beer in hand. "Anybody want to tell me who this Jim Jim is?"

Katarina twisted until she was facing all of us, the biggest Kool-Aid grin on her face I'd ever seen. "Jim is a man from our kickboxing class. He's a financial analyst at T. Rowe Price, owns a townhouse in Canton on the harbor, and has a yacht." She scanned the table. "Oh, and he's thirty-four, single, and most importantly, he doesn't have any kids." Katarina leaned back in her seat, folded her hands on the table, and upped the wattage on her smile.

I exchanged looks with Meagan and Ann.

"Isn't that great," Katarina insisted. "He's a professional. And he makes a lot of money. A townhouse in Canton, guys! A yacht!"

Ann rolled her eyes. "But how does he look?"

Though the question was directed at Katarina, both Ann and Meagan had their eyes glued to me. "He's good looking," I said. About six feet tall, dark blonde hair, blue eyes, nice body," I shrugged, and added, "not bad on the eyes at all."

"So what's wrong with him?" Meagan asked impatiently.

Katarina shook her head. "Nothing. He's perfect."

"There are no *perfect* men, Katarina," Meagan said, "Take it from me, I know."

"Well Jim is. He's perfect, sexy, and we're going out on Saturday night."

The waitress brought our entrees, refilled our waters, then retreated behind the bar where a clan of gorgeous forty-something's had gathered to see and be seen.

"So where are you and Mr. Wonderful going?" Ann asked.

"Dinner at Ruth's Chris Steakhouse, then dancing at Club Blue."

Ann froze, fork midway to her mouth. "Come again?"

"We're going to dinner--"

"No, I got that. That other part, the Club Blue part."

"We're going dancing at Club Blue. It's some trendy new club a few blocks south of The Belvedere."

"Club Blue isn't new, babe. It's been there for years."

"I've never heard of it."

Ann grinned. "You wouldn't."

As though sensing something interesting happening, Meagan set her fork down. "What's up with Club Blue?"

Ann chuckled to herself. "What a bunch of prudes. Club Blue is a fetish club."

"What kind of fetish?" I asked.

"Fetish as in BDSM. Bondage, domination, sadomasochism," she translated for those of us still confused.

My mouth fell open and Katarina simply stared. "You're lying."

"I don't lie about sex."

"Well maybe I heard him wrong, or I misunderstood."

"There you go," Meagan concluded, pretty much summing up what the rest of us were thinking. "There's his imperfection. He's gonna take you to dinner then beat the crap out of you."

Ann laughed. "What I wanna know is if he's a sub or a Dom."

Katarina, looking too much like a deer caught in headlights, darted panicked looks around the table. "I've never been to a fetish club. They won't expect me to *do* anything, will they?"

"Only offer your body up to the Doms for their pleasure?" Katarina frowned. "I hope you're kidding."

CHAPTER TWO

Journal entry 1/14/05, 8:19 a.m.
Katarina is a dead woman. That's all I have to say on the subject.

Can you believe she had the nerve to not show up for class today, leaving me alone to deal with Crazy Jake?

Since I mentioned Jake anyway, I have a few questions regarding his behavior, which is, in a word, odd. When had Jake started taking such an interest in my "form"? Aren't there thirty-three other people in class besides me that he could bully?

How come every time I made a mistake, Crazy Jake was right there to acknowledge and correct it?

Was he touching me more than necessary, or was I losing my mind ... I'm probably losing my mind.

Was Crazy Jake getting better looking by the day? As crazy as this sounded, I think so.

With my mind full of thoughts of Jake, I pushed through the outer doors of Fit For Life and stepped onto the sidewalk, only to find the skies had opened and let loose with a deluge of ice cold rain.

Shaking my head in growing ire as my ankle-length, leather coat was pelted with rain drops, I cursed Katarina again for not coming to class. Had the little hussy shown up, I wouldn't be standing on the sidewalk getting drenched with a three block walk ahead of me.

NOTE TO SELF: Must buy a car.

I was stepping into the rush of foot traffic on the sidewalk when somebody called my name.

"Stella!"

Argh! Have I said how much I hate hearing my name shouted?

"Stella!"

Dear God, would he--whoever he was--stop.

I looked past the throngs of people rushing to and fro in front of me and spotted the speaker sitting in a car idling at the curb. When I realized who the driver was, I gaped.

Jake drove a Jag. Not just any Jag either, but a black Jaguar XJR. Damn! He was gorgeous when he was inside the gym, but sitting in a black Jag, he was downright irresistible.

"Looks like you need a ride," Jake called to me. One leather-clad arm was visible as he leaned out his window and motioned me over.

Squinting against the flecks of rain spilling over my hood and plopping fatly on my face, I shook my head. "I only live a few blocks north. I can walk."

Don't ask me why I said this because I've no idea. As soon as the words were out, I damned myself in seven languages for being a fool.

"I'm heading that way anyway. Get in."

My mind raced. Did I want to get in a car, alone with Jake and let him drive me home? Well, why wouldn't I? I'm attracted to him and there's the smallest of chances he's attracted to me. Who knows what could happen. Maybe I could get a dinner date out of the deal. I'd have to put my "man vacation" on hold but that wasn't a big deal.

That mean inner voice we all have, the one that seemed to revel in putting us in our place just as we're beginning to feel good about ourselves, said, "You can't go because you'll probably say something stupid, like, gee Jake, from what I saw on Monday you have a huge cock. Can I see it?"

"You're getting soaked," Jake advised me unnecessarily. It was pouring so hard there was a white mist hovering in the air.

Deciding to take Jake up on his offer, I walked to his car and got in the passenger side. I'd scarcely shut the door before Jake rocketed away from the curb and into traffic.

The car was unbelievable with a leather interior, heated seats, and every amenity a guy could want. Sitting in Jake's car was like melting into butter, or at least how I imagined melting into butter must feel.

"Where to?"

I used the sleeve of my coat to wipe water from my face. "Mount Vernon. I live a few doors down from the Washington Monument."

We drove the short distance in silence, which was more than a little frustrating. In the few seconds it had taken me to walk from the doors of Fit For Life to his car, I had envisioned a number of possible erotic encounters. His silence, however, spoke volumes. An interested man would initiate conversation, attempt to get to know more about me. Instead, Jake stared out the windshield as he drove and didn't utter a sound. On the bright side, I supposed it was good to have my fantasies dashed early on.

"Your friend Dev is really nice."

Jake glanced at me from the corner of his eye. "He said the same about you."

I tried not to seem too thrilled to know Dev mentioned me. "Have you been friends long?"

"A few years. Hey, do you mind if I come up and use your bathroom?"

"Bathroom? Oh, make a right turn here. It's that building there, the brown one."

"Too much water this morning," he explained.

At first I thought he was referring to the rain, but then I realized he was still talking about using my bathroom.

As he spoke he drove past my building, apparently looking for a parking space. He found one, across the enclosed square in the center of my street, and did an expert parallel parking job that somehow made him seem even sexier than he had five seconds before. (I'm not even going to attempt to explain this.)

"Yeah, you can use my bathroom," I said, hoping to God I hadn't left dirty socks lying on the floor this morning.

Ten minutes later he emerged from the half bath off my family room and stepped into the kitchen where I'd just put on a pot of coffee. He seemed incredibly interested in my décor. He was surveying his surroundings as though he were contemplating purchasing everything in sight. "Coffee?"

"No thanks." He came around the center island toward me. A sudden desire to flee swept through me, but I managed to control the urge. Jake seemed too big, entirely too male to be in my kitchen. The flowers I kept on the island, the ornately decorated plates and glasses I kept displayed on the breakfast bar, even the bright pattern of my tiles seemed suddenly less feminine with him around.

He'd removed his coat and the sight of that body in tight jeans, boots, and a black T-shirt nearly undid me. He was too good-looking for his own good ... and for my own good. It was inevitable that I'd say something stupid if he stayed too long, or *do* something stupid.

"It's always interesting to see how someone decorates their home."

"To you maybe, not to me."

He stood so close I could feel his body heat. The delicious, musky aroma of him filled the air around me. His hair, pulled into a wet braid, smelled like sweet apples. Everything about him was intoxicating. It was impossible to be within ten feet of this man and not get turned on. My panties felt damp between my thighs, trickles of arousal saturated the soft cotton. My body hungered for Jake.

He hadn't done or said anything to merit my response, still, a churning of excitement deep in the pit of my stomach had me biting my inner cheek and struggling for control. Being this close to this man was enough to send my hormones into overdrive. I thought if he actually touched me, I'd orgasm on the spot.

"Want some tea?" I offered in a voice I barely recognized.

"Did you eat anything this morning?"

"I can't work out on a full stomach."

His emerald eyes bore into me. Again, they roved my body as casually as if he owned it. My breasts, my thighs, my hips. More disturbing, his hungry gaze made me feel indescribably carnal.

"You're too thin," he decided. "For a woman your height you should weigh a hundred and twenty-five pounds at least. What are you, one-fifteen? One-seventeen?"

Though I was still aroused, I rolled my eyes. "Too thin is one-ten, one-oh-five. I'm one-twenty and I think my body is fine. Anyway, I thought men *liked* that waif look."

"Hmm, a woman with no hips, no thighs, and no breasts. Let me think about that." He paused, then continued, "Stella, the only men who want a woman without hips, thighs, and breasts are men who are into twelve-year-old boys. A woman should look like a *woman*, not a little boy."

I eyed him. "So you're saying I look like a little boy?"

"No. But you could stand to gain some muscle. You're too weak, an easy target."

Again, I rolled my eyes. "Not this again."

"You are. You should at least think about taking my self-defense class."

"I don't want to take your stupid self-defense class, Jake. I don't need it. I carry pepper spray with me at all times."

"Pepper spray?" he repeated, incredulous. "What's pepper spray gonna do when you're confronting a guy my size?"

"Stop him dead in his tracks."

"You have to be near the guy to be sure you get the spray in his eyes. Get close enough, and even if you spray him, there's a chance he'll get his hands on you."

I turned away from him and filled my mug with coffee.

"Nice ass," he said, almost to himself.

I stiffened, decided the best route to take with that comment was to completely ignore it. I pretended I didn't hear him. "I know how to handle myself."

"Really? Okay, let's try something." He walked to the breakfast bar and lifted my key chain from the counter. "Take them," he said, offering the keys with the pepper spray dangling from a key ring.

Reluctantly, I walked to the bar and took them. "What am I supposed to do with these?" I asked.

"Where do you usually carry it? In your pocket?"

I shrugged. "Yeah."

"Good. Put it in your pocket, the way you would if you were outside."

"Why?"

"Just do it."

I shoved the pepper spray into the pocket of my jeans then stared at him. "Now what?"

"Now, we play a little game. I want you to walk around your house. Walk anywhere you want, look at anything you want."

"And what will you do while I'm strolling?"

"Wait. When I think you're at your most vulnerable I'm gonna attack you. When I do I want you to pull the pepper spray out of your pocket and try to spray me. That's all you have to do. Once you have the pepper spray out of your pocket and pointed at me, the game ends and you win. I'll never say another word about the self-defense class again."

I studied him for a moment, sure I'd missed something. "Let me get this straight. You want me to pretend to be some woman walking around the city streets and you're going to pretend to be a criminal who attacks me? Then you want me to spray you?"

"Don't actually spray me, just point the spray at me ... if you can. I want you to see how useless pepper spray is if you don't know the basics of how to defend yourself."

I considered his challenge and grinned. A morning spent wrestling with Jake? There were far worse things in the world I could be doing, like push-ups, kickboxing, and exercising in general. But I doubted I could find anything else that would be half as interesting. "You're on."

He smiled at me. "You seem confident."

"All I have to do is point this stuff at you. It's not the most difficult thing I've ever had to do."

"What do you say we up the ante then?"

"Up the ante? How?"

"If you win, you only pay for classes through June, the rest is free."

I think my mouth fell open. I don't remember exactly if it did, but it must have. "If you win?"

"You go out with me on Saturday night."

Of their own accord, my eyes darted down to his crotch then up again. "Why don't you just ask me out on a date if you want to go out with me?"

"Because that would be boring. My way is more fun."

"This date thing, is that why you've been all over me in class?"

He snorted. "I haven't been all over you. I've been doing my job."

Starting to feel a bit cocky, I shook my head. "You've been all over me. Julianne is beginning to give me dirty looks."

One of Jake's rare smiles spread across his face. "So I may be giving you a bit more attention than the rest of the class," he shrugged. "I can't help it, you need the most help. Plus, you're oddly appealing."

"And you need to learn how to compliment a lady. Oddly appealing doesn't do it for me."

"You're like Halle Berry on acid." His smile broadened when I frowned.

"I think you should stop while you're ahead." Jake had a sense of humor ... who knew!

"So what do you say?"

I considered his proposal. Could I go through with this? Could I go on a date with Jake if I lost the bet? Was this something I wanted to do? Yes, yes, and yes! Besides, Jake was right, this would be fun. And it wasn't like going on one date with him--if I lost--constituted a serious breach in my vacation plans.

I stared into his eyes and gave him a slow, deliberate nod.

He grinned. "Go on then. I'll wait in here a few minutes then come looking for you."

I nodded again.

By the time I was standing in front of the sofa table in my living room I was wondering if I should purposely lose. But as tempting as he was, only having to pay for a half year's worth of gym use was too good to turn down. I'd have to go with the discounted gym rate. If Jake liked me enough to try to win a date, there was no reason why he wouldn't ask me out properly later.

I scanned my living room from the golden-colored walls to the thickly stuffed sofas, looking for someplace to mount a defense. I considered grabbing the poker from my fireplace but decided against it. If I were walking the city streets I wouldn't have a poker with me.

I also considered making a stand in the sitting room by my piano. I had a heavy, faux crystal candy dish on it that would definitely make a great weapon should I need one. I could pretend the dish was something else, a large bit of debris maybe, or even a--

"Don't move."

Jake's voice startled me so much that I nearly jumped out of my skin. I tried to run. Unfortunately, the sofa table hadn't moved in the last five seconds. Instead of running forward, I ran smack into it, slamming my head so hard against the edge I saw stars. I slid to the floor and landed on my back. I was quick about flipping onto my knees though. I turned over and began to crawl away but was stalled by a hand on my ankle.

The surprise of his voice coupled with my unexpected fall made me a little more jumpy than the situation merited. Logically I knew the hand could only belong to Jake, but emotionally I felt it could belong to anyone.

I screamed. And I kicked.

Neither had the desired effect though. The hand on my ankle--the strength of it stunned me--began dragging me away from the sofa table and across the floor.

Damn, I thought. I had to do something, and fast. The competition couldn't end so quickly. It had barely started. If I lost too easily, he would think I lost on purpose just so I could have a date with him. That would be too embarrassing for words.

The hand was joined by its mate and Jake gave me a tug hard enough to make my arms go out from under me. I fell flat on my stomach.

Pepper spray.

The words flashed in my head like the answer to a prayer. All I had to do was grab the pepper spray, point it at him and the game would end. I would be the winner.

Struggling to fight him off with a series of quick kicks, I reached down for my pocket. I let out a gasp of surprise when sudden weight came down on my prostrate body. All at once I couldn't move or even breathe. I tried to roll over but realized I was being pinioned to the floor by the weight of Jake's body.

For a moment the weight disappeared as Jake crawled my length.

I had barely decided on a plan of action before he completely threw me for a loop by flipping me onto my back. What was left of my air was crushed out of my lungs as he straddled my chest, his two hundred plus pound body pinning me to the floor.

It wasn't too difficult to see I was on the losing end of things. I should have been angry. But I wasn't. With Jake atop me, the muscles of his inner thighs flexing as he rode my writhing body, anger was the last thing on my mind. A potent rush of lust surged through me. I hungered for attention, and was suddenly quivering with the need to be touched. I realized that I wanted Jake to do more than wrestle me into submission. I wanted him to spread my thighs and impale me. I was desperate to know what it was like to be made love to by such a man, to feel the stiff flesh of his erection moving inside of me.

Determined to put up a good fight despite my inner yearnings, I kicked and tried to twist, but the man was as solid as stone. I struggled like a mad woman and he effortlessly took my hands, one by one, and pinned them beneath his knees. In this position, he didn't have to do anything but sit and wait for me to give up and admit defeat.

"Still think you can handle yourself, Stella," he taunted. "What good is your pepper spray now?" To prove his point, he pulled the pepper spray from my pocket and waved it in front of my face. "I could spray you with it."

Even with my arousal, the smug look of satisfaction on Jake's face made me long to get a hand free so I could slap him.

Hands on hips, secure in his domination, he gazed down with a huge smile on his face. "You lose, Stella. Admit it."

I took in a deep breath then pushed up with all my might, hoping to unseat him.

Nothing happened.

"What about class?" I asked. "How are we supposed to behave in class if we go out on a date?"

"Us going on a date is not that big of a deal. Nobody's gonna track us down and tar and feather us. It's just a date."

I raised my head enough to bring my face within inches of his crotch, stared at the bulge in his pants, and then I looked up at him. He didn't move.

"I find that happens a lot when I'm around you," he indicated his hard on.

I nearly offered myself to him. Instead, I dodged. "Still, I think we should keep the fact that we're seeing each other to ourselves."

"If it makes you feel better it'll be our secret."

His jeans were incredibly tight. His cock, solid as a rock, strained against the material. I realized if I leaned far enough up I could touch it with my lips. On the heels of that thought, a sudden desire to kiss it overcame me. Damn it to hell, I wanted this man in a bad way.

"So we're on?"

I opened my mouth to respond, but didn't get a chance. My doorbell chimed.

Jake stiffened and I stared up at him, wide-eyed. "Damn!" I glanced at the clock and saw it was nine-thirty. "Damn!"

"Who is that?"

"A client. My nine-thirty appointment." The bell chimed again. "Get up," I said, struggling to roll from beneath him.

"First promise me Saturday night."

"Get up!"

Casually, he set his hands on his hips and gazed placidly

down at me. "I'm waiting. Tell me what I want to hear."

"My client's gonna leave, I have to answer the door!"

"I want to see you, Stella. On Saturday."

I was about to agree, but remembered I'd--along with Ann and Meagan--promised Katarina to meet her and Jim at Club Blue. "I can't do Saturday, I have plans."

"What plans?"

The bell chimed, this time more insistently. "I'm going out with my friends."

"Where?"

"Club Blue," I blurted before thinking better of it. As soon as that knowing smile crossed his face, I knew I'd made a mistake.

"You're not collared are you?"

"Collared?"

"Collared, as in, belong to a Dom."

I stared at him a moment, unable to answer. "Belong to a Dom? What the…No! I don't belong to anyone."

"Good. I'll meet you there then."

Panic surged through me as I wondered how I'd explain to Katarina why I was meeting Jake at a fetish club. She'd go through the roof. "No!"

"Yes."

"No!"

"Yes." He rose to his feet and offered me his hand.

I didn't think I could move let alone stand. Somehow, I managed.

"No, Jake. I'm only going to be there for a little while anyway."

"Good, then we'll go someplace private for drinks afterward and maybe a little more wrestling."

"I can't."

"Why are you putting me off when you and I both know you want to say yes?"

My face heated, but he had a point. Still, I didn't think he'd understand about Paul the Prick and my mini-vacation from men. I'd only just vowed on Monday to stay away from men, and here I was, four days later, already giving in.

The doorbell chimed again.

"What do you want from me?" I turned from him and started for the door. I could hear his heavy footfalls close behind.

When I got to the door and pulled it open it was to look out onto an empty space. "See what you've done? I've lost a client. That's four hundred dollars!"

Jake stepped past me, moved into the hallway and pointed.

I stepped over the threshold and glanced down the hallway in time to see the back of David Maxwell's head bobbing toward the stairs. "David!" I called. "Sorry, I was … busy."

David turned then started back. "I figured you'd been called away unexpectedly."

I stepped aside to allow David in. He gave me a shy smile then made the mistake of turning to look at Jake who was frowning with obvious displeasure at David's arrival.

"Go on and wait in the office, David. I'll be there in a minute."

Once David was out of earshot Jake advanced. I retreated until the unyielding surface of the wall stalled any further movement.

"See you Saturday. Don't worry. I'll bring a collar for you."

"I won't wear it. Collars are for dogs, not humans."

He threw his head back and laughed. "Enjoy your day, Stella." He stepped back, then made his way down the hall.

* * * *

1:04 p.m.

I've just had lunch with Ann to tell her of my morning with Jake. She seemed very impressed with my ability to attract a sexy, fitness, guru type. Also, she's looking forward to meeting him.

We called Meagan and told her about my coup.

"What of your vacation?" she wanted to know.

"I've decided I'm on a vacation from my vacation." And I figured that was all that needed to be said about it.

Both have promised not to say a word to Katarina but left me to tell her.

I'm so excited and cannot wait for tomorrow to arrive.

CHAPTER THREE

Journal entry 1/15/05, 8:37 p.m.

I walked up Charles Street, heading in the direction of Club Blue. I walked briskly, albeit a little uncomfortably. The latex mini dress I wore was so tight I could barely breathe let alone walk. I'd nearly worn a pair of stiletto heels with the ensemble but decided against it. Instead, I'd donned a pair of stiletto Mary Jane type boots I'd spied this afternoon in a boutique. Now, as I crunched through snow, I was glad I had. The boots were far easier to maneuver around in, plus they supplied the added benefit of covering my calves.

I didn't know if Jake would really show tonight, but if he did, I didn't want to do anything stupid. That's why I'd gone out tonight without shaving my legs. No way in hell I was having sex with Jake with stubbly legs.

When I neared the club I could hear techno rock music blaring from within. Whoever the band was, they were royally pissed off. Their music was raucous, and I supposed, appropriate for a fetish club. Beneath the dueling guitars and computer generated bass I couldn't hear much else.

At the entrance to the club I flashed my ID at the door and stepped inside, bringing white swirls of wintry powder in with me. After giving the crowd a quick scan for Ann, Katarina, and Meagan and coming up short, I decided the place was too packed to notice any one individual face. Under a festive disco ball, people--all dressed in black--jockeyed for position on the dance floor. Many had given up the effort to actually dance and simply bounced up and down in place on beat. It looked as though every eligible single in Baltimore had fled the snow and sought refuge here.

Oh well, I thought, slipping my coat off and stepping into the fray.

Boisterous laughter rose around me as I made my way to the bar. I could feel the clammy skin of the people who brushed by me and smelled cigarette smoke in their clothes. I had to quell a desire to go to the ladies room to wash their sweat off.

Mentally, I ran down possible drink options in my head, noting that I couldn't have anything too strong. Mixed drinks were out of the question, as was beer since I couldn't drink just one. How did that joke go? *Officer, I've only had one drink. One after another.* If Jake came, I wanted to be sober.

"Well wouldn't you know it," the blonde behind the bar said when I squeezed in. "New blood. What can I do you for, honey?"

Her eyes were narrowed and she gave me a smile that caused the lines around her mouth to deepen.

"I'm that obvious?"

"Hell yeah! But we can change that."

I scanned the bar for a spare stool.

"Don't bother," she advised. "Full house tonight. You're lucky to have what you got, even if it is standing room."

I gave the bar another look. It wasn't promising. "I think you're right. Hey, I thought this place was a fetish club. It looks like a dance club ... a dance club with an all-black dress code."

"It is a fetish club, honey. Upstairs we dance, downstairs we play." She grinned. "Know what you want in the drink department? No. I'll catch you next time 'round then, once Bradley throws another good one on," she said, referring to the music. The techno song had ended and a rather large crowd was making an exodus toward the bar. "For now," she eyed the crowd with pleasure, "I've got drinks to serve."

She did a slow groove to the other side of the bar where a group of leather-clad guys were waving bills in the air, hoping someone would take notice.

"Stella?"

The sound of my name spoken gently against my ear sent a shiver of anticipation up my spine.

He was here.

I froze for a moment, too startled to move. All day I'd been unable to do anything but think about Jake and yesterday morning in my house. I'd been looking forward to tonight, hoping against hope that he'd show. I promised myself I wouldn't be too devastated if he blew me off. God knows he didn't give any indication he was interested in me at class this morning.

Slowly, I turned to face him.

He was dressed in leather. Black leather pants, no shirt, and a Matrix style leather trench coat that hung to his booted ankles. His nipples were the lushest shade of pink I'd ever seen. They were puckered from the cold and looked hard as pebbles. Just looking at them made my mouth water. His sable mane was loose and falling in gleaming waves over his shoulders and down his back. It was the first time I'd ever seen it loose. He looked completely at ease. He absolutely glowed. His honey complexion seemed golden under the flashing lights.

He was gorgeous.

And he knew it.

Worse, he knew I knew it.

He snaked his arm around my waist. The cold leather of his coat chilled my skin, making me jump. The force he used to propel me forward was gentle but insistent. I found myself gliding a step toward him before I realized what was happening.

"Hello Stella," he said against my ear.

The peach fuzz hairs on the back of my neck stood to attention. "You came."

"I said I would."

I strove for calm though my heart was doing flip-flops in my chest. "I thought you were just being difficult. I didn't think you were into this sort of thing."

"You have no idea what I'm into."

I considered making a caustic remark but decided against it when he bent and whispered in my ear. "You avoided me in class today."

"Me? *You* were avoiding *me*."

"I wouldn't dream of avoiding you." Abruptly, he stepped back. He let his eyes roam my body, from head to foot, a slight smile tugging on the edge of his lips. "Now look at you. Stella, Stella. I can tell I'm going to have a hard time being a gentleman tonight. You look beautiful."

Breathless, I whispered, "And I'm going to have a hard time wanting you to be a gentleman."

Someone called my name in a deep, plaintiff voice, interrupting our conversation. "Stella! Stella!"

Argh!

Jake whirled around. "Who the hell is that?"

I twisted around and saw a familiar face. Ann's boyfriend, Gerard, looked as boyishly handsome as ever, despite his forced smile. Still, his eyes said he was genuinely happy to see me. He looked tired though. His blond hair hung limp at his shoulders, and his gray eyes were rimmed in red. The black jeans and shirt he wore were wrinkled, as if he'd pulled them from the bottom of a hamper and threw them on. His black leather jacket was the only unmarred piece of clothing he had on.

I leaned into his embrace, noticing how strong the smell of beer clung to him. "Saw you standing here," he yelled over the music, then eyed Jake with undisguised hostility. "Thought I'd come over."

I glanced at Jake who was pointedly staring at Gerard.

"It's a mad house in here," I said. "Are the girls here yet?"

"Yeah. Everyone's here. You're the last." Still staring at Jake, Gerard motioned in Jake's general direction and asked, "Who's this?"

"This is Jake. My kickboxing instructor."

"Her date," Jake added, detaching himself from me long enough to offer his hand.

Gerard studied the proffered hand for a moment, then took it in his own and shook.

"This is Gerard," I told Jake. "One of my good friends."

"Come on," Gerard said. Grabbing my wrist, he hauled me through the crowd behind him.

Jake, holding tight to my other hand, followed close on my heels.

I noticed with some surprise that Gerard had his cane with him tonight and was leaning heavily on it. This made our progress through the crowd awkward. I'd rarely seen him use it. Most days he left it at home, but tonight he was looking a little uneasy on his feet, not to mention how unkempt he was.

Back in high school Gerard had run track. He'd apparently been very good at it. Unfortunately his track career had contributed to his present problem. He had weak knees. There were nights when moving was a chore for him. Nights when too much drink and too much sadness conspired to make walking difficult. Looked like tonight was one of those nights.

I wondered how much he'd had to drink. A drunken Gerard was always a sure sign that Ann had broken things off with him--again. I had to wonder why he was always so surprised when she broke up with him. After so many years of this, how could he be? He was a nice enough guy, very good-looking, but if he wanted to keep Ann's interest he'd have to learn how to play hard to get. Instead of getting wasted after she dumped him, he should make a point of looking better than ever. Be a little stand-offish; make her question her decision of leaving him. She might wonder if she'd made a mistake if he didn't make it so obvious that their breakup had devastated him. At the rate Gerard was going, the only thing Ann would think when she caught sight of him was, 'Thank God, he's out of my life.' Gerard simply couldn't handle being dumped.

A line of booths spanned the wall to my left. I spotted the girls as we reached the end of the row. They were sitting on a rise against a large picture window, the thick panes frosted from the cold. Gerard led us to the circular booth and motioned Jake and I up the stairs.

"You made it," Katarina announced to the table at large. Her smile, however, wavered when she saw who was standing next to me. "Jake?"

"Katarina," he said with a nod.

Katarina's eyes narrowed with disapproval. I had meant to bring the subject of Jake up with her, but somehow, the time had never seemed right.

"We were beginning to think you changed your mind." Meagan eyed Jake and gave me a smile. "So this is the kickboxing instructor. Glad to meet you, Jake. I'm Meagan."

"Stella," Katarina interrupted, "You remember Jim, don't you?"

Considering Jim was the reason all of us were here, how could I forget him? I didn't say this. Instead, I gave Jim a winning smile and scooted into the booth.

"Jim, you already know Jake," Katarina continued.

The two men nodded to each other.

"And this is Peter." Meagan motioned casually to her drop-dead gorgeous date.

Peter had the kind of dark good looks that had made Taye

Diggs a star--milk chocolate skin, midnight eyes, and a smile that made a woman want to faint. We shook hands. I was a little disappointed I wouldn't be seeing much of him after tonight. Meagan had a way of scaring off men. So far, no man had been able to deal with the pressures inherent in dating a woman as beautiful as Meagan on a long-term basis.

Jake eased into the booth next to me. Once we were situated he transferred his hold on my hand to my thigh. This had the direct result of sending a wave of dizzying pleasure through my body. He gave my thigh a squeeze. Then, with the tips of his fingers, he stroked my skin, staring hungrily at me the entire time. I can't say exactly what it was, but there was something about his level, green-eyed stare that made the woman in me yearn for his touch.

"I didn't know you were coming, Jake. I didn't know you and Stella were seeing each other."

Jake transferred his hypnotic eyes to Katarina, who seemed unimpressed with his dark good looks. "Stella and I have been seeing each other for a couple of days now," he explained.

"It's nothing serious" I added. "I didn't think I had to make an announcement."

Sitting at the end of the table, Gerard poured beer from one of three pitchers into two mugs. The first mug he handed to Jake, the second he took a swallow from, and then passed to me. "Yeah, yeah, Stella, I know. No beer on a first date. But you know you want one."

I accepted the proffered drink and sniffed delicately at the glass. "This smells generic. You know I hate generic beer."

"What a princess," Jake said, letting his fingers dance up to the edge of my very short mini-dress.

"You have no idea, Jake," Meagan began. She proceeded to spend a good thirty minutes regaling us with tales of my princessly behavior, from my refusal to sleep on anything less than three hundred thread count sheets as a child to my inability to use drugstore shampoos and conditioners on my hair as an adult. I tried to tell her Jake wasn't interested but he only shushed me quiet.

Ann, Katarina, and Gerard even threw in a few anecdotes of their own. How encouraging it is to have friends that are always ready to embarrass you in front of possible boyfriends.

"It's always so comforting how some people never change," Meagan finished.

Jake fixed me with those eyes, a slight grin pulling up the corner of his mouth. "Why mess with perfection."

I smiled stupidly and let loose with a ridiculous sounding giggle.

Okay, so this was the lamest come-on ever, since he'd said I was weak and underweight on Monday. Still, I indulged myself. It wasn't every day a sex god of a man set his sights on me.

Ann held her beer mug up and gave him a slight bow over the table. "Nice. My kind of man." She'd said the latter while staring at Gerard who promptly flipped her the bird.

Rolling his eyes as he set his hand back in his lap, Gerard grabbed the half-empty pitcher in front of Ann. The liquid looked dark and syrupy. He politely emptied the offending mug he'd given me earlier in three large swallows and replaced the former liquid with the darker brew. "Dogfish Head," he said, as he again set the mug before me. "Their Indian Brown Ale."

I sniffed again, approving of the chocolaty aroma. I hadn't planned on drinking beer, but I couldn't be rude to Gerard when he was already feeling down in the dumps.

"Jim," Katarina beamed, "why don't you tell us about your yacht."

Pleased to have been brought into the conversation, Jim sort of swaggered forward in his seat and reached in his back pocket. He came up holding a wallet, which no doubt held pictures of said yacht. "I got this baby when I was...."

* * * *

10:33 p.m.

We sang *Breathe* with Prodigy, giving the air some serious hip action. I really shouldn't have been dancing in such a brazen manner with Jake, but since my three best girlfriends were there I couldn't seem to stop myself.

Ann and Peter held their beer mugs aloft as they danced, sloshing liquid this way and that, while Meagan and me bumped the sides of our hips together. Jake, his arms fastened around my waist, rocked with me. I was very pleased to see he had rhythm.

"We should do this more often," Katarina yelled over the

music, bouncing up and down and holding Jim's hands above her head.

Ann nodded. "This place is great."

"We should go downstairs!"

"Believe me Katarina, you're not ready for downstairs. Hell, I'm not ready for downstairs."

Rocking precariously back and forth on his crotches, Gerard nodded. "I took Ann down there once and she was cross-eyed for a week."

Jake took my hand and spun me so I twirled awkwardly under his arm. I wasn't very graceful and knew I looked silly, but I didn't care. I was having too good a time to care. Giggling, head reeling from the spinning, I nearly lost my footing when the music slowed and Jake grabbed my hips and pulled me to him. "Finally, a slow one."

"As slow as this place gets." I let my body relax against his.

His muscles flexed when he wrapped his arms around me and pulled me tight against his sweaty chest. "This is nice."

"Have you ever been here before?"

Instead of answering, he kissed my ear, brushing his lips over the sensitive skin. Desire made my loins give a reflexive heave as intense need surged with a force strong enough to bring me to my knees. His lips were moist and wet, and I could smell French wine on his breath.

His fingers fluttered over the exposed skin of my back. "You look incredible tonight, have I told you that?" I focused on breathing, and then stiffened in surprise when he nudged the hollow of my throat with his nose. "And you smell wonderful." He pressed his lips against my skin, gentle, but insistent. His free hand began a languid descent over the swell of my breasts.

I did nothing to stop him. I wanted to feel this, to know his touch and the pleasure he could provide. I'd been fantasizing about it since I'd met him.

We swayed to the music, my thigh nudging between his powerful ones. Being with Jake like this, feeling the slick skin of his chest against my face when I ground against him was nice.

The music was loud, but I couldn't hear the voices of those around me anymore. The world had narrowed, had evaporated until all that existed was Jake and me.

Intoxicated with the feel of him, drunk on the thought of being with him, I reached between his legs and gave his cock a gentle squeeze. Almost immediately it swelled in my palm.

He groaned. "Stella, that feels good. You shouldn't do that."

I rubbed the engorged length, closed my eyes and imagined what it would be like to have him hard and hot inside of me. "You're hard."

"If you knew how much I wanted you right now you wouldn't tease me. You should stop before you do something you'll regret."

I swallowed. Hard. I'd never done anything like this before, never been so bold with a man. It was invigorating, and scary as hell. Nevertheless, I gazed into his eyes. "I won't regret anything."

Even as I said this, he was easing his hand between my thighs. With deliciously slow strokes, he moved the pad of his thumb over my damp panties. "You're soaked." My knees went weak, but he held me against him. "You want me bad, don't you?"

I ignored the arrogant tone his voice had taken and gave him another squeeze.

"Come home with me tonight, Stella?"

In the span of two minutes I'd become so aroused I was actually contemplating going home with him, unshaven legs or not.

"Would you like that?" he asked. "Like me to take you home?"

I moaned despite myself.

I should've been worried of the spectacle we were making, but the club was so crowded, nobody seemed to notice. Plus, I supposed this type of thing went on there all the time.

"Come home with me," he insisted.

Was I ready to be alone with Jake again? There was no telling what I was likely to do if left alone with this man. I wasn't doing a very good job at playing hard to get. But then again, why shouldn't I? I'd never been one to play games. I was more the "if you like him, tell him" type of girl. Besides, I was an adult. There was no reason why I couldn't handle an adult relationship with Jake, even if he was the most gorgeous man I'd ever known. He was gorgeous, and he seemed to be taking our budding relationship very seriously, which was a plus.

"Okay," I said with a decisive nod. "Let's go."

"Go where?" Katarina sashayed next to me and raised her brows.

"A private party for two." Jake reached for my hand.

Gerard, who'd been standing in the middle of our circle rocking back and forth, stilled. "I think you should stay, Stella."

I couldn't see Jake's expression, but apparently it was convincing enough to inspire a change of heart in Gerard. Or so I thought. As I followed Jake away from the dance floor, Gerard held my arm long enough to whisper, "People aren't always what they seem Stella. Be careful."

CHAPTER FOUR

Jake opened the passenger door of his Jag, waited while I eased inside, then shut the door with a single thrust of his hip.

In the seconds it took him to walk to the driver's side, panic set it. Was I really going through with this? I'd never gone home with any man I wasn't dating, and despite what Jake said to the contrary, we weren't formally seeing each other. What would we do once we got to his place? Okay, I knew what we'd do, but could I actually do *it* with Jake? What if I wasn't good at *it* tonight? And what would we talk about before we did *it*? Would we have anything to talk about?

And most importantly, what had Gerard meant by that ominous little statement? People aren't always what they seem? What the hell was that supposed to mean?

Shit!

Shit! Shit! Shit! My legs!

Shit! I hadn't shaved them!

Jake opened his door and slid inside. The sound of his leather encased ass gliding over the leather seat made me suddenly ravenous with need to have a taste of him. A shiver of anticipation danced up my spine even as I decided I'd have to think up an excuse and make my escape. I couldn't have sex with Jake with hairy legs.

"You know what," I forced myself to say.

Jake shifted in his seat, put the key in the ignition, and twisted. The car purred to life. "You're not going anywhere, Stella."

First of all, how the hell had he known what I was gonna say? Second, who died and made him boss?

As if that was all to be said on the matter, he put the car in reverse and backed out of the parking space.

"Wait a minute, Jake. I'm having second thoughts."

He cruised to the parking attendant and pulled a twenty from the ashtray, pausing a few seconds to fix me with his green eyes. "You're not going anywhere, Stella," he said again. This time he was careful to speak more slowly, enunciating every word carefully so I couldn't possibly miss his meaning.

A betraying rush of pleasure surged through me, followed closely by a less potent rush of confusion. What the hell was going on here? What was wrong with me? He couldn't talk to me like that. Could he? I'd never allowed anyone to level orders at me. I can't stand bossy people.

Why was I letting Jake get away with it? When I'm at class I have to do what he says because he's the instructor. But I didn't have to take his crap beyond that.

"Until I say otherwise," he continued, conversationally, "that nearly nude body of yours belongs to me."

Again, pleasure surged through me. My stomach felt so light and airy, I wouldn't have been surprised if I'd floated away on cloud nine that very second. And my panties were so damp, I'd been squirming around on my seat, trying to find a comfortable position since I'd sat down. I'd never wanted a man more than I wanted Jake right then and there.

I bit my inner cheek hard. I had to get control over the situation again, and fast. If I went through with this, Jake would have full control over everything--including my body. "My body," I squeaked. After allowing myself a few seconds to clear my throat, I began again. "My body," I said an octave lower, "belongs to me."

He crossed Pratt and drove up Light Street, a slight smile playing on the edge of his lips. "You say one thing, Stella, but your face and your body tell me something different."

"My face and my body are saying that I've changed my mind. My face and my body are saying--"

He inhaled. "I can smell your desire."

I clamped my mouth shut as heat rushed to my face. Embarrassed, I closed my eyes and faced my window.

"It's nothing to be ashamed of, Stella. Knowing how much you want me ... knowing how much I turn you on...." his voice began to waver so he let the sentence go unfinished.

"Where do you live?"

"Change of subject? Okay, I'll play. I live here. Harbor Towers."

He turned left then made another series of quick turns. By the time I'd opened my eyes and gotten a look around, the car was descending into another parking garage.

Still, I didn't need to study my surroundings to know where we were. "Harbor Towers," I said. "Impressive. And expensive."

He shrugged. "They're not so bad. I own a condo here. And it's close to the gym."

Harbor Towers was the nicest, most exclusive residence in all of Baltimore. Built on the Inner Harbor, Harbor Towers has its own private yacht club, restaurant, and sports complex. Impressive didn't begin to describe the luxurious compound.

"Stella?"

I was jolted back to the present and realized he'd parked the car and now stared at me.

"What?"

"Come here."

I felt the tip of his finger on my chin a moment before he drew me forward, closer to him.

The kiss was slow, hot, and so sensual I practically melted into the seat. His tongue was wet and tasted as sweet as honey. Even as he delved deeper, I opened to him, welcoming him, losing myself in him.

He settled a hand on the back of my head and pulled me closer, moaning into my mouth as he deepened the kiss. "I'm gonna fuck you so good, baby," he vowed. "So good you'll never want any other man between your thighs."

I sighed, forgetting my fears, my hairy legs, and Gerard's admonition. "Promise?"

He pulled away from me and let those emerald eyes rove my face. "What do you think?"

I don't remember walking into the lobby or the trip in the elevator to the top floor. All I remember is the nearly overwhelming need I felt as we traversed fifteen floors knowing I had to maintain my decorum.

After we walked through his front door, I was pressed firmly against the wooden frame with Jake's body against mine.

We kissed again, touching each other in a frenzy of desire. His bare chest scorched the exposed skin of my breasts, but the heat barely registered in my brain. I was lost in the thrill of finally being alone with Jake again.

"My room," he said against my lips.

He shoved off of the wall, pulling me with him.

I tried to scurry across the foyer beside him, but I slipped on the slick surface of the marble tiles. The heel of my boot skittered ahead of me and I would have fallen had Jake not bent and scooped me up into his arms.

Then his lips were on mine, possessive and ravenous, as he walked down a hallway. We broke contact long enough to mount the spiral staircase that led to his bedroom.

Deep hues of green and maroon gave Jake's room a brooding ambiance. A mahogany four-poster bed dominated the large space. Complete with sheer curtains set into richly carved rails, the bed was ornate and looked luxurious. Jake was the first single man of my acquaintance to show such extravagance in decorating his home.

He'd just settled me on his comforter when I remembered my earlier misgivings.

My legs were hairy as a yeti.

I bolted upright on the bed and let out a yelp of dismay. "Wait!"

"I don't think I can."

My mind raced. "You have to. I'm not on the pill," I said, making this up as I talked. "I have to put in my whatsamajiggy."

"Your whatsamajiggy?"

"Yeah, you know. My contraceptive thingy." Damn it all, what the hell was that thing called?

"You mean a diaphragm?"

"Yes. That's it." I hopped off the high mattress, purse in hand. "Where's your bathroom?"

Obviously sensing defeat, he settled on the bed, legs wide, and motioned at the door on the far side of the room. "Through there."

I nodded and sprang for the door.

Once inside, I shut and locked the door, cursing myself silently for my stupidity. After all, I had gone to a fetish club tonight hoping to meet Jake. Common sense should've dictated that I shave my legs just in case anything happened, not to *prevent* anything. But damn it, I was charting new territory here.

"Razor blade," I muttered, scanning the bathroom.

The obvious choice was the medicine cabinet. Where the hell was it? In every home I'd ever lived in the medicine cabinet was within a mirrored or a shuttered door.

There were no cheesy shuttered doors in this bathroom, but there were mirrors a plenty. Mirrors were over the sink, mirrors positioned artfully around the sunken bathtub, and mirrors were just outside the shower stall. There were friggin' mirrors *everywhere*.

I started with the mirrors above the sink, but struck out.

"You okay in there?" Jake called from the bedroom.

"Yeah," I said, checking for mirrored doors around the tub, "just need a few more minutes."

No mirrored doors, I decided a minute later. Who the hell had a bathroom with no mirrored doors? Where was the medicine cabinet?

That's when I noticed it, a single door on the far side of the bathroom. I ran to it and pushed it open. I found myself on the threshold of the biggest walk-in closet I'd ever seen.

Could any one person possibly own so many clothes? I felt I'd somehow stumbled into a small designer clothing boutique. This wasn't a simple walk-in closet with four walls; this oversized clothing sanctuary had rooms.

Curious, I entered, promising myself I'd only stay a second. Hopefully not long enough to attract Jake's suspicion. I walked down the main aisle, passing room after room of clothing. None of the rooms were overly large, perhaps five by ten, but the sheer order of the space astounded me. Every room had mahogany shelves and racks, and every one was full of male clothing. Business suits took up one room, casual button up shirts and trousers took up another. Then there was the room with all the jeans and T-shirts, a room for shoes, and a room for ... leather.

I took a step inside this last room and stared, open-mouthed. There was a rack of leather pants and a shelf with all sorts of leather boots. Then, on the far wall I saw shelves containing masks, handcuffs, fur restraints, and other items I couldn't quite name. Beside those were an assortment of paddles, riding crops, and whips hanging on the wall.

Not thinking beyond curiosity, I walked further into the room and touched a riding crop. From the look and feel of the leather, the implements of punishment were well made and cared for.

For reasons I couldn't explain at the time, the paddles were of particular interest to me. One was covered in rows of blunt-edged spikes that I imagined were horribly painful when applied to flesh. I lifted, tested it against my thigh, then set it back in place.

I lifted a different paddle off the wall and tested it against the palm of my hand. I'd only struck lightly but the sting of pain had me replacing it fast. Though it wasn't covered in spikes, it had less give than the other. I didn't imagine this paddle would feel any better than the last when wielded with enough enthusiasm.

A bright red paddle hanging on one of the bottom rungs caught my eye. It was smaller, more delicate than the others, and in addition to being more colorful, Jake's name was etched in cursive script on the side facing me. Seeing his name on the paddle, I imagined what it would be like to be bent over his lap as he used it on me. The thought made me take a step back in surprise. I'd had fantasies about such scenarios before, however I could never actually picture myself submitting to such treatment.

I lifted it from the wall then ran my hand over the carved forms of naked bodies that twisted and writhed along the length of the handle. How would being whipped with something like this feel? Would it sting or would it hurt?

The thought had been in the back of my mind, but now it spilled into my consciousness. What kind of man had a collection of paddles in his closet?

"See something you like?"

I jumped about two feet into the air and dropped the paddle on the floor. When I was grounded again, I found I was suddenly frozen to the spot, unable to move.

"I knocked on the door for a good minute," he was saying from behind me. His voice grew louder as he closed the distance between us. "When you didn't answer I unlocked the door from the outside and went in. I thought something had happened to you."

What could I say? I was looking for a razor blade but found these instead. Somehow that hadn't seemed like the right approach.

"Hasn't anyone ever told you it's impolite to go snooping around someone else's things?"

I couldn't gauge his emotional state from his tone. He didn't sound angry, but some were at their most dangerous when they took on that silky smooth, butter-don't-melt-in-my-mouth tone. Silence seemed the most appropriate course of action at this particular juncture, so I didn't say a word.

He bent to the floor and picked up the paddle I'd been holding.

I stiffened.

When he set his hands against the wall, effectively caging me in, I tried to make myself smaller.

"Do you like my paddles?," he continued silkily.

I didn't move or utter a sound.

"Cat got your tongue?"

"No," I managed to squeak.

He took a step back and let his hands fall to his sides. "Turn around. Look at me. I'm not gonna bite your head off."

Yeah, but I just might die of embarrassment on the spot. I'd been stroking the paddle, practically drooling over it and he'd seen me. Unfortunately I didn't drop dead. My heart kept up its incessant clatter in my chest and I remained in Jake's closet where I'd been caught red-handed.

"Turn around Stella."

Slowly, head down, I turned. "This is so embarrassing. I'm sorry. I don't usually go snooping through people's closets," I said to his boots.

"Look at me."

I focused on getting air into my lungs and then out again.

"Look at me." He accented the demand with a whap of the paddle against his thigh.

I not only looked at him, I stood to attention and barely managed to keep myself from saluting.

He grinned. "Better. I thought that might get your attention. Why are you in my closet?"

I was so nervous I couldn't think straight. Before I even considered making up a lie, the truth tumbled out of my mouth in a rush of words.

His only response was to raise an eyebrow and ask, "You were looking for a razor blade?"

"Yes."

He turned, and walked down the aisle toward a waist-high chest of drawers. From a narrow top drawer he pulled a sleek black razor blade and a can of shaving cream.

He crooked his finger at me. "Come here."

Still feeling embarrassed beyond belief, I sidled over to where he stood.

"Razor blade, shaving cream. Help yourself."

I stared at him for a beat, at his outstretched hands, then back at his face. Was he really going to let this go so easily?

I tried a smile but his eyes remained level and sober.

I took the proffered items and started toward the bathroom.

"Did I say you could leave?" he called, stopping me in my tracks.

Damn. Damn. Damn. "No," I said aloud.

I turned and saw, much to my dismay, he'd picked up the paddle he'd set on the top of the chest of drawers. "Come here."

I considered making a run for it but decided that would be undignified. Reluctantly, I stepped in his direction.

Whapping the paddle against his thigh again, he said in a steady voice, "In this house, Stella, there are rules. You've been here ten minutes and already you broke one. Though, I can't say I'm displeased."

"You don't think I'll let you beat me with that thing," I blurted.

"I think you're dying for me to do just that. I saw the way you were looking at it."

"I could leave."

He shrugged. "You could, but you won't. You want to be here."

Lust, overpowering and all-encompassing, raged inside of me at his words. I realized quite suddenly he could do whatever he liked to me. Knowing this should have heightened my fear, but it didn't. Instead, desire warred with common sense, and I had to force myself not to throw my body to the floor at his feet and beg him to take me right there and then.

"But I'm not a sadist," he said. The hungry way he looked at me seemed to argue against that statement. "I'll give you a choice. One, you can bend that luscious body of yours over my knee and take the twenty paddles you have coming."

"Or two," I said, helpfully.

"Agree to stay with me, here, all night."

I laughed before I could stop myself. "That's easy."

"As my personal sex toy."

That brought me up short. "Sex toy?"

"Sex slave," he clarified. "You do whatever I tell you. All night. Those are your options." Saying this, he edged past me and out of the closet. "You have five minutes to think about it. I'll wait for your answer in the bedroom. Go on and shave your legs while you think."

In the bathroom I did just that. Sitting on the counter by a sink full of water with shaving cream smoothed out over my legs, my mind raced over what I should do.

I hadn't wasted any time on contemplating leaving. Jake was right, I wanted to be there. He had also seemed to know his offer of being a sex slave or receiving a paddling would excite a desire I'd only ever contemplated in secret. As I ran his razor blade over my legs I realized there really wasn't any decision to make. I'd known what I would do as soon as he set the options before me.

I walked out of the bathroom five minutes later to find him reclining on his bed, staring into the fireplace. He'd taken his coat off and his chest seemed impossibly muscular in the dim light of the flames.

"Decided?" he asked, not looking at me.

I nodded. "I'll do the sex toy thing."

"I figured you would."

"But what all does it entail?"

"It entails whatever I want it to. But don't worry. I'll make sure you enjoy yourself. Now for the fun," he said, and got to his feet.

One moment he was resting easily against the pillows, the next he was inches from me, chest rising and falling in time with his rapid breaths. I was relieved to see he'd discarded the paddle, but a little scared when I saw the look of anticipation on .his face. More disturbing, I realized he wasn't exhaling so much as he was panting. He was breathing so fast, I worried he would hyperventilate.

"I need to see you, Stella. I need to see you naked."

"But shouldn't we talk or something first?"

"Conversation is beyond me right now. We can talk later."

"Okay." I bit my lip. "Maybe we should--"

"Take your dress off, Stella. *Please.*"

Since the dress was small it wasn't difficult to remove. It was lying in a puddle at my feet in less than a minute. The panties followed.

I felt so exposed, so laid bare standing in front of him naked. I thought I should cover myself with my hands, fold my arms over my breasts, something ... but I didn't. I stood stark still, hands at my sides and waited.

He drank me in with his eyes, took in every inch of my body, my breasts, my legs, my face, and the juncture of flesh between my thighs screamed for his attention.

"Hairless," he said with approval. "See you remembered to shave something."

My face heated and I looked away.

Abruptly, he turned and went to the bed. He began arranging the pillows. At first I didn't know what he was doing, but then I realized he'd positioned the pillows into what looked like a hill on the edge of the bed.

"Come here, Stella."

I went to him, barely able to breathe. I was so turned on.

He held me by the waist and positioned me over the pillows. I'd felt exposed before, but I was downright open to the elements now. His comforter was soft against my cheek, yet I couldn't say I was as comfortable with the placement of the rest of my body. Tail end risen in the air, I felt I should shove the pillows aside so I could lie flat on my stomach.

Then he touched my thighs and I felt the press of his erection at my opening.

Airy tingles flowed through my body.

"I've wanted you like this since the first day you came into my class," he said. "Gorgeous and at my mercy." He edged closer, ran his finger down my spine. A series of chills had me shivering. "That feel good, Stella?"

"Please Jake," I begged, "I can't wait."

"That's it, beg me for it." He shifted his hips and let his erection glide over my clitoris. The pleasure of this simple movement had me pressing my face into the mattress to staunch my cry of delight.

I thought for sure he'd ease into me then, but he didn't. Instead, he rocked his hips back, letting his cock glide over my sensitive nub a second time.

I bit into his comforter and moaned, so aroused I could

already feel an orgasm building deep inside. It pulsated and teased, lingered just beyond my reach.

His fingers pressed into the flesh of my hips as he rocked forward again, repeating the torturous movement that had so nearly undone me a second ago.

"Please, Jake. I can't take anymore teasing."

Slowly, he rocked back again, drawing the orgasm closer. "Tell me how much you want my dick inside of you."

"I do."

He pressed forward, this time accenting the torture by squeezing my nipples between his fingers. No pressing of my face into the mattress or biting the comforter could staunch the cry that erupted out of me. I writhed beneath him, struggled to rub my clit against his cock, desperate but unable to come.

"Say it," he insisted.

"I want your dick inside of me," I cried out against my arm.

"Now say it so I can hear you."

He eased back, rubbing his thumbs over my erect nipples and sending waves of erotically charged heat through my body.

"I want your dick inside of me," I screamed in frustration.

He plunged into me with one, strong thrust. Even before he started to move within me, the orgasm that had been hovering just out of my reach erupted. I screamed his name as I rode the climactic ecstasy.

He pulled back and thrust inside, fast and hard. His need to be satiated was so strong, he moved with an animalistic hunger that had desire rousing my body even before the last shudders of my orgasm dissipated.

Hands clasping my hips, fingers biting into my flesh, he drew back and sank into me again. Drew back then drove in, sure and deep. He grunted like a beast, groaning as he drew his thick length out of me. "Oh, Stella. Oh, Stella," he said, then began murmuring my name.

I couldn't talk, couldn't think. I received the most delicious coring of my life.

My fists clenched in reflex with every thrust, the comforter was soon crumpled and wrinkled within my grasp.

Without warning, he wrapped his hands around my waist

and lifted me. One moment I was kneeling on the bed in front of him, the next he'd shoved the pillows off the bed and pressed me flat on the mattress. He came down atop me, still riding me hard.

I gloried in the feel of his body on mine, and his sweat drenched chest pinning me to the mattress beneath him. Never had I felt so alive and completely filled by a man before.

He drove into me harder and I pushed against him, matching him thrust for thrust. Liquid fire oozed in my loins and snaked through my body.

He moved faster, moaned louder.

"You feel so good Jake," I managed to say. "So good. Don't stop." I let out a yelp of surprise when I felt his lips against the back of my throat, felt his tongue glide over my damp skin.

"You belong to me, Stella," he said into my ear, then licked at my earlobe. "Say it."

He ground his hips and drove deeper inside of me. "I belong to you, Jake," I agreed breathlessly.

His lips closed over my throat and he sucked hard as he quickened his pace. With every withdrawal he panted into my ear. Every possession brought me closer to the edge, approaching the precipice.

I gloried in this pleasure, in the feel of his body's demand for mine.

"Fuck me this is good," he whispered and drove in hard and deep.

Bright light danced behind my closed eyes as a second orgasm ripped through me. I bucked beneath him, writhed. I realized he was coming too when he entwined his hands with mine and squeezed.

For a moment we were frozen, pleasure too intense, too strong to overcome. We hovered on the edge of sanity, hovered, then returned to earth with matching sighs of bliss.

CHAPTER FIVE

Journal entry 1/16/05, 12:37 a.m.
"What do you want?"
I sat at the breakfast bar while he was opening cabinet doors searching for possible food items.
"What do you have?" I asked, surprised that I wasn't merely hungry but famished. It was just after midnight and I wanted to eat a four-course meal.
He stood from the cabinet he'd been perusing and gave me a smirk. "Let me show you." As he moved across the kitchen to the refrigerator I watched the muscles in his thighs flex and release. It was enough of a sight to make me feel light-headed with desire all over again.
After we roused ourselves from his bed, he'd donned a pair of loose, black jogging shorts that rode low on his hips. The simple shorts on any other man would not have been anything spectacular, but on Jake the sight was enough for my hormones go on full alert.
His chest was slick with sweat from our recent lovemaking, as was his hair. It hung in shimmering waves down his back and over his shoulders. His lips looked as though he'd rouged them deep mauve, simply the effect of kissing. Most alluring was the sight of his hipbones peeking from the low-riding shorts he wore. The man was a walking, talking advertisement for sex.
"How about pasta?" He pulled the refrigerator door open to display the inside stuffed with food. I saw celery stalks, carrots, fresh broccoli, and lettuce, but I also saw casserole dishes--presumably full of food--a whole chicken, two gallons of two percent milk, some thick red substance I supposed was a juice of some sort, and lots of other stuff.
"I didn't think a fitness guru like you would eat this much," I said, rising from the bar stool and meeting him at the door.
"I'm six-five and I weigh about two thirty. If I didn't eat this much I wouldn't make it through the day."
"Well, you're a foot taller than me and you outweigh me

by a good hundred and ten pounds. I'll be fine with a salad." I reached inside the cool interior for the bag of lettuce I spied from across the room, only to have my hand slapped. I pulled back and glared at him.

"You're gonna need a lot more than a salad to keep you going tonight. Sleep is the last thing I'm letting you do. You can sleep tomorrow after I take you home."

"So you're taking me home. So I'm not your prisoner indefinitely?"

He edged me aside with his hip and pulled one of the casserole dishes out. "We'll see how well you follow orders." He grinned at me, carrying the plate to the center island.

I trailed behind him, curious as to what he'd feed me on what was to be a marathon night of sex.

"Ravioli stuffed with smoked salmon, artichoke hearts, and crab meat," he announced.

"I'm not eating that. You know how many calories are in something like that? And never mind the cholesterol."

"What cholesterol?"

"The cholesterol in whatever sauce you made to go with it. No doubt some cheese sauce."

As I spoke, he examined the casserole dish, eyed the dishes he'd removed from the pantry, then settled on heating the entire pot. He took the casserole to the oven, set it inside, and turned it on to three hundred and fifty degrees.

"That should be about fifteen minutes," he said. "And no, I didn't make a cheese sauce. For your information the sauce is low cholesterol, lots of calories, which is exactly what I want right now."

"I want a salad."

"Too bad."

Twenty minutes later we were settled on plump sofas in the living room sharing an oversized bowl of raviolis. He'd started another fire, more to set a mood, I imagine, than for heat since the room was nice and toasty already.

"Take my robe off," he said quietly. "I love looking at your body."

"Aren't you worried we'll get sauce on your couches? They're beige, not exactly a color that'll blend well with--"

"Take the robe off or I'll take it off."

I took it off.

I laid the robe across the sofa before sitting again, unwilling to mar the cushions with sauce--or anything else.

As I got comfortable I reflected on all I'd done this week. I was more than a little shocked by my own behavior. I was actually spending the night in Jake's house. Never, ever could Katarina know about this. Never! She'd kill me.

"So what happens Monday at class?" I asked, wondering how I could ever behave casually with him again.

His fork hand paused and he lifted his head to look at me, an eyebrow raised. "I thought I'd leave a note on the bulletin board about us, letting everyone know that not only are you habitually late to class but you're also being fucked by the owner of the gym."

I gave him an eye roll. "You're crude and I'm serious."

"So am I."

I took up my fork and studied the pasta. Not only did it look good but its tangy fragrance had been torturing me since Jake brought the bowl out of the kitchen. Even though I hadn't wanted to eat it and had actually only agreed after much discussion, arguing, and debate, the delicious smelling concoction made my stomach growl in demand to be fed. While I wasn't crazy about eating such a dish so late at night, Jake was very persuasive. The sight of his erect cock and his promise of what he'd do to me after we ate didn't hurt his cause either.

"Anyone ever tell you that you're bossy?"

He nodded. "It's what women love about me."

"Is that so?"

He nodded, and then held his fork to my mouth. "Open up and say ah."

I let him place ravioli between my lips. I could feel the hot sauce glide over my tongue as the taste of smoked salmon filled my mouth. Not only did this smell good, but it tasted wonderful. "Someone's been telling you lies, honey," I said of his earlier statement.

"Really? You're saying you don't like domineering men?"

"No, I don't. I don't like anyone telling me what to do."

"Mmm," he said, placing another ravioli in my mouth. "Then what were you doing at the club?" Before I could answer he interrupted me. "I know, your girlfriend was meeting someone there. Big deal. You didn't have to go dressed in latex."

"Everyone was wearing latex there. And leather," I added.

"Yeah baby, but your dress couldn't have been more sub if you tried. Though I suppose that was the point."

I reared back as if slapped. "Sub, as in submissive?"

He grinned. "What else?"

"Screw you! I'm no sub."

"You're no Dom."

"I'm no sub. I was only in that stupid club in the first place for--"

"Katarina," he finished. "Come on. There's just the two of us. You're telling me you've never fantasized about having some man...." He stared towards the ceiling and frowned. I suppose he was searching for just the right words. "Dominate you," he finished, and then shrugged. "You'd be surprised how many women do."

I considered this for a moment.

Sure, I'd had the occasional kidnapping fantasy where some sexy, swashbuckling type came along and claimed me for his own. Then there was that police officer fantasy where I'm speeding down the highway and get pulled over by a sex god of a cop who gives me a citation that makes my toes curl. Then there were the spanking fantasies I'd harbored since I was a teenager. I still couldn't figure out what they were about. But they were all just fantasies, not things I'd ever consider doing in real life.

"Okay," I admitted. "Maybe I've had a few. But so what?"

"I saw how you were looking at those paddles in my closet. Baby doll, you have sub written all over you."

"Do not," I said petulantly.

"Admit it. I saw how excited you got in the equipment room when you got down on your knees in front of Dev. What were you hoping he'd do to you?"

"That wasn't excitement."

"It was excitement. Admit it." Jake leaned back and stared at me.

"Okay, so maybe I was a little excited. So what? It doesn't mean I'm a sub or that I want to be whipped. It just means...." I floundered for a likely explanation. "I like kneeling in front of sexy men. Maybe it's a penis thing." Ha, that sounded like a *good* explanation in my ears.

"Why don't you give it a try tonight, with me."

"The sub/Dom thing? With you? I'm not crazy, Jake, I've been in your class, remember? No way I'm letting you near me with a paddle."

"Class is one thing, this is something else. I'm an experienced Dominant. I know what I'm doing. Who better to experiment with than me?"

Jake was a Dominant...why wasn't I surprised? "I don't know. I've never done anything like you're proposing."

"You give it a try and we keep this between the two of us. Nobody else needs to know."

I gazed at the fire, uncertain of how to proceed.

"And I'll respect your limits. If you say no to something or tell me to stop, I stop. It's all about making you feel good."

It was a fantasy I'd had for a long time and Jake was gorgeous. What harm could come from experimenting? "You promise you'll stop if I say stop?"

Jake nodded. "All you have to do is say Orangutan and I'll stop."

I tried to keep a straight face but couldn't manage it. I busted out laughing. "Orangutan?"

"Yeah. It'll be our *safe* word. No chance you'll say Orangutan on accident."

"All right. Let's play."

Jake didn't move. He reclined on the sofa, forking food into his mouth. After a few seconds of silence he asked, "Did you enjoy the pasta?"

I frowned. Pasta? Thought we were having a sexy conversation here. "Yeah, it was good."

"Good. Go upstairs and wait for me in my bed. I'll be up shortly."

Rising from the sofa, I grabbed his robe and wrapped it around myself.

"You better be naked by the time I come up," he admonished.

* * * *

2:48 a.m.

I lay on my stomach, my body still humming from the pleasure of being so thoroughly satiated. If anyone had told me this morning I'd be making love to the sexiest man I'd ever seen, I would have thought them mad.

Abruptly, the bed dipped. When I glanced up I saw one

leather boot pressed into the mattress inches from my face. I yawned and stretched languorously.

"Wake up, sleeping beauty, this night's just getting started."

Crap. Guess I had fallen asleep. "Why don't you come down here and play," I purred.

"Since you're a virgin submissive I think we should do this carefully. I find role playing to be the best way of initiating a virgin submissive. It's far easier to submit if you're pretending to be someone else."

I rolled onto my back. "So who do you want me to be?"

"I don't want to get too elaborate. Let's just say that I'm a wealthy Spaniard and you're my little harem girl. I've caught you eyeing my driver with lascivious intent in your eyes and am about to punish you with twenty paddles to the ass."

"Twenty?"

"Twenty. And make sure you put up a bit of a fight. It's no fun when a sub throws herself on the floor and readily submits to my punishment. Actually, behavior like that bores me."

Put up a fight, I could do that. I could put up a really good fight if that's what he wanted. "All right. I won't go down easy."

One booted foot resting on the mattress, he stared down at me. He held the red paddle I'd been examining earlier in one hand, and he was repeatedly smacking it against his thigh as he gazed at me, an insidious smile on his face. One look at the thick bulge in his leather pants told me he was more than ready to play. "You remember the *safe* word?"

I nodded. "Orangutan."

"Good. It's play time, Stella." He crooked his finger at me. "Come here."

Time to play hard to get. I rolled away from him and out of the bed and found to my vast surprise it was rather easy to slip into character. "Hell no!" I roared.

He grinned. "You don't think you can run away from me, do you? Where you gonna go?"

"You're not beating me," I said, hoping to God he'd catch me fast.

"Who's gonna stop me?" Even as he said this he stepped onto the bed and walked across the mattress toward me, slapping the red paddle into the palm of his hand. I guessed the point was so I could hear the crack of leather meeting flesh. The sound made my poor, sensitive skin crawl. "Are you gonna stop me?"

I searched the room for someplace to hide, but came up empty. I couldn't elude him long enough to hide. He'd see where I went and simply follow.

Still playing hard to get, I asked, "Can we discuss this, sir?"

He stepped off of the bed and advanced on me. "What's to discuss? You have twenty lashes coming to you and I can't wait to give you what you deserve."

I retreated until I felt the glass of a window. I yelped at the unexpected cold against my bare back. "I said I was sorry, sir. I didn't mean anything by looking." I wrapped my arms protectively around myself and gave him my best, come hither, smile. "He was very good looking and I...." but I couldn't finish my thought. Jake was getting nearer. The *whack-whack* of the paddle sounded louder than ever.

"This won't be the last time I beat you, princess, so you might as well get used to the pain now. You'll be needing a lot sweetheart, I can tell." He closed the distance between us and reached for me.

I drew back my leg and kicked him square in the shin as hard as I could. When my bare toes came into contact with the leather boot, and more importantly, the hard bone beneath the leather, pain shot through my body like a flash of lightning.

"Yow!" I howled, grabbing my injured toes while simultaneously trying to hop away from his grasping hand.

I was well aware of how ridiculous I was, hopping around on one foot wearing nothing but a robe and a scowl, but it couldn't be helped. Jake had said I couldn't let him paddle me without putting up a fight.

"Twenty-five then. No kicking."

"You'll never take me alive!"

A second later he had me. He set his arm about my waist and lifted me off of my feet. Even though I punched and kicked him, he didn't have trouble bringing me to the foot of the bed where he'd already attached two ropes to the posts in preparation for my punishment. He must have done this after I dozed off.

"Put me down," I demanded, half-heartedly.

He set me between the posts and made ready to secure my left arm, but as soon as my feet touched the floor I spun around and decked him in the gut.

For a moment he was too stunned to react. Precious seconds ticked by as he stared at me. Seconds were all I needed to take advantage of his temporary paralysis by running to the bathroom and locking the door. It wasn't that the blow had hurt him, in truth he'd probably hardly felt it, but it had been such a surprise. I had completely caught him off guard.

I was still congratulating myself on my quick reflexes when I heard him call to me from the other side of the locked door.

"You don't think this door can stop me from coming in to get you, do you?"

My heart quickened at the sound of his voice. I'd fantasized about just this thing a million times. Still, the reality of it was proving far more stimulating than any fantasy I'd ever had.

My fantasies were often about some domineering male who was able to master me, but I had always been in complete control. I'd done all manners of things for my fantasy Dom, secure in the knowledge that he would never push me too far. I had no such control over Jake. He could do anything to me. Not only was he domineering, he was also large enough to carry out all of his intentions. Lust, need, and feminine yearning flared inside of me with such sudden and powerful force it left me stunned. I wanted Jake to paddle me and was prepared to submit to nearly any sexual desire he gave voice to. This was the realization of years of fantasy, the culmination of every wanton urge I'd ever been afraid to give voice to.

A quiet clicking sounded from behind the door. In the next instant the door swung open and Jake appeared in the opening, an evil grin splitting his face.

"I see I have my work cut out for me," he said as he stepped into the room.

"Did I tell you how much I like the candle stands in here?"

"How nice for you."

"They're very pretty. And it smells wonderful in here."

He let the paddle dangle over his shoulder and stood with his legs spread. His body completely blocked the exit.

"You know you want this. Your body is positively begging for it." He pointed to the floor directly in front of him. "If I have to come and get you, it'll go far worse for you."

I took a step back. "But sir, surely--" I screamed and hopped back another step when he suddenly came at me. There wasn't anywhere to run. The bathroom was large, but not so large that I could escape. Even if I wanted to escape.

Before he could grab me, I threw myself to the floor and wrapped my arms around the toilette.

His laughter echoed off the walls. "This! This is all you could come up with."

"You'll never take me alive."

He crouched to the floor beside me, still laughing. "What a baby," he said as he wrapped his hands around my waist and gave me a gentle tug. "Were you this much of a baby as a child?"

"Shut up!"

"Had you allowed me to do it, the entire event would have been over by now."

I clung to the porcelain, trying to find a ridge where I could ensure my grip, even as he pulled me free of the structure.

"Oh, I'm gonna beat you senseless," he promised through gritted teeth. He hurled me up and off of the floor by one arm, kicked the toilet seat down, and forced me onto my stomach over it. "You know you want this." He lowered himself until he was sitting astride my back, a move that effectively pinned me to the toilet beneath him.

I struggled to unseat him. Already I could feel his cock rising to attention.

"Let's see you run away now," he said.

Even as he spoke I felt his cock grow harder still.

Lust churned inside of me. It was a struggle not to beg him to set me on the bathroom floor and fuck me right there. He wanted to, was desperate to and I knew it. I could only imagine how I looked bent over the toilet beneath him, my ass poised between his knees.

I tried to struggle from beneath him but the effort quickly exhausted me. He didn't even have to fight me, his weight was enough. My breasts were squashed against the toilet seat and my stomach wasn't faring much better. The simple act of breathing proved to be a feat in itself. When he grabbed my arms and twisted them up and behind me so they were bent and pressed against my lower back, I decided the jig was up. Worn out, I let my body go limp beneath him.

"You will learn to obey me," he said too quietly. "Or I'll have to keep punishing you. Would you like that?"

Before I could respond he fell on me with a torrent of blows that had me screaming bloody murder. He wasn't even using the damned paddle either, he was doing it bare handed. One hand was secured about my wrists so I couldn't move my arms while the other did its evil work. The sharp pain of his hand against my rear was almost too much to be borne. When the last slap stung my buttocks he brought his hand to rest passively against my stinging flesh.

I gasped for breath. Trickles of sweat slid down my temples and I could feel long strands of my hair sticking to my face like an adhesive. I was pushed to the limit of endurance, but still, I felt a stirring between my legs.

"So then," he said cheerily, "are we ready to be a good girl?"

Before I could answer he gave my backside a pinch and I yelped in pain.

"Well?" he asked. This time though he ran a finger between my cheeks, skimming the surface of my skin until he reached my cunt. I was dripping wet with excitement.

I writhed under his touch.

"Mmm," he moaned, "I knew you'd enjoy it."

He slid a finger inside of me and I bucked beneath him. I was rocking my hips in intense pleasure as he moved his finger slowly in and out.

"I ... I didn't enjoy it, you beast."

He eased a second finger inside and I groaned.

"Beast is it?"

His weight suddenly lifted off of my body but I was too exhausted to take advantage of the reprieve and move. I was flattened like a pancake and didn't know if I'd ever move again. I let my arms, loosened from his vice-like grip, slide from their bent position at my back and hang at either side of the toilet. I had no idea what he was doing right now and I couldn't generate enough energy to care.

"Stick a fork in me," I murmured, "I'm done."

Then I screamed, tried to sit up, and collapsed back onto the toilet. The second time he dragged his tongue over my clit I bit my lip to stop the second scream from erupting from me.

"You taste like heaven," he said.

Then he entered me with the tip of his tongue. I thrust my hips toward him, desperate for release. I bucked. Had I thought myself too exhausted to move before? Well, I'd just had my second wind.

He drove his tongue inside me, slid it out, and then lapped up my moisture.

"Feel good, baby?" He asked.

"Yes."

He sucked my nub into his mouth and stroked it with his tongue.

I went positively crazy. I gasped and twisted, begged and pleaded, and nearly went out of my mind from how good it felt. Needing release, hungry for another orgasm, I moved my hips against him. When he abruptly pulled back I protested loudly.

"Like that?"

"Please don't stop."

I heard him get to his feet, and saw from the corner of my eye that he was standing behind me, hands on hips, surveying my upturned backside. I probably should have felt more self-conscious than I did, but I was too turned on to feel anything other than out of my mind horny.

"Right now there's the matter of your punishment that needs to be taken care of."

Finding sudden strength in my arms, I pushed up from the toilet seat and twisted around to face him. "Do what? What was that you just did if it wasn't punishment?" I opened my mouth again to protest further but wisely shut it before I could say anything that would add to the punishment.

He turned and started out of the bathroom. "Follow me."

He halted at the foot of the four-poster bed and stared at me, pleased to see I had followed him from the bathroom. Folding his arms over his chest, he leaned against a post. "Are you ready to do as I say or do you need another lesson in obedience?"

"I'm ready."

"Good girl. Come here."

With all of the conflicting emotions raging through my body, it took me a moment, but I managed. I walked to the spot he indicated and stood.

"Raise your arms over your head so I can bind you to the posts."

I wanted to protest. Despite my desire, everything inside me wanted to turn and flee the room, yet, I raised my arms as ordered. One by one, Jake bound my arms to the posts, securing them tight enough so I couldn't move them but not so tight as to hurt me.

"I'm not going to bind your legs, but don't think that means I won't if you prove yourself incapable of following direction. Got me?"

I gave him a quick nod.

Quietly, he stepped behind me. A second later I shivered as he ran his hands gently up and down my spine. "You're so beautiful, Stella," he whispered against my ear. "Tell me if I truly hurt you and I'll stop. No questions asked." Gently, he tangled his fingers in my hair and drew my head back until it rested on his shoulder. The kiss was long and deep. Lust flowed through me. I was so frantic to have him inside me again I thought I might faint. When he pulled away from me I did all I could do to remain standing. My legs felt like jelly.

"I've decided to go easy on you, Stella. Ten strokes," he said, then took a step back.

I flinched at the *whap* of the paddle when he slapped it against the side of his thigh.

"Any last words?" he asked.

Before I could say anything, he brought the paddle down squarely on my ass. Quickly, he followed the first strike with two more. The pain sliced into my tender flesh, so intense that I gasped for air. I couldn't breathe, couldn't even scream, couldn't do anything but writhe in my restraints and try to get away from the paddle. Unfortunately, the binds were too sure. All my squirming seemed to do was annoy him.

"Don't you dare move," he ordered, with steel in his voice. "Spread those legs and stand straight."

"Can't," I gasped when the paddle came down again.

"Oh you can. And you will or I'll keep beating you until you do."

"Please. I can't. It hurts too bad."

He stepped back and let the paddle rest at his side.

"I'm not hitting you very hard," he said. "Nothing I've done tonight will cause you any harm, but you're screaming and wailing as though I'm killing you. What a sniveling little baby you are," he said when he'd stepped closer. He grabbed a handful of my backside and squeezed. I flinched. "Isn't this what you've always wanted?"

For a moment I was breathing too heavy to answer. When I finally replied, I'm sure he had to strain to hear me because I was talking with my face pressed into the crease of my arm.

"It hurts."

"Hurts or stings?"

I considered this for a moment. He really wasn't whapping me very hard, it was more the surprise of the paddle striking my flesh than it was actual pain. "It stings."

"Of course it stings. How did you think it would feel?"

I didn't have an answer for that. Tears stung my face and my hair was a disheveled mess atop my head, however, there was a part of me, a secret part of me that had begun to come alive under the paddling. I could feel the churning of lust deep inside. I was afraid of the stinging, true, but those last few lashes hadn't been unpleasant. There was something else there, something I wanted to examine deeper.

"Do you want me to stop?" Jake was asking.

"No," I said, quicker than I would have thought myself capable.

"Good girl. Now stand up straight and don't you dare try to pull that ass away from me."

I forced myself to stand erect then braced for the coming blows. When they came I pressed my face into my arm and bit down on my bicep to staunch the screams. After two more good whacks I was screaming openly again, no longer concerned with decorum. The uppermost thought in my mind was how best to withstand this punishment. I didn't dare squirm away from the blows anymore. I'd accidentally done that one whack ago and earned myself another three.

Each time, he brought the paddle down with deadly

precision on my tender backside. Each time, I screamed for mercy. The sting was sharp, intense, and inescapable, but over time it began to take on layers. There was the burning pain as the paddle smacked hard against my skin, but there was something else just under the surface. At first I couldn't describe it, but as the blows continued I noticed how the pain, begun on my backside, resolved itself between my legs. As the paddle came down the pain was slowly being replaced with an intense pleasure I had never known. Despite the sting, my screams were accented with low moans of desire.

"Eight, nine, ten," Jake counted.

I panted between strikes, my body accustomed to the rhythm he had set. I burned with want. I'd never known such raw desire.

When he had finally reached thirteen I had indeed done a lot of begging, bargaining and pleading. My ass throbbed. I could feel a trickle of moisture tickling at my thighs as it seeped from my folds. Not only had I been beaten to within an inch of my life, I had enjoyed it. I didn't know if it had been from the beating or from the heady feel of being completely dominated by Jake. Never in my life had anyone took control of me in this manner. No man had ever done this to me before. This feeling, this submission to another, was a new sensation.

He undid my arms one by one. When I was loosed from the ropes I collapsed into his arms, panting.

He allowed this for a few delicious moments. I took the time to gaze up into his face.

His green eyes were aglow with pleasure. A thin sheen of sweat covered his face and he was smiling wickedly. All at once I was desperate for him to kiss me.

Seeming to sense my need, he bent and gave me a peck on the forehead, then settled me onto the bed. He went around to the other side and settled himself on the edge.

I weakly stood and followed.

For a moment I wondered if my limbs would be strong enough to hold my weight. Right now they felt as strong as spaghetti noodles. But once I had my full weight on them they proved sturdy enough.

"Did you enjoy that?" he asked.

"God help me, yes."

"I knew you would."

I lowered myself between his splayed thighs, breathing in the leathery scent of him and glorying in the feelings he evoked in me. The sight of him enthralled me. Then there were the tight leather pants and his cock, solid as a rock and straining against the animal skin.

I can't explain this phenomenon, it had happened earlier this week, the irresistible need to kiss his erection. Previously I quelled the desire, tonight I didn't. Before I thought to stop myself I was leaning forward on my knees. When I closed my lips around the material over his erect cock he sucked in a breath and stiffened.

The taste of leather filled my mouth, but instead of this being a turn off, it heightened my arousal. I ran my tongue over the length of him, loving the way the harsh material felt against my tongue.

It only took Jake a moment to mentally shift from spanking to sexual gratification, and when he did, I knew. He gripped the back of my head tight and repositioned so his legs were spread wide around me.

"That feels good," he said. "Don't stop."

I didn't have any intention of stopping. Instead, I stretched my lips wide in an attempt to wrap them around the full girth of him. I lapped at him hungrily, trying to fill my mouth with the slick material encasing him. All the while he massaged the back of my neck. When he began rolling his hips against my mouth I fought to maintain my sanity. I was engulfed in the scent of him, lost in the feel of having him all around me.

"Music," he said a little breathlessly.

It only took him few seconds of fumbling to find the remote control on his bedside table. After he had it he stretched his arm and pointed the remote toward the stereo. A moment later Kim Waters' "Never Leave Me" was playing. It seemed the perfect soundtrack for us.

He spread his legs wider and rocked his hips in rhythm with the music. Reaching down a moment later, he loosened his pants with one hand then pulled his engorged cock free. It bobbed in front of my face. "Suck me," he whispered. "I want to fuck your mouth."

An uneven sigh escaped his lips when I took him in and swallowed every inch.

I wanted to eat him alive, to fill myself with him. The head of his cock slid deep into the back of my throat then glided nearly free in rhythm with his thrusts. He leveled himself up with one hand, grabbed the back of my head with the other, and began pumping his hips against my mouth. "That feels so good," he said again. "Fuck me, what are you doing to me?"

I nipped him gently with my teeth then wrapped my lips around his girth, running my tongue along his length. When he set his legs over my shoulders and pulled me deep into his crotch, I sensed he was near to release. A moment later he stiffened.

"Stop Stella." He spread his legs, gripped my shoulders and forced me away from him.

"Why?"

"Get on the bed," he said in a hoarse voice.

I guess I didn't move fast enough. He reached down and scooped me up, rolled over with me in his arms so I was splayed beneath him on the bed.

"Check out the He-Man routine," I said, smiling.

He settled between my thighs and grinned back at me. "Impressive, eh?"

I'd begun to say 'very,' but the word metamorphosed into a moan of pleasure.

He eased into me with one, slow stroke.

"Oh, yeah," lips against my cheek, his voice sounded muffled when he spoke. "This is what I want." He pulled back then slid inside again, the feeling so intense he had to bite his lower lip to keep it from quivering. "Feel good?" he asked, rocking his hips against mine.

In answer I wrapped my legs tight around him and pulled him close. The feel of his body on mine, of the slick warmth of him as he glided in and out was nearly too much. I bit my own lip, gasping with every delicious thrust.

Our mating earlier tonight had been savage, carnal, but this, this was something different. Something I couldn't quite name. It was more intimate. I felt as though he were showing me a secret side to himself, letting me know that tonight was more than sex to him.

Eyes locked to his, I could feel my body turning to liquid fire beneath his touch. I reached for him, gripped him by the shoulders and ran my tongue over the hollow of his throat. I wanted to feel him everywhere, to have the taste of him on my lips and on my tongue. I couldn't get enough of him.

"You feel so good, Stella."

I tried to smile but couldn't manage. "You too."

I nipped the tender skin of his throat, swirled my tongue over his damp flesh and tasted him. He was spicy and sweet, hot and cold, and more perfect than I ever could have imagined.

He rotated his hips and plunged deeper.

"Dear God, you're killing me Jake."

"Baby, this is nothing." Easing his length slowly out of me, he paused long enough to make me want to scream in frustration. When he drove into me this time, the movement was so slick and smooth, so fierce and deep, I felt it in my belly.

I screamed. My body bucked beneath him, rocked, hungry for more of the same.

And he gave it to me.

I felt his hands close over my wrists, pinning them to the bed. He reared back then drove into me hard and fast. His hair fell in a curtain around his face, shielding him from view. When he pulled back and entered me hard and fast again, I was ready for him, meeting him with a thrust of my own.

He gave his head a shake to get his hair out of his face. "Like that, do you?"

"It feels so good."

"I bet it does." His grip on my wrists tightened even as he lowered himself atop me, pinning my body beneath his weight.

I let the heel of my foot graze his thigh, marveled at the thick bands of muscle I felt. I wanted to feel all of him, to touch all of him.

"Look at me, Stella," he said.

He was beautiful. Green eyes intent, his hair was wet and sticking to his face and his full lips were open, and they were hued a sexy cherry red.

I leaned toward him and he fell on me.

Thrusting hard, he kissed me with a hunger borne of a starving man. His tongue plundered my mouth even as his cock pummeled me into a euphoric stupor. He tasted me, nipped my lips, then sank in deep and froze.

Bright electric sparks of pleasure exploded behind my eyes. The orgasm tore through my body, making me spasm even as Jake fell atop me, groaning his own ecstasy. Wave after delicious wave rolled over me until my body felt as pliable as a bowl of Jell-O. I shuddered, moaned, nearly cried because it felt so good.

When it was over we lay still, content and thoroughly satiated as our hearts slowed and our breathing returned to normal. After a time, Jake hiked himself onto his elbows and stared down at me. "That. Was. Fucking. Amazing."

I beamed.

CHAPTER SIX

Journal entry 1/16/05, 8:34 a.m.
I am a sexual pioneer, traversing uncharted territory with the panache of Christopher Columbus sailing into the new world. Have had the most exciting night of my life, *and* Jake and I have vowed to do this again ... soon. I should very much feel like a sexual deviant. Instead, I feel like a sexual virtuoso.

What now? How do I follow up a night of mind-numbingly great sex?

I'll go home and languish in my tub for hours, reading Cosmo, sipping a mimosa, and live like the sexual pioneers who have gone before me. I won't over tax myself today since I had a very busy night.

My thighs are slightly sore and my insides feel like Jell-O. Overall, I feel like a conquering warrior.

Walking up the stairs to my home, I couldn't help smiling like a silly schoolgirl who just got a love note from the most popular boy in class.

Was there any man more perfect than Jake? Doubtless.

Would I do it all over again if given the choice? Hell yes!

I got off the stairs and headed toward my front door, recalling the decadent breakfast he'd made for me this morning, *and* served me in bed, pancakes topped with fresh fruit, whipped cream, and strawberry syrup. Somehow most of the cream had ended up on yours truly ... wonder how that happened. But Jake was very good about licking every bit of it off. Just the memory could make my toes curl. Then we put on *Fox and Friends*, curled up together, and made love. He rode me slow, kissed me tenderly, and murmured in my ear how beautiful I am.

Must call Ann and tell her everything.

Jake is awesome!!!!

CHAPTER SEVEN

Journal entry 1/18/05, 8:05 a.m.
Where the hell is Jake?
He wasn't at class today. AGAIN!
I haven't seen any news that a sexy gym owner was run over by car or truck. It would be just my luck to finally meet a perfect man and have him struck by lightning.

* * * *

7:54 p.m.
Peculiar. Jake didn't call today. I'm very worried for his safety. Hope nothing bad happened to him.

* * * *

Journal entry 1/19/05, 5:53 a.m.
Can't sleep so I've checked all the phones in the apartment. They seemed to be working fine. Cell phone appeared okay as well. Maybe telephone lines went down yesterday ... and cell phone towers ... or maybe not. Maybe he just hasn't called yet. Probably he's busy. He is a business owner.

Should I call him? No, that would seem desperate. Besides, I didn't get his home phone number. But I could get it from the gym ... maybe.

Hopefully he'll be at class today.
Can't wait to see him.

* * * *

8:07 a.m.
Where the hell is Jake!?
Is he avoiding me?
I shouldn't have stayed at his house Saturday night. He must think I'm easy or that I'm a cheap whore. Must think I'm ... shit! What if he thinks I'm a bad lay? What then? He seemed to enjoy himself but maybe he was acting. Why do it four times though if it was not enjoyable to him?
I hate men.

* * * *

4:24 p.m.
Gerard called again today. It's the fourth time he's called

me in three days. What the hell does he want? I'm in no mood to hear him whine incessantly about Ann while simultaneously trying to convince him that, no, I cannot convince her to give him another chance.

I'm in my own misery.

* * * *

8:05 p.m.

I hate men! Men suck! Men are liars! Say they'll call you but never do!

Have spoken with Ann who suggested we go to his place and relieve him of his prick. Perhaps he'll keep promises better without it.

"They're all assholes," Ann advised. "It's how they're made."

"But why are they so nice to begin with?" I complained into the phone. I was sitting in my bedroom in the dark, staring out my open windows at the lights of the city beyond. In the street below I could hear the clatter of people as they made their way through the streets, merrily going to covert meetings with their lovers no doubt. All this sex shouldn't be happening when I was suffering such hell.

I considered going out tonight, but had decided against it. Ann seemed to think a night out with the girls would make me feel better, but I had my doubts. The only thing that would definitely make me feel better right now were my hands around Jake's throat. "Why say they'll call if all they want is a one-night stand?"

"They think it's what we want to hear. I say screw 'em. Literally and figuratively." I sighed, but she continued. "You screw them before they can screw you."

"I'm not that kind of person."

"Well, hon, you better become that kind of person. Nothing appeals to a man more than a woman who doesn't want him."

I sighed again. "Like Gerard."

It was her turn to sigh. "No, not like Gerard. What you need is to attract a man you want."

"There's nothing wrong with Gerard, Ann. I don't see why you treat him so badly."

Ann grunted. "We're back together so give it a break."

"Good. You know, he's been calling me. Did something happen between you two again?"

The line went silent for a moment. "Shit, you didn't talk to him did you?"

"I haven't talked with anyone."

"It doesn't matter. What I think--"

"Has he done something to you, Ann?"

"No."

It wasn't like Ann to keep secrets from me. Then again, I'd been feeling so down in the dumps lately that she wouldn't want to burden me with her problems. "Because I'm fine, you know. If something's wrong you can tell me."

A long hissing sound spilled from the earpiece as Ann gave voice to her annoyance. "Gerard's such a little shit sometimes. I wouldn't give any credence to what he says."

"What did he say?"

Another sigh. "He claims he's seen Jake before, claims Jake is dating the singer of some Goth-rock band."

I closed my eyes against the barrage of emotions that threatened to engulf me. Shame, embarrassment, humiliation. How stupid could I have been to do all the things I'd done with a man I hardly knew? He'd played me like a fiddle. He had known just what to say and what to do to get me to fall into bed with him. How stupid could I possibly be?

"Stella?"

"I'm here. Who is she? What band? Is she blonde and blue-eyed?"

Ann hesitated. "Not exactly. Look, I'm not even sure Gerard knows what he's talking about. You know how threatened he gets by other attractive men."

"Stop blowing smoke up my ass, Ann. Tell me what he said."

"Okay, fine, but don't say I didn't warn you." She paused, seemed to consider how best to start then simply threw decorum out the window and blurted it all out. "The singer of the band isn't a she but a *he*. And he isn't a blond but a brunette. I don't think I should give you the name of the band because they've just gotten back into town this week after playing some shows in New York. Stella? You still there? Stella?"

"A man," I squeaked. "Jake is in love with a man." My voice was gradually becoming louder as I spoke, as well as more crazed, but I couldn't help it. "I've been obsessing over a homosexual. You're telling me Jake is gay?"

"Well, technically not gay. If he spent the night with you that would make him bi--"

I screeched into the phone. "I've been dumped for a man!"

Ann waited a few seconds before starting again. "Come on Stella, it was one night. Apparently he's been seeing this guy for a while."

"It was one *amazing* night."

"What you need is to get dressed and get out of that house. Put on some makeup, a nice dress and meet me for drinks at The Oak Room. Once you see yourself made up, you'll feel better. You always do. Nothing like looking good to put a smile on your face."

"Not tonight, Ann. I've just found out that my lover's in love with another man. I don't feel up to being social just now."

"Come on. I'll call the girls and we'll all meet. You need your friends more than ever right now."

"No! I don't want Katarina to know about this. She'll kill me if she finds out I slept with Jake. Jake, our gay kickboxing instructor."

"Hon, do you plan to keep going to his kickboxing class?"

I stood from my bed and went to the window to stare down at the traffic easing through the square. Everyone seemed to be having a good time tonight--but me. Wonder what Jake was doing tonight. Probably out with his Goth-rock lover having sex. The bastard.

"Stella!" Ann called into the phone. "Stop thinking about him. He doesn't deserve to have you think about him."

I groaned noncommittally into the phone.

"Get dressed. I can be at your place in fifteen minutes."

I took in my frayed jogging pants, tattered tank top and sighed yet again. True, I could change my clothes, but right now my hair was so knotted and out of control just the thought of combing it exhausted me. I simply didn't have the energy to deal with trying to look good tonight. "Maybe tomorrow," I suggested.

Ann was quiet for a moment as she considered this. "All right," she agreed. "Tomorrow. I won't take no for an answer."

"I said maybe tomorrow."

"Okay Stella, here's the deal. Tomorrow night Jake's lover's band is playing at Hammerjacks. What do you think about us heading out to have a look at him?"

"Think that would make me look desperate, like I'm stalking Jake," I whined.

"Hell no. We're there to see a show, if we happen to run into Jake and his boy toy, oh well."

"Son of a bitch."

"Fucking bastard," Ann agreed.

"I hate men."

"Me too."

"Okay I'll go. But no Katarina--"

"Yes Katarina. You're dropping the class anyway so you'll have to tell her why sooner or later."

Damn. Hadn't thought about that.

"Okay. Tomorrow."

* * * *

Journal entry 1/20/05, 3:07 a.m.

Phone seems to be working. Maybe some bizarre phone company bug where only a certain number was unable to make calls to my house has occurred. Maybe Jake has been trying desperately to reach me for days to tell me of his homosexual lover but has been prevented from doing so by the evil telephone company. Maybe I gave him the wrong number. Maybe I inverted the three and the nine. That must be it. I must track him down and fix my error.

* * * *

8:09 a.m.

I'm not explaining any error to a bastard male who thinks with his dick. I hate Jake! Jake is an idiot! Jake sucks! Jake the Jerk is no better than Paul the Prick. They're all the same.

Must go, Katarina's calling me.

Still haven't told her about Jake. I'll tell her tonight.

* * * *

9:05 p.m.

I've decided that Ann was right. I've done nothing wrong. The fault rests with Jake the Jerk, not me.

I've put on my sexiest dress. It's backless, comes to my thighs, and has a low-cut bodice. The slinky black number and my black stilettos are just what I need tonight. I've also managed to get my hair under control. No longer do I look

like Lion-O from *Thunder Cats*.
This was progress.

* * * *

10:37 p.m.
Katarina shrieked from beside me. When she had our attention she shrieked again. This time it was a name. "Trent Reznor! I love this song." She began mimicking Trent singing "Closer," trying to sound sexy and failing miserably. Somehow Katarina wasn't convincing in her vow that she'd fuck anyone like an animal. At least not half as convincing as Trent Reznor.

She gave me a push. "Come on, I have to dance to this." I gave Gerard a shove. I didn't know whether or not she truly loved this song, but I was grateful for the diversion. So far the night out with the girls had fallen flat as a means to brighten my spirits. Everyone, including Katarina, was so busy trying to soothe me that I'd ended up feeling horribly sorry for myself. On top of that, Gerard kept insisting all night that if someone had told him sooner that I was seeing Jake, he could have saved me the heartache. Still worse than this, I'd not seen any sign of Jake tonight.

I waited as Katarina pulled Ann and Meagan from the booth. None of us asked Gerard if he wanted to dance. As we jogged down the stairs to the main floor I realized I didn't want to dance with a male anyway. Men were stupid. You'd never catch a group of guys dancing together. Especially not to Nine Inch Nails. Women were so much more enlightened.

We were just hitting our stride on the dance floor when the lights in the club went dark, the stage filled with cloyingly sweet smelling fog, and screams erupted around us.

"Maverick's about to go on," Meagan said, grasping my hand. "Do you want to go back upstairs to the table or get closer?"

"Let's go upstairs," I said. "People are starting to rush the stage."

We had to push our way through the throngs of females heading down the stairs. Apparently Jake's lover was popular among the ladies. Wonder if they knew their beloved rock star preferred to play in the boy's room?

"He'll probably appear onstage dressed in tights," Ann

scoffed.

"Or a miniskirt with combat boots on," Meagan agreed.

We settled at our table. Though we were on the second floor, it was open and railed and looked down onto the first floor. From our vantage point beside the rails we could gaze down on the stage and see the members of the band far better than if we'd stayed on the main floor.

"Maverick! Maverick! Maverick!" the crowd began to chant.

I rolled my eyes. "What's his name?" I asked Gerard.

"He calls himself Cinder but his real name is Devlin."

I whirled around. "Devlin, as in Dev? Gerard you idiot, that's not Jake's lover, that's his friend. I've already met Dev."

Gerard took a swig from his glass of bourbon. "I'm telling you Stella, Cinder, also known as Devlin, also known as Dev, is Jake's boyfriend."

I didn't respond. I didn't think I had to. The thought that Jake and Dev, two of the most masculine men in Baltimore, were lovers was too ludicrous for words.

Some idiot sauntered onstage and began talking up the band by way of introduction, as if that were necessary. Already the crowd was behaving like rabid beasts.

"Maverick!" the announcer finished, one fist held aloft as he gazed triumphantly into the audience.

A moment later everything went pitch black.

The crowd went wild. Females shrieked, males howled and hooted. It was all very embarrassing.

Quietly at first, gradually building in volume, a synthesizer began playing a dissonant melody that put me in the mind of a horror movie. A moment later a throbbing, syncopated, jungle beat started from the back of the stage where I presumed the drummer was. The combination of the two was oddly erotic. Without realizing, I'd begun rocking slowly in my chair. By the time the bass player began plucking notes on his guitar, the entire crowd had begun to rock back and forth, gyrating against each other as though the music was some kind of sexual stimulant.

When the lead guitarist appeared, fingering arpeggios and moving slowly in time with the music, the dark stage began to pulse with soft blue light. I supposed we, the audience, should have been impressed that sometime after the lights had gone dark the band members--save Cinder of course--had tiptoed onstage.

Despite my annoyance at being misled by Gerard, I had to admit the music was strangely appealing. It invoked images of sex and made one want to writhe around on the floor with my legs spread wide in the manner of a cat in heat.

I jumped ten feet into the air when an explosion set the entire club ablaze in bright, orange light. Flames danced at the sides of the stage, blue lights burst into flashing strobes of white light.

A tall figure, garbed in black, seemed to materialize center stage. The figure didn't move, didn't acknowledge the adoration of his fans, he stood still as a statue staring sullenly out at the audience. Just when I'd begun to think Cinder was a no-show and the members of Maverick had set some dummy onstage to take his place, the figure spread his legs and arms wide and trilled some inhumanly high note into the microphone.

A group of frenzied Maverick fans rushed the stage.

The stage lights rolled across the stage and focused on Cinder, giving me my first true view of him.

I stared, transfixed. The man on the stage was indescribably sexy. He wore leather pants and a loose net shirt that hung low on his wrists. Where Jake was tan, this man was pale. His brown hair hung to his shoulders in unruly waves.

He was gorgeous. He was Dev. This *was* the man I'd met at Fit For Life. Still, the fact that Dev was onstage didn't mean he was Jake's lover.

When he lifted the mic to his mouth and began to sing, a thousand monkeys having sex on the floor at my feet couldn't have torn my attention away from him.

I watched the show in a daze I would happily fall at that man's feet and offer myself to him. In the manner of a cat in heat.

I couldn't hear the conversations going on around me, couldn't see anything save the man on the stage. I felt mesmerized, transfixed. Bamboozled.

When he sang the final notes of their last song and disappeared from the stage a pang of regret drew me to my feet to stare over the railing, hoping to catch another glimpse.

"Stella?" I felt someone tugging on the seam of my dress. "He's gone. The bastard," they added loyally. I didn't have to look at the speaker to know it was Ann.

Quietly, I returned to my seat.

After I'd sufficiently collected myself, I studied my friends. "Did that man look gay to you?" I asked.

"Honestly?" Meagan wanted to know.

I nodded.

"That could be the sexiest man I've ever seen. No way he's gay."

"He's gay," Gerard insisted.

"No way."

"I'm telling you guys, he's gay."

"I don't know, Gerard," I said. "He flirted with me at the gym, told me I was beautiful."

"Well he is gay."

I wasn't convinced Gerard knew what he was talking about. The entire time Maverick had been onstage, Dev had flirted shamelessly with every female in sight. There was no way he was gay.

"Someone wanna come with me to get a drink?" Katarina asked.

I didn't answer because I was lost in my thoughts. Dev not being gay brought up a more disturbing explanation for Jake's defection. If Jake wasn't gay and in love with Dev that meant the reason why he hadn't called had to do with me. He simply didn't like me. Wasn't interested in me. What we shared had been a one-night thing for him, nothing more.

I didn't know which was worse, being dumped for a man or being dumped out of disinterest.

"Stella, come with me to get a drink."

I looked up to see Katarina was staring at me. Absently, I nodded and rose.

As we descended the stairs and made our way to the bar Katarina chattered about how much she enjoyed the show and how surprised she was by this.

"That Cinder guy is sexy. I don't know, Stella, if I was a guy I'd be tempted by Cinder too. That is if Jake is actually gay."

As the bartender made her drink Katarina informed me of the many fine attributes she'd spied on Cinder, namely the impressive bulge in his pants. "They're good," she said, sipping her drink as I waited for my own. "I don't know if I'd believe Gerard if I were you. Besides, if Cinder was Jake's lover, wouldn't Jake be here tonight?"

"He is," I said.

And he was. I'd just spotted him standing in the hallway near the backstage door. There was a small crowd gathered in front of the hallway where he was standing. I hadn't seen him at first, but he stood a full head taller than most people.

Katarina twisted around and stared in the direction I indicated.

"Crap, I think you're right," she decided.

Suddenly an all-encompassing rage seared me. Blind with fury, I shoved away from the bar and pushed my way through the crowd toward him. I could hear Katarina's voice, almost as one hears background noise when watching a movie, calling for me to stop. I continued forward, shoving through the bodies that blocked me from my destination.

As I neared the backstage door, it opened and the beautiful man I'd just seen onstage twenty minutes earlier, stepped halfway out of the door. I figured it was lucky for him that most of the people in the club were too busy dancing and drinking to look this way. Had any of Cinder's rabid fans realized how close he was, they would've charged him for sure.

As I watched, Jake moved to the door, leaned in and whispered something into Dev's/Cinder's ear.

Who knew Jake was such a funny man? Whatever he'd said had Dev reeling back a step and throwing his head back with laughter.

In and of itself, this scene wouldn't have meant anything. At least it wouldn't have meant anything if Dev hadn't stepped further into the hall, looped a finger in the waistband of Jake's pants, and pulled him close. The kiss was slow and hungry, so hot it scorched me from ten feet away.

It was true. Gerard hadn't been telling stories. Jake was gay.

I closed the distance between us, murder on my mind. When I was scarcely a foot away from him Jake didn't have a clue that I was standing there. It was Dev who finally noticed me, Dev who pulled away from Jake and focused his attention on me. He tilted his head to the side when he saw me, gave me a cocky sort of grin and raised a brow in question. "Ah, it's you."

Jake, who suddenly realized he wasn't alone with his lover, turned to see what had caught Dev's attention. He stiffened when he saw me, and then had the audacity to smile.

Powered by rage, given courage by my fury, I stepped closer to him, close enough to smell the apple-scented shampoo he used.

"Dev," Jake began, "you remember Stella--" was all he got out because at that precise moment I drew back and landed my knee as hard as I could into his crotch.

His eyes bulged; he stiffened, then slowly descended to the floor.

"Bastard!" I finished.

I'd half expected Dev, the faithful lover, to retaliate. But he didn't. When I twisted around to meet his gaze I was surprised to see he was smiling. Not laughing, but he did seem amused. "Good for you," he said.

I turned then, common sense returning in a rush, grabbed Katarina--who seemed frozen with shock--and fled. I ran for the exit with Katarina close on my heels. I figured we could call the others from the car and let them know we were ready to leave. Jake was a large man, after all. There was no telling what he'd do once he found his feet again. I'd been on the receiving end of his punishment and figured I was a good judge. The best move I could make was getting the hell out of Dodge.

CHAPTER EIGHT

Journal entry 1/21/05, 1:36 p.m.
Jake called again. I presume he believes that if he calls me enough I'll get tired of hearing his stupid messages and pick up. I won't though. I don't want to hear his excuses and stupid explanations.
The bastard.

* * * *

Journal entry 1/23/05, 8:07 p.m.
I simply can't face Jake, not over the phone or in person. I haven't been back to class since the night I saw him with Dev. The entire Jake experience is simply too humiliating for words. I'm never, never, never, going to do anything that stupid again.
Next month will be better. As long as I keep my distance from men.
Men suck!

CHAPTER NINE

Journal entry 2/1/05, 8:14 p.m.
I miss Jake.
Scratch that. I hate Jake.
Jake is an arrogant ass.
But I miss him.
Argh!
It's all over between us and has been for a week. Ann says it's unhealthy to obsess over a man I only spent one night with, and I know she's right, but it was one amazing night.

He stopped calling last week, but I can't say I'm pleased. Guess he got tired of talking to the answering machine.

You tell me. Is finding out your lover is gay grounds enough for refusing to see him again? Wait. Don't answer. Not only is Jake gay ... bisexual, but his lover could very well be the sexiest man to ever walk the earth. Could I fault Jake for loving a man I found irresistible and sexy as hell?

There's the phone. Gotta run. I'm supposed to be meeting the girls at The Oak Room in about ... *Argh!* I was supposed to be there ten minutes ago.

* * * *

10:32 p.m.
"What you need is to go out with someone else, Ann." Meagan lifted her wine glass and held it poised for a toast. For a moment, firelight danced across the shiny surface and reflected a rosy tinge onto her café au lait skin. Her golden brown curls fell in waves over her shoulders. "To new beginnings," she said when Ann and I hefted our drinks.

We sat at our favorite table in The Oak Room having cocktails, something we did often. There was a blazing fire in the hearth a few feet from the end of our table, and the glow of soft red light overhead, casting a welcoming ambiance over the lounge. The lulling sound of the conversations going on around us blended into the background with the smooth jazz of George Benson, crooning to us from speakers positioned around the room. The Oak Room was like a second home to us. Of late, however, our usual group had dwindled to a threesome--Meagan, Ann, and myself. Occasionally, Ann's on again, off again boyfriend, Gerard--the current object of derision--made an appearance. Katarina was a no-show more times than not these days.

Our bitch-fests simply weren't the same without Katarina's voice of reason to console and calm us. Without Katarina's reassuring presence, our nights became a series of one bitch-fest after another.

"Fuck new beginnings," Ann slurred, obviously feeling the affect of drinking four glasses of wine in an hour. "And where the hell is Katarina? She said she'd be here."

Meagan shrugged, and then took a sip from her glass. "Don't ask me. As far as I know, she's still coming."

"It's that damn Jim, again. I just know it."

"Maybe you shouldn't have anymore to drink, Ann."

Ann rounded on Meagan, eyebrows furrowed. "What you talking 'bout, Meagan?" Ann said, and then exploded with laughter.

The Gary Coleman impersonation had been funny the first time she'd done it, mildly amusing the second and third time, but the joke had gone stale by the fourth. I love Ann, but when she drinks, she's an absolute menace.

Still grinning, she took another swallow of wine. "See there. I'm perfectly fine." As if to mock her words, Ann's brown hair flared wildly about her shoulders. Her neat, semi-bang had sometime in the night decided to stand on end. With her eyes rimmed in red and her usually smooth skin blotchy and pale, Ann looked anything but fine. "Who does she think she is anyway?" Ann continued, clearly warming to her theme. "Ditching us for that damn Jim. I'd never ditch you guys for a man."

"That's 'cause you don't have a man," I offered, then mentally kicked myself.

Ann narrowed her eyes at me. "Fucker."

Meagan gave up any effort of toasting to new beginnings and glared in my direction.

I sighed. "I'm sorry, Ann. I keep forgetting."

"Fucker!" Ann said again.

Had I thought she was referring to me I might have been offended. Since I knew Gerard was the fucker in question, I took no offense.

"It won't last," I said.

"What does he see in her?" Ann wanted to know.

"It won't last."

"How could he have done this to me? I hate Gerard ... and I love him. But I hate him more."

Meagan and I exchanged looks over the table. Ann had been like this since Gerard broke up with her a week ago and announced he was seeing someone else.

Seeming at a loss for what else she could do to soothe Ann, Meagan placed her arm over Ann's shoulder and gave her a squeeze. "It's his loss, babe."

"I love him," Ann blubbered again.

This was one of the annoying things about having three best friends. There I was wounded from the Jake fiasco, and I had nobody to listen to me whine about my broken heart. I was in need of some serious comfort. Meanwhile, all Ann wanted to do was talk about *her* problems. She had been going on and on about Gerard for a good forty minutes. Okay, so Ann and Gerard had been together a lot longer than Jake and me, but at least Gerard ditched Ann for a *woman*. Besides, if Gerard hadn't dumped Ann she would have dumped him. It's what Ann did and what Gerard expected. He simply beat her to the punch this time.

"I'm tired of talking about Gerard," Ann declared. "Let's talk about Katarina and how this is the third time she's ditched us for that damn Jim."

This seemed to animate Meagan. "He's not even all that cute."

"He obviously makes Katarina happy," I said, hoping to bring the conversation around to me.

"Who cares?" Ann said. "He doesn't make us happy. Least she could do is pick a man we like."

"I like Jim."

"Speak of the devil." Meagan eased forward on the sofa and gestured toward the door.

I had to twist around on my seat to see who she was talking about.

Arms interlocked as though their lives depended on it, Katarina and Jim strolled into The Oak Room. Tonight she had let her blonde locks fall loose down her back, a look Jim preferred.

"They look like friggin' Siamese twins," Ann complained. "You think they're attached at the hip, or is that the way they walk now?"

With their matching heads of blonde hair, lithe figures, and pale complexions, they kind of looked related. "At least she didn't ditch us again," I said.

"She didn't have to bring him. I can't believe she brought him."

I nearly pointed out that Gerard often came to our "girls' night out" get-togethers, but managed to stall the words before they slipped off my tongue.

"Be nice," I said in a low voice before Katarina and Jim reached our table.

In stark contrast to my admonition, Ann rocked forward on the sofa and glowered at Katarina as soon as she reached our table. "How very nice of you to join us," she slurred. "We've only been waiting two hours."

Knowing the signs, Katarina smiled at Ann as she settled on the sofa next to me. "They broke up again?" she whispered into my ear while simultaneously prodding me with a hip to move over and make room for Jim.

"Gerard broke up with her this time," I confided.

Katarina raised her brows at this and pursed her lips. "I'm sorry I'm late," she said to everyone at the table. "Jim and I had to stop by his parent's house to--"

"I don't care," Ann interrupted. "I'm having a nervous breakdown."

For the next thirty minutes we all listened while Ann described, in detail, all of Gerard's bad qualities. When Katarina finally broke in to change the subject I was happy, until I realized her topic of choice was Jake and his refusal to stop billing her for her gym membership, even though she'd cancelled it.

In retrospect, Katarina's idea that we could meet our future husband's by joining Baltimore's most popular gym seemed extremely ridiculous. Even if I hadn't slept with Jake, I probably wouldn't have met anyone I would want to marry. As it was, Jake was the only man I'd been remotely interested in. Though, that probably wasn't accurate. When Jake was in a room, other men ceased to exist.

As far as Katarina and Jim--who met at the gym--we'd have to see how long their relationship lasted.

"He won't stop billing me," Katarina complained.

"Did he actually say he wouldn't stop billing you?"

"Yes. I finally got him on the phone today."

I got a bill too, but I hadn't called the gym myself, yet. I'd been procrastinating, too afraid I'd get Jake and be stuck having an awkward conversation with him. But maybe I should call anyway. Membership at Fit For Life wasn't cheap.

"Don't even think about it," Meagan said, pulling me from my thoughts.

I looked up to see that everyone was staring at me. "What?"

"You're not calling that man. You're just looking for an excuse to talk to him."

I shook my head and proceeded to lie through my teeth. "If I wanted to talk with Jake I would have done it all those times he called me." In reality, the only reason I hadn't picked up the phone when he called was because my ego was bruised.

"Let Katarina handle this."

"I can't," Katarina said, "I've tried but he won't budge."

"See," I said. "And I might not have to deal to Jake. I'll go to the general manager and see if he'll help me."

Already a plan was forming in my mind. I'd go to the gym tomorrow and see what was going on.

CHAPTER TEN

Journal entry 2/2/05, 6:57 a.m.

I don't know what it is about having people stay overnight that makes me go all domestic. I simply don't understand this phenomenon. Nevertheless, there I was, hot pink apron tied over my Tom and Jerry PJ's, flipping pancakes and frying sausages. It wasn't even seven yet and already I had a pot of French vanilla coffee brewed. *Fox and Friends* was on the television, the kitchen and family room were filled with the homey scent of coffee and food, and I was feeling no pain. It was uncanny.

"I feel like shit."

I whirled around and gave Ann a bright smile. "Pretty much how you look. Bet you wish you'd listened to me now."

Shuffling to the breakfast bar, she collapsed onto a stool and moaned. "Why didn't you stop me from doing those tequila shots?"

"I tried."

"Not hard enough. My head feels like a train … like two trains are racing around inside."

I piled two fluffy pancakes and two sausages onto a plate and carried it to her. "You'll feel better after you eat."

She frowned at the offering. "I cannot eat sausages. But I think I could do with some pancakes. Any tea?"

"How about coffee? I brewed a pot for us."

Ann paled. "I couldn't stomach coffee. Just give me some tea if you have it."

I filled the teakettle with water and placed it on the stove, turning the temperature to high.

"So what's the plan for today?" Ann asked after I set a steaming mug of chamomile before her.

"Dr. Chester Taylor is coming at eight thirty to have a resume and cover letter done. It's a rush job, he needs it done in a week, so we'll make a nice chunk of change off him. After that I'm going to Fit For Life to see about getting the gym billing stopped."

"Her name is Candace and she works at Chevy Chase Bank. In Laurel."

I'd settled at the breakfast bar beside Ann, poised to eat. At her words I looked up from my plate and stared at her. "Gerard's new girlfriend, I presume."

She nodded. "I just wanna see her. Just once."

"It won't do you any good."

"I have to see her, Stella."

"Why. You wanna torture yourself?"

"Hey, when you wanted to see Devlin, a.k.a. Cinder, I was right there beside you."

I sighed. Of course she was right. But somehow seeing my lover's boyfriend and Ann seeing her ex-boyfriend's new girlfriend didn't seem quite the same.

It hurt knowing the man I'd been hoping to start a relationship with was in love with another man while he was sleeping with me. But I sort of preferred Jake being in love with a man instead of a woman. This way it wasn't a slight against me. Jake may sleep with women from time to time, however he'd chosen to share his life with a man.

I nodded. "Okay. We'll go after my eight-thirty leaves. But I have no idea what you're gonna do once we get there."

"I only want to see her. Just once."

* * * *

9:40 a.m.

"You mentioned dive certifications earlier," I said to the attractive man opposite my desk in my home office. "Can you name them for me now?"

He gave me a slow smile, as though I'd offered him my body on a silver platter instead of asking for his certifications. I should have been offended, but I wasn't. He'd been flirting with me for the last hour and I was enjoying the hell out of it.

Dr. Chester Taylor was a good-looking man. A *very* good-looking man. Not at all what I'd expected. While he wasn't drop dead gorgeous like Jake, he was pretty damn close. Dressed in gray slacks that hugged his long, muscular legs, and a black ribbed turtleneck sweater, which offset his tan skin, the doctor was an incredibly sexy man. His hair was sun bleached blond, something I knew since he'd just arrived in Maryland from a diving trip in Hawaii. He had the kind of California good looks that would make him stand out in any crowd.

Still grinning at me, Chester said, "PADI Basic Open Water Scuba Diving, June 1999. PADI Advanced Open Water Scuba Diving, July 2000. PADI Rescue Diver, August 2000...."

As he spoke, I typed his information into the Client Information Form on my desktop computer. "Was it the love of history, water, or adventure?" I asked when he finished, surprising myself by giving voice to what I'd been wondering from the moment this man started talking about himself.

"Diving?" he asked, arching one bushy brow in question.

I nodded.

He eased back in the chair and crossed his legs, an ankle over one knee. With my desk between us I couldn't see the actual movement of his legs, but I could see his knee come into view when he began to bob it up and down.

"Why do you ask?"

"Nautical archaeology. You sound like an underwater Indiana Jones. It sounds dangerous ... and exciting," I finished, hoping desperately he hadn't heard the Indiana Jones comment. Dear God, why couldn't I shut myself up before stupid things like that slipped out?

"All of the above," he said with a shrug. "And I love animals. All kinds. Grew up on a farm so I've always had them around me." He paused to lick his bottom lip. "Cats, dogs, cows, pigs, horses, chickens, you name it. Even tried to tame a deer once when I was twelve." He shook his head and laughed. "Don't have to tell you what a disaster that was."

"The deer didn't fancy the idea of being your pet?"

"Not one bit. See, I was twelve but I'd done some roping before. Mostly calves, so I thought I could do the same with a deer. They have those big eyes and gentle faces. They seem harmless."

The image of an over eager, twelve-year-old, Dr. Taylor trying to rope a deer had me chuckling. "Doesn't sound like a very good idea to me."

"Well see, you're a city girl. You'd be afraid to rope a calf. When you grow up in the country your view of animals is different. Not so much fear as respect."

Damn! Even as he spoke I could feel it happening. All the signs were there. Throbbing loins, a fluttering heart, and a ridiculous need to tilt my head to the left and sigh every time he did something I thought was cute. I tried to remind myself that I was taking a vacation from men. A long vacation, but somehow my mind couldn't compute the information.

Damn it to hell, I was falling in lust with Dr. Taylor ... my client.

I'd learned nothing from the Jake fiasco. Apparently I was still a glutton for punishment.

I was unstoppable and uncontrollable!

"As far as that deer goes," the doctor continued, "I never got a chance to use the rope I'd carried with me into the forest. Soon as I got within twenty feet, the damn thing charged me. I nearly cracked a rib trying to get away from it."

I swallowed hard, smiled, then crossed my hands and settled them on my desk. This was my professional pose, my "let's get down to business" pose. "Okay," I said in my, "let's get down to business" voice. "We've covered professional background, education, licenses, certifications, special skills, memberships, awards, publications, speaking engagements, references, and your objective. Is there anything else you'd like to add?"

"Well Ms. Rice, I really like the idea of taking you out sometime."

I had to bite my inner cheek hard to keep from smiling. At that moment I knew I wasn't supposed to be with Dr. Taylor as Stella Rice, the woman. At every client consultation I was there as a representative of AIR, and as such, it was my responsibility to keep this meeting professional. Least that's what I always told Ann anytime I found her flirting with a client. It had always seemed like a reasonable request when I advised Ann. However, at the moment, keeping things on a professional level didn't seem all that important or reasonable. After all, I could still do a kick-ass resume and cover letter for Dr. Taylor even if I went on a date with him. One date wouldn't ruin my level of professionalism. I supposed it wouldn't ruin Ann's either.

"Is that so?" I asked, trying to sound nonchalant, as

though California type heartthrobs always tried to pick me up.

"That's so," he agreed. "What do you say?"

For reasons I couldn't explain, I thought of Jake. We weren't together and hadn't shared anything but one night of great sex. Jake was a non-issue. Still, by going out with another man I felt that I was permanently closing the door on any possible reconciliation.

"You don't date white men?" he asked, mistaking my silence for a refusal.

"No, it's not that," I began to say.

"You aren't seeing anyone else are you?"

Damn if his Southern drawl wasn't the cutest thing I'd ever heard. This man was downright lethal. He had "golden boy" good looks with a down to earth, Southern charm that had me near to drooling.

"No, I'm not seeing anyone. But I don't date clients. It's one of my rules."

"Haven't you ever heard that rules were made to be broken?"

"I'm not a rule breaker." I pushed back from my desk and got to my feet, determined to end this meeting before I did something stupid. Or, God forbid, said anything more idiotic than the Indiana Jones comment.

"Sorry to hear that," he said, rising as well. "You've got the prettiest brown eyes I've ever seen. But just now they look like that deer's eyes; wide and spooked. So I'll back off, but I want you to promise me you'll think about it."

"Think about what?"

We both turned as Ann strolled into the office.

AIR's office was housed in what was supposed to be my den. The room was large enough for two desks--set at opposite ends of the room--two client chairs, and a bookcase. Clinging to her third cup of tea, Ann moved behind her desk and sat. Though she hated the formality, especially on days like today when she wasn't feeling good, she had gone into my closet and put on a blue and red pantsuit. With her short, chestnut hair pulled back and held in place by a clip at her nape and the bit of makeup she'd put on, she looked almost human again. I could barely tell she was suffering the results of an all night drinking binge.

"Going out with me," Dr. Taylor explained before I could

maneuver him out the door.

Ann depressed a button on her CPU and the motor whirred to life. She looked at me, at the good doctor, then back at me. "A date?"

"Yes," he said at the same time I was saying no.

"I think it sounds like a good idea."

"Nobody asked you," I informed my turncoat of a friend.

Ann let loose with a snort. "The rule?"

Dr. Taylor nodded. "Good to know it isn't just me."

"Oh no, it's not." Ann assured him. "Stella's a stickler for rules. I think she has a rule for everything. When to wake up, when to eat, when to take a sh--"

"In any case," I interrupted. I placed my hand gently, but insistently on his lower back, leading him out of the office and toward my front door. "You said you need your resume in a week. I'll have it and your cover letter done by Monday. You can pick it up Monday morning. What time is good for you?"

Though he allowed me to propel him forward, he came to a halt in the foyer. Turning, he smiled down at me.

My heart skipped and I took a step back.

This man was more than lethal. He was positively toxic.

He set his hands on his hips and shook his head. I was amazed that such a simple movement could look so sexy.

"Think about it," he said, then pulled my front door open, stepped into the hall and turned to face me again. "You can tell me Monday morning at eight-thirty five, five minutes after you give me my new resume and cover letter and I pay you the remainder of your fee. Deal?"

I considered arguing the point but figured the quickest way to get rid of him was to agree. "Agreed," I said.

"Because five minutes after you give me my new resume and cover letter," he continued, "I won't be a client anymore."

I smiled. "Touché."

"See you Monday." That said, he turned and walked away.

I had to force myself to not peek into the hall and watch his progress. Instead, I shut the door, locked it, and went in search of Ann.

CHAPTER ELEVEN

5:47 p.m.
Why! Why! Why!
Why do I get myself into these stupid situations? Better question, why do I surround myself with loonies? All of my friends belong in loony bins. And I belong in a loony bin for associating with them.

"I just want to see her, Stella," Ann had explained. "I just want to see if she's better looking than me." And I was fool enough to believe her.

Mistake 1. Agreeing to go to Laurel to have a look at Gerard's new girlfriend.
Mistake 2. Not having a car of my own for this little expedition.
Mistake 3. Agreeing to get into a car with Ann behind the wheel.

So there I was, sitting innocently in the passenger's seat of Ann's monster SUV, wondering how bad the twenty-five mile drive back to Baltimore from Laurel would be during rush hour while Ann the nut pulled into the Chevy Chase Bank parking lot.

Okay, the first sign of trouble was the fact that the bank wasn't the sort of bank I'd been expecting. I had envisioned something with cash machines, drive-through banking, and an interior filled with tellers who doled out cash to customers. What I got was a one-story brick building, sans the usual bank paraphernalia, and two security trucks sitting in front of the main lobby. This wasn't a customer service bank; this was the bank's corporate office.

I stared out my window, a niggling of dread forming in the pit of my stomach. "We can't go in there, Ann."

"I know, but it's almost four thirty."

The dread grew. Nevertheless, I asked, "What happens at four-thirty?"

"She gets off work. All we have to do is drive around the

parking lot until we find her car, and wait."

I began gesturing out the window at the security trucks. "Drive around the parking lot? We can't drive around the parking lot. This place has security guards."

"Big deal. For all they know we have business here. We could be perspective employees looking for a job." She gave me a wink, a gesture clearly meant to calm me.

It didn't.

"Promise me all you want to do is look."

She raised her right hand in the air, an unmistakable sign of good faith, and proceeded to lie through her teeth. "I promise Stella," she said. "All I want is a look. There's her car. The red Jetta."

I didn't ask how she knew what Candace drove. I didn't want to know.

Five minutes later, when Ann looked solemnly at me and said, "If something bad happens, you got my back, right?" I knew I was in trouble.

I stared for a moment, unable to respond.

"Right?" she repeated.

"What could happen?"

Ann shrugged. "I don't know. Probably nothing. I'm just asking if something were to happen, you got my back."

I suddenly felt like I was in high school again, a period of my life you couldn't pay me to repeat. There were so many things I hated about high school I hardly knew where to start. But if I *had* to pick a starting point I'd say it was those days I went in knowing sometime during the day I'd be forced to fight because somebody did something to upset one of my friends. The other girl's friends would inevitably get involved which, of course, meant my girlfriends and I had to get involved. Threats would be bandied about for the better part of the day, there'd be much trash talk and posturing--I would be doing more than my share of both--while all the time I was silently praying nothing would happen.

I hated fighting. I *loathed* fighting. I simply wasn't very good at it and didn't fancy the idea of finding myself in a parking lot brawl at the age of thirty.

I supposed this was part of friendship, watching your girlfriend's back no matter how much of a nut she acted.

"Of course I have your back. That doesn't mean you

should start a fight with this girl, Ann."

Ann snorted. "I'm a grown woman, Stella. This isn't high school. I don't start fights."

The sigh of relief had barely escaped my lips when, from the corner of my eye, I saw Ann throw herself at her horn. The loud *honk* seemed to echo for seconds after Ann pulled back.

"What the hell are you doing?"

"That one there." Ann pointed toward a statuesque blonde who'd been about to step into the Jetta. Her hair was long, swept away from her face and held in place by a pink clip. The clip was the perfect match of her high-heeled pumps and floral dress.

She was very pretty. In fact, she seemed perfect. Not a hair out of place, not a stitch of clothing rumpled. This girl was, in a word, the "Anti-Ann."

Along with the other people who'd exited the building, this woman turned to see where the noise had come from.

Ann waved a hand at Gerard's new girlfriend, a bright smile affixed to her face. "Come here," she pronounced carefully, so the girl could read her lips.

"What the hell are you doing, Ann?"

"Shh." Ann said.

The woman looked around for a moment, unsure of what to do. But when Ann waved again, motioning for her to come over, the blonde seemed to come to a decision.

Cautiously, she started for the truck. When she got to Ann's open window, Ann offered her a shake. The bright smile remained in place.

"I'm Beverly," Ann said.

I groaned. Whatever was about to happen, I was sure I wouldn't like it.

"Candace," the girl said, clasping Ann's hand and shaking it.

"I'm sorry about this," Ann began, "but I figured you should know."

"Know what?" Candace asked.

"I'm Gerard's ex." Ann waited for a reaction. When none came she continued. "I broke up with Gerard last month because he gave me chlamydia."

Candace, who'd been leaning into the car, abruptly straightened and took a step back. "What did you say?"

Ann nodded. "The bastard didn't say a word about having it."

Candace's mouth opened, shut, and then opened again. "Who are you?"

"We were dating seven months before I found out. Anyway, I thought you should know."

"Gerard hasn't said anything about having a health condition."

Ann gave Candace a condescending smile. "He goes to the block," Ann said of Baltimore's sex district, "and sleeps with strippers. He did it the entire seven months we were together. The bastard only admitted it to me when I confronted him about the chlamydia."

"Gerard's not like that."

"I doubt he's changed."

"I don't believe you."

Ann shrugged. "I just thought you should know. Don't want what happened to me to happen to you. Wish somebody had told me about it before I slept with him." Ann paused, gasped, and clutched her throat. "You haven't slept with him, have you?"

Obviously dazed by this encounter, Candace shook her head no and took another step away from the truck.

"Good. Don't." Ann smiled. "Have a nice day." Mission accomplished, Ann put the car in drive, gave Candace enough time to take another step back, then pulled out of the parking spot.

For a long time I didn't say anything. I stared at Ann as she maneuvered the truck through the stop and go traffic on I-95 and would have remained silent had I not seen the slight quiver of her lips when she was pulling onto Pratt Street. "She's gorgeous," Ann finally said.

"So are you."

Ann snorted. "She's perfect though. Like something out of a movie. No way Gerard's breaking up with her."

A lone tear slid down Ann's cheek and plopped onto her shoulder.

"Why don't you stay at my place again tonight. We'll watch movies, eat junk food, and stay up all night."

Sniffling, she nodded. "I'll swing by my place and pick up some clothes." She paused. "I hate feeling like this. I absolutely hate it."

CHAPTER TWELVE

Journal entry 2/4/05, 7:45 p.m.

I've spent the last two days avoiding the phone. Katarina has called a bazillion times about Fit For Life. I know I was supposed to go there on Wednesday, but I didn't get a chance.

After leaving the bank in Laurel and seeing Candace up close for the first time, Ann was devastated. "Why did she have to be so pretty?" She'd wanted to know. And, "Why did she have to drive a Jetta while I drive a man truck? Why did she have to have such perfect hair and such a perfect body?"

I'd spent most of the night commiserating and trying to comfort Ann. When the task seemed too much for me I'd called in reinforcements. Katarina and Meagan arrived on the scene with a stack of DVDs, ice cream, and munchies. Though the movies had helped distract Ann for a while, they weren't enough to get her feeling like her old self again.

Today I've been dodging calls from Katarina and, surprise of surprises, Gerard. He wants to know why I let Ann tell Candace he slept with strippers and had STD's. I didn't have an answer for Gerard so I let him talk to my machine.

In any case, I'm too mentally exhausted to even consider going to Fit For Life today.

Maybe tomorrow.

* * * *

Journal entry 2/6/05, 4:57 p.m.

Had I really thought Jake had it in him to be reasonable? Had I forgotten how persuasive he could be? Yes and yes!

Purposely, I waited until two in the afternoon to go to the gym. My hope was that by waiting I'd prevent a run-in with Jake. I knew from experience that on a typical day, Jake showed up at five in the morning and was gone for the day by one. I left an extra hour in there for safety's sake, figuring that by two he'd be long gone.

At two p.m. sharp I sauntered through the lobby of Fit For

Life, headed to the front desk, and asked to see the manager on duty.

The guy behind the counter, a mega-sized man, gave me a gap-toothed grin and attempted to arch a brow. It was probably then that I should've turned tail and fled. Clearly this man knew who I was. I didn't flee though. Instead, I scolded myself for being paranoid and made myself remain calm and impassive. I could handle this. I'd come prepared. I was dressed in a severe, black on black business suit, designer pumps, and showing just enough leg to titillate and tease. Decades earlier, women had mastered the art of looking professional and aloof while maintaining an in-your-face sex appeal. All women knew how off kilter this made a man, and I wasn't above using this look to my advantage.

My confidence lasted for about five seconds. The act crumpled as soon as Mega-Man said, "Ms. Rice, Jake is waiting for you. He said to bring you to his office when you got here."

My mouth fell open.

"This way." Mega-Man stepped from behind the counter and walked through the archway that led into the gym. He'd gone a good twenty feet before he'd realized I was still in the lobby. He paused, turned to look at me, and gave another go at raising his brow. "Coming?"

I considered the question then nearly told him no. I thought better of it, reasoning that sooner or later I'd have to face Jake. Baltimore wasn't the largest city in the world, and we were likely to come across one another in a restaurant or lounge one day. Either I turned tail and ran away from him today, dodge him the same way I'd dodged his calls, or I could be a woman and face him. After all, I hadn't done anything wrong. He was the one who'd slept with me knowing he was involved with someone else. He was the one who'd pursued me until I gave in. He was the one who should be ashamed and running scared, not me.

Deliberately, I held my head high and started forward. "I'm sorry," I said to Mega-Man as he led me through a side door I hadn't noticed on my earlier visits to the gym. "I didn't call Jake to tell him I was coming so hearing he's been expecting me caught me off guard."

Mega-Man grunted. I wasn't sure what I was supposed to

make of that, so I fell silent and followed him up a stairwell. As I stepped onto the first landing, I realized this would be the first time I'd get to see Jake's office. Jake had two managers and three assistant managers at Fit For Life to cover the hours of operation. I'd been in the day manager's office when I signed the Fit For Life contract, but that was down on the main level.

The stairs led up to the second floor and ended abruptly facing a plain white wall. To my left was another white wall, but to my right was a door. Mega-Man rapped on the door three times then retreated down the stairs. He paused long enough to wink and give me another grunt.

My stomach writhed. I was about to see Jake for the first time since the night at Hammerjacks when I'd caught him locking lips with his boyfriend, Cinder, a.k.a. Dev. How on earth could I nonchalantly demand this guy break a fitness contract with me when last month I'd been tied to his four-poster bed being paddled to within an inch of my life and loving every second? I'd explored my fetishes with this man, done things with him I'd never contemplated doing with another. I had oral sex, swallowed his love juice, been made love to while I intermittently moaned and screamed his name. Dear God, my entire family would live in shame if they knew half of what I'd done, and the sad truth was, I wanted to do every one of them again. And with Jake.

That thought led me to a second realization--the true reason why I'd been avoiding Jake. My pride was wounded and I was angry, but not enough to *not* repeat past mistakes if given the chance. The only way I could be sure I wouldn't sleep with him again was to stay far away.

The door swung open, pulling me from my thoughts, and I found myself staring up and into Jake's face.

As always, his beauty stunned me. He told me during our night together that he was half Algonquin from his father and half Puerto Rican from his mother. This ethnic mix explained his exotic good looks, but not the potent effect they had on me. His emerald eyes bore into me as I stood looking at him, momentarily paralyzed to the spot. His lush, pink lips quirked into a knowing grin and he stepped back, motioning me inside his office.

I reminded myself that I had to behave with decorum and dignity. I was there with a goal. And that was the only reason I was there.

"Come in, Stella," he said, when I remained in the doorway.

The sound of his voice sent tingles of anticipation rippling down my spine. He had a sexy voice, like melted cream. It was silky and intoxicating, and brought back memories of him confessing all of the perverted things he wanted to do to me.

I could feel my face heat at the remembrance.

Staring purposely at my feet, I stepped into his office.

CHAPTER THIRTEEN

The office was spacious and as decadently decorated as his home. A large, mahogany desk was the focal point, and it was set atop a maroon and forest green area rug. Two chairs sat opposite his desk, there was a bar in the far corner of the room, a sofa, and another door that led ... I didn't know where. The wall to my left was made entirely of glass. From the gym below this entire wall appeared as one large mirror, but that was a façade. From here in his office, Jake could oversee everything that happened in Fit For Life.

Once I was inside, he closed the door. I heard the unmistakable sound of a lock slipping into place.

Goose flesh popped out along my arms.

"Have a seat," he said, from behind me.

I glanced at the sofa, then at the pair of visitor's chairs facing his desk. I opted for a chair.

As I walked across the room I felt Jake on my heels, moving so close that the scent of him completely engulfed my senses. He smelled *good*. Even after kickboxing class, sweaty and mussed from exertion, Jake had always smelled yummy.

I sat in a chair, crossed my legs, and struggled to remember why I was there. It wasn't to have sex; however, that thought was the preeminent one filling my mind.

"I knew you'd come," he said, resting his hands on my shoulders from behind me and squeezing. "Katarina's been calling every day, demanding I break her contract."

Katarina. That was it. The contract.

He'd begun to knead my shoulders. His fingers on me felt so right, so welcome that I had to stop myself from leaning into him. Instead, I slid forward, ending the contact.

"You have to break the contract, Jake," I said, proud of the resolve I heard in my voice.

"Do I, now?"

"Yes."

He stood in front of me then hiked one jean-clad hip onto

the edge of his desk. His foot rocked back and forth and I noticed he was wearing black work boots today. They looked damn sexy on him.

"Give me one good reason why I should," he said, easing further back on his desk, knees splayed.

Damn it to hell, he was hard. Not just hard either, but solid as a rock. His erection pressed against the crotch of his jeans so forcefully I wouldn't have been surprised to hear the material rip and see his cock come spilling out amid a tangle of dark hair.

I forced my eyes away from his erection and swallowed hard. "Because it's the right thing to do?" I hadn't meant it to come out as a question, but Jake had me so unnerved, and that's exactly what it sounded like. A question.

"I'll tell you what," he began, grinning insidiously at me. "You come to my place on February fourteenth--"

"Valentine's Day?"

"Yeah, Valentine's Day. You stay all night and I'll break Katarina's contract." Then, he added as an afterthought, "And yours."

When I managed to collect my thoughts, I got to my feet. Outrage made my voice quiver. Thrusting my finger into his chest, I accused, "You want me to spend the night with you? That's the only way you'll break our contracts?"

He nodded.

"I'm not a whore. I won't sell my body for two stupid contracts."

"You won't be selling your body. The contracts are an excuse. You want me just as much as I want you. You can use the contracts to justify it to yourself."

"You arrogant ass! Why the hell would I want to spend the night with you? You're a liar and a cheat. And you're gay."

"I never said I wasn't attached. You never asked. And I'm not gay, I'm bisexual."

"With the way you came on to me I naturally assumed you were unattached."

"If you had asked I would have told you. Did you really think all those clothes in the closet belonged to me?"

As a matter of fact, I had. "I suppose Dev is going out of town again and you don't want to be alone on Valentine's Day."

He shook his head. "No, Dev is gonna be home."

I frowned. "So why do you want me there?"

"Not just me, Stella. Dev wants you to spend the night too. It'll be the three of us."

I gulped. "Let me get this straight. You expect me to stay at your house for Valentine's Day? Overnight, with you and your lover?"

He nodded. "And this time, Dev gets to play too."

"Have you lost your mind? "First you brow beat me at gym class, then you sleep with me and never call me, now you want me to be you and your boyfriend's whore. Screw you, Jake."

He lifted a hand in protest. "I did call."

"Yeah, after I caught you red handed."

"No, don't leave. Please Stella, sit, let me explain."

"I don't want to hear it."

"Please. Five minutes. That's all I ask."

I folded my arms over my chest and began tapping my toe. "You've got three minutes."

Jake exhaled heavily. "All right. I'm not sure how to say this so I'll just come out with it." Another exhale.

"Spit it out already, Jake."

"All right. I wasn't supposed to sleep with you."

I rolled my eyes. "You've gotta do better than that."

"Just hear me out." He pushed himself further back on the desk and attempted to smile. It was the most pathetic thing I'd ever seen. "I've always been attracted to you, Stella. From that first day when you walked into my class in that ridiculous pink body suit with your hair in a French twist." A sincere smile tugged at his lips. "You were so beautiful and so unaware of it. You were clumsy and silly…you made me laugh."

"I've never seen you laugh in class."

He acknowledged this fact with a nod. "True, but I was laughing on the inside." The smile disappeared and his face took on its usual sober expression. "I mentioned you to Dev. When he came to class that day he knew who you were." He paused and began tapping his fingers against his thighs. "As soon as I saw the two of you together I knew Dev was attracted to you too. When I got home we talked about you. Talked about how it would be nice…that it might be fun…Hell, we decided we'd like to have a go at you."

"A go at me?" I repeated, incredulous.

"I know that sounds bad, but we didn't mean it in a bad way. We'd talked about sharing a woman before but had never found the right one, until you joined my class."

"What about me made you think I'd be open to being with two men?"

"Nothing. I couldn't guess how you'd feel about being with Dev and me so we agreed the best course of action was for me to approach you and feel you out. That's all I was supposed to do. That's why I insisted on going into your house that day, then insisted you go out with me Saturday night. Problem was that every time I was alone with you things got out of hand. And that night...." He ran a finger through the loose strands of his hair. "Long story short, when I told Dev I'd gone on ahead without him he was pissed."

"Was he jealous of me or you?"

"Both of us. He was furious. I couldn't call you when he was like that. It would have sent him through the roof."

"So now he's forgiven you?"

Jake nodded. "Now he's forgiven me."

"And he wants to ... resume the plan?"

He didn't answer, at least not with words. I felt the heel of his boot glide over my calf as he hooked his leg around mine. A moment later he dragged me forward into the circle of his thighs.

The kiss was slow, tentative at first, but as I relaxed into him, it deepened. His tongue moistened mine, his lips tasted sweet as honey, and I was doing precisely what I said I wouldn't do. But it felt too incredible, and I didn't want to stop.

Determined to get control over the situation, I eased my arms between us and gave Jake a shove.

Nothing happened, save Jake exerting more strength to hold onto me.

"No," I tried to say against his lips.

He pulled back and uttered, "Yes." He wrapped his legs around my waist and locked me in place. When his lips meant mine this time, I knew there was no going back.

Moaning hungrily, he drew my tongue into his mouth and sucked. A jolt of sexual awareness danced from the juncture between my legs to my nipples and back down again. I rubbed against him, pressing closer, needing to feel him all over. I suddenly wanted him so much I could scarce stand on my own two feet.

"Dear God, Jake," I said when he eased me away and slid off his desk. "What are you doing to me?"

"Binding you to me," he said. His voice was hoarse, barely audible above the pounding of my heart.

He moved to stand behind me, set his hands on my waist and nudged me forward until I was pressed against his desk. "Wait a sec." He said. He retreated but returned in seconds. "Lean on this." He eased a pillow from the sofa under my hips so the angled edges of his desk wouldn't cut into me.

Thoughtful and considerate.

"Now, take off your shoes so we can get those pantyhose off," he said.

Matching words to action, he crouched while I slipped my feet free of their leather confines. He set his hands on my thighs and began to slide the pantyhose off. I'd never had a man handle me in such a way, so gently while primal hunger was evident in the way his hands shook when he touched me.

Tossing the pantyhose aside, he stood to his full height and loomed over me. "Bend over, Stella," he ordered, giving me a helpful prod.

The next moment I was chest down against his desk, cheek pressed to the cool, dark wood, hair splayed around me. He eased the skirt of my suit up around my waist.

"Do you know how bad I've wanted to do this?" he asked. "How many times I wanted to go to your place, kick down the door, and make you admit you want me?"

I didn't answer. I couldn't if I wanted to. I was lost in the feel of his fingers grazing my skin as he grasped my panties and drew them down just enough to give him access to my throbbing center.

I was bare from the waist down, naked and unprotected. The warm air of his office tickled my clit as I lay waiting. I shivered.

"Do you know how many times I've fantasized about finding you in The Oak Room and making you come home with me? Making you submit to me again?"

"And what about Dev?" I asked, wondering what Jake's lover would've thought of this.

In answer, he slid into me slow, careful not to press too fast and hurt me. "Fuck, you feel good. Dev won't believe how tight you are. He'll die when he feels you, Stella. He'll die on the spot, that's how good you feel."

He pressed in further and I bit my lower lip. A guttural groan slid from my lips.

"How do you want it Stella?" he asked after he'd eased his cock into my core. "Slow and easy or fast and hard?"

I didn't think I had the patience for slow and easy just now, so I told him a little hoarsely, "Fast and hard. Real hard."

"Hold on, then." Without saying another word, he eased back excruciatingly slow, paused, then thrust into me faster and harder than I would've believed humanly possible. The sudden force of the movement had me sliding along the slick surface of his desk. I was thankful he hadn't removed my shirt and bra. Had I been naked from the waist up I didn't doubt my breasts would've been brush-burned.

I didn't have time to catch my breath before he was withdrawing from me. My insides felt sore from the sudden intrusion, unaccustomed to being so thoroughly filled. I was beginning to doubt the wisdom of my fast and hard request. After going a few weeks without sex, slow and easy might have been the better choice.

Before I could say as much, he drove into me, sending riotous sensations surging through my body. I wasn't entirely sure if it was pleasure or pain I was feeling, or if it was a bizarre mix of both.

As he eased back again I levered myself onto my elbows, hoping to control his thrusts.

"Jake?" I asked, a little breathlessly.

"Am I hurting you?" he asked, plunging into me a third time.

The force of his thrust made me collapse onto the desk, a low moan in my throat. All-encompassing ecstasy teased in the pit of my stomach. Tempting, even as it stayed just beyond my reach. Every time he surged deep, the delicious sensation intensified. It grew until I was shoving into him, forcing him to drive deeper.

He drew back and thrust, setting a rhythm I was powerless

against. Each possession left me desperate; each withdrawal had me eager for more.

"That's right," he said. "Give in to me."

Unable to form words, I sighed.

I felt around for something to cling to, something to anchor me against the jarring force of his hips moving against mine. My hands found purchase on his desk, so I gripped the edges and hung on for dear life, riding his cock all the while.

I could tell by our hunger that this wouldn't take long. We were both too needy to take our time, too frantic for a lingering coupling.

He kept his hands on my hips, fingers digging into my flesh as he moved my hips in time with his thrusts.

On the very edge of control, hovering on the precipice of unfulfilled desire, my climax danced just out of reach.

"Fuck, I'm gonna come, Stella."

He pounded into me and pulsed. The sensations engulfed me, raged through my body at double-time, the pleasure descending too fast to control. I didn't want to orgasm yet. I wanted more. Still, when I felt him ejaculate, the orgasm that had teased, delivered. A fierce spasm shook my body. I forced my buttocks against his hips even as he wrapped me in his arms and held tight.

He fell backward into a visitor chair, pulling me along with him into his lap.

After three more thrusts, we were both done ... and well satisfied.

* * * *

"A word about Dev," Jake said, pulling me more firmly onto his lap a few minutes later. "He's a closet actor. He loves performing. And not just on stage for an audience."

"I haven't said I agree to your Valentine's Day proposal."

He gave me a squeeze that made the muscles in his arm ripple. "You'll come." And we both knew he was right. "Anyway, about Dev. He's always dreamed of being an actor. Our closet is full of costumes he's worn onstage with Maverick. He gets a rush out of incorporating his leather gear into sex. See what I'm getting at?"

I stared at him. "I haven't a clue."

"Dev loves sex. Dev loves performing. But what Dev really loves is to combine his passions. Get me?"

"He sings while he has sex?"

Jake rolled his eyes. "Sex skits. He gets a rush out of thinking up wild scenarios, pretending to be a character in the situation, and fucking."

I tried not to laugh but it was difficult. "Like playing Doctor? We sort of did the same thing that night at your place."

"I guess you could say that. Except Dev's set-ups are much more elaborate."

"I don't know whether I should be aroused or afraid."

"Definitely aroused. Dev gets off on sex games." He watched for my reaction. When I continued to smile he went on. "Dev's a great fuck, Stella. The more turned on he is the more fun you'll have."

"What about you?"

"I'm gonna have a hard time sharing you."

* * * *

9:07 p.m.

"You did what?"

Ann, Katarina, and Meagan all shared matching looks of alarm. I chugged some more Sam Adams and tried to seem nonchalant about the whole affair. All afternoon I'd been practicing my, 'I have sex on desktops all the time' face. "I had sex with Jake today," I said again. "In his office. On his desk."

"You did what?" Katarina repeated.

Had we gotten stuck in a conversational loop? It felt like we'd all somehow become broken records. I could hear the words, "*On his desk*," echoing over and over in my head, followed closely behind by, "*You did what?*"

"In his office?" Meagan eyed me up and down. "I'm impressed. I didn't think you had it in you."

Katarina shoved a blonde strand from her face and frowned. Her disapproval radiated off of her like body heat. "Well I'm not impressed. What were you thinking, Stella? You can't go around having sex in men's offices."

"Was it good?" Ann wanted to know.

A memory of my body splayed across his desk, Jake standing behind me, impaling me, flashed in my mind's eye. "I've never done anything like that before," I said, still stunned stupid by my own behavior. "It was amazing. It felt so carnal. I can't remember ever being so turned on."

"What about my money?" Katarina wanted to know.

"Screw your money," Ann said. "I wanna know more about the sex. Gerard and I used to have exciting sex. We did it at a concert once. Standing up, right in the middle of the auditorium. Best sex I ever had."

"How're you ladies doing?"

Ann grinned unabashedly at the waitress, not in the least bit embarrassed that the woman had overheard Ann telling us about another of her and Gerard's sexual escapades.

"Another MGD," Ann told the lady.

Katarina shook her head. "I'm meeting Jim for drinks later. I don't want to be drunk before I get there."

"I'll have another Margarita," Meagan said. After the waitress was out of earshot, Meagan leaned over the table, careful to keep her long curls away from the flickering candle flames, and confided, "I did it at an concert once too. It was an outdoor concert. And we did it on a blanket. It was amazing. Just me, Tim--or was it Jason--and the stars."

"So who here besides me isn't an exhibitionist?" Katarina wanted to know.

Okay, so I'd had sex on a desk. I didn't think that made me an exhibitionist. "I was in a locked office. I don't think that makes me an exhibitionist. And anyway, sex in his office isn't the oddest thing about our meeting. The real kicker has to do with our contracts." I paused to make sure I had everyone's attention. And I did. Beside me, Katarina's expression was one of trepidation. Across the table, Ann held her beer aloft, waiting to drink until I said whatever it was I had to say. Meagan simply stared. "Jake said he'd break our contracts, no questions asked, if I'd spend the night with him on Valentine's Day. With him," I continued, "and his boyfriend, Dev, a.k.a., Cinder."

As expected, I'd struck another chord. For a good fifteen seconds, nobody said a word. However, there was much gasping, throat clasping, and offended grunts emanating from our section of the lounge.

Ann was the first to speak. "Do what?"

"Spend the night with them. They want a woman to share, to play with I suppose. And they've elected me." I shrugged. "Go figure."

"You said no, right?" Katarina's manicured fingers

clenched into a fist. "Tell me you kneed him in the balls."

"The two of them!" Ann added.

Meagan gasped again, shaking her head. "Was he serious?"

"Jake doesn't joke about sex."

"What about you? You think this is funny? You think you're up to having sex with two men at the same time."

"I told him I'd think about it."

Katarina's fist came down on the table, making us all jump. She bared her teeth and curled her lip. "What's there to think about?"

"Come on," I said. "You guys saw Dev. The man is gorgeous. Jake is gorgeous. When will I get another chance to have sex with two men who look like that? And at the same time to boot. A Jake and Dev sandwich."

"Dev?" Katarina repeated, incredulous. "Since when did Jake's lover become Dev?"

"That's what Jake calls him."

"Ménage a Trois," Meagan said. "If you do this, you'll have to remember, it's just sex. Don't mistake it for anything else and get hurt."

Katarina's head swung around to face Meagan. "You can't be serious. You're not seriously telling Stella this is an okay thing to do."

"It's Stella's choice."

"This is crazy. Come on, Ann. Back me up on this."

Ann downed some MGD then shook her head. "I think I'm with Meagan. As long as Stella doesn't get emotionally involved, this could be fun. Hell, I'd do it."

"Why doesn't that surprise me?" a male voice asked.

We all jumped when a cane materialized in the air above us, descended, and struck the table with a loud *whap*. The *whap* was followed by a string of curses and unflattering comments that had the blood draining from Ann's face. Only as the spray of spittle began to dissipate was I able to identify the speaker, and only then when the tide of his anger had lessened to an extent that his words no longer resembled that of an enraged chimpanzee.

"Gerard," Ann said, once she'd composed herself sufficiently to stare down her nose at him. "What the hell are you doing here?"

Why she asked him that instead of being nice to him, I'd

never know. She'd only spent the last week crying and moaning about him. If this was the best she could do to win him back, I didn't think she had a chance in hell.

"Stay away from Candace," was his short, but passionate retort to Ann.

"Candace? Candace who?"

I tried not to snort at the ridiculousness of this question.

Gerard's lip curled. I feared he was about to let loose with a fresh torrent of expletives. Instead, he rested his fists on the table and leaned closer. His blond hair fell over his forehead, making him seem younger, more innocent, less pissed off. "I know it was you, Ann. You and Stella." I felt his eyes flash on me as he said my name.

"Hey," I said, throwing up my hands in defense, "leave me out of this."

"Stay away from Candace."

"Drop dead," Ann replied.

"If I find out you've been harassing Candace...." he paused. No doubt he was trying to think up a suitable punishment.

"Don't you dare threaten me."

Unable to come up with anything good, Gerard stood erect and said, "Stay away." Then he turned and stomped out the front doors.

We were silent, unsure if it was safe to speak yet. We knew the precarious position we were in. One wrong word, one casually spoken phrase could be enough to push Ann over the edge. None of us wanted to see her attempt to drown her misery in tequila again, so we waited and tried to gauge her emotional state.

It didn't look promising. As she reached for her beer her lips had already begun to quiver. Her eyes looked moist and disbelieving and her nose was turning red.

She finished off her beer in a few gulps, raised a hand for our waitress, and ordered herself two tequila shots.

"Ann," Meagan was the first to say.

"I hate him," Ann declared.

I reached across the table and gave Ann's hand a squeeze. "Tequila won't help."

"Oh yes it will. It'll make me numb."

"Remember how awful you felt Wednesday morning after drinking all night?"

"Yeah," Meagan agreed. "Don't let Gerard do this to you."

As the waitress set Ann's tequila shots on the table, Ann nodded her thanks, hefted one shot glass, and swallowed. She didn't bother with the salt or the lime, all she cared about was the booze. "Just shut up and let me drink," she said.

And that pretty much capped off our night.

CHAPTER FOURTEEN

Journal entry 2/7/05, 8:35 a.m.
Oh, the tangled webs we weave.

If I had thought the doc was going to forget our conversation of last week, I was destined for disappointment. Okay, so maybe disappointment isn't the right word here because I wasn't really disappointed. I was pleased, enthusiastic, but I was not disappointed. I was feeling guilty, though. Why I should feel guilty was anybody's guess. Okay, so I'd had sex with Jake again. Big deal. It wasn't like having sex with Jake meant anything serious was happening between us. Sex with Jake was just that. Sex. Jake was involved with someone else. Our date on Valentine's Day aside, the important thing was that I owed Jake nothing and he owed me nothing. I was a free agent, able to date whomever I pleased.

Least that's what I kept telling myself.

Dr. Taylor arrived promptly at eight-thirty in black slacks and a lemon-yellow, button-up shirt. He stepped into the office behind Ann, slipped out of his coat, and waited.

Somehow I didn't remember him looking this good. He could've stepped off the cover of a romance novel and into my office. If I didn't have such a strong grip on reality I would have thought that was exactly where he'd come from--that Ann had gone out and grabbed some erotic novel and shaken the doc loose from its pages.

He smiled, almost shy and boyish, and held out his hand when I started toward him. It took a second, but reality settled itself on me again and I lifted my own to meet his. Our palms touched and I nearly yelped in surprise. His skin was so hot that it seared. And rough from years of hands-on work.

Slipping my hand free, I nodded to Ann who quickly retreated from the room--grinning like a loon--and shut the door. The usually large office suddenly felt too small to hold the two of us.

He brushed against me as he crossed the room, then

settled in the seat opposite my desk.

When I gave him the resume and cover letter I'd spent the last few days working on, he spent exactly two minutes looking them over. He paid me the remainder of my fee, grinning as he signed the check and placed it in my hand. It was all very professional and above boards. A minute later, he said, "What about that date?"

I stared at him and considered turning him down flat, then threw that idea out the window. Jake belonged to someone else, he'd never belong to me. For my own well-being I had to see other people. "I don't know," I said, knowing damn well that I had every intention of saying yes.

"Come on. It'll be fun."

"When were you thinking?"

"Saturday."

"Let me check my schedule," I parried, trying to sound busy and important. "I'll call you tonight and let you know."

"I'll be by my phone, waiting with bated breath for your call."

I escorted him to my foyer and out the door.

Dear God, I hope I'm not making a mistake.

* * * *

8:46 a.m.

Desperate to get back in Katarina's good graces after last night, I rang her the moment the doc left. "Guess what?" I practically shouted into the phone.

Katarina, who was currently in her downtown office, probably staring out the window asked, "What?"

"I have a date. No, don't groan. It's not Jake and Dev. It's a former client. His name is Doc--"

I could almost see her perking up when she interrupted. "He's a Doctor?"

"Not the kind you're thinking of. He's a Nautical Archaeologist and *fine*."

"So when are you going out with him?"

"Saturday."

"Doing what?"

"I don't know. I haven't told him yes, yet."

"Good for you, Stella. Let's hope the date goes so good you forget about Jake."

In all honesty, I didn't know if that was possible.

CHAPTER FIFTEEN

Journal entry 2/9/05, 10:36 a.m.
Since Gerard's departure from Ann's life, she seemed to be a permanent fixture in mine. She slept in my home, ate my food, and drank all my tea. Don't get me wrong, my home is always open to any friend or family member in need of emotional comfort. This is, of course, assuming said friend or relative is sane. At present, sane wasn't a word I'd use to describe Ann's mental state. Angry, desperate, and irrational were better descriptions. And at times, when she was guzzling my "Awake" tea and had way too much caffeine flowing through her veins, crazier than a shit-house rat.

Last night she'd sat at her desk for hours, downloading every song she could find that reminded her of Gerard. After amassing a suitable number of songs to ensure hours of heartache and despair, she burned them onto a CD, then she showed up at my bedroom door armed with it, a bottle of tequila, and time to spare.

It wasn't a good night.

This morning she'd allowed me the privilege of holding her hair while all of last night's tequila revisited her.

I can't go on this way. And Ann definitely can't go on this way. She'll kill herself with alcohol poisoning if she tried.

I have to do something!

"I'm a mess."

I looked up to see Ann walk into the office. She came around my desk and slumped in the client chair across from me. I took in her wet hair, rumpled jogging pants, and her pale face, and nodded. "You have to pull it together."

She nodded. "I have to get Gerard back."

"No, you have to forget about Gerard. Move on. Date someone else."

Ann grimaced and shook her head. "I'm not interested in anyone else."

"Then spend some time on your own. You don't need a man to complete you."

"Not any man. Gerard. I feel lost without him."

Okay, so I liked Gerard too. He was a great boyfriend whenever they were together. He was devoted, caring, loving, and affectionate. If I was going to be honest, this breakup wasn't Gerard's fault at all. It was Ann's. Whenever they broke up it was always her fault.

"Why?" I asked, suddenly. "You get him back and then you'll break up with him again."

Ann slumped lower. "I won't. I appreciate him more now."

"Honestly, Ann. If I was Gerard, I would've broken up with you too. After a while a person gets tired of being dumped all the time."

"Oh great! Now you're turning on me too. I can't take this any more. My life is falling in on me!"

I phased out Ann's ranting as a thought occurred to me. What if this was what Gerard wanted? Could the only reason he'd broken things off with her be to give her a taste of her own medicine?

The beginnings of an idea began to form in my head. It was risky, not a definite, but if it worked out, it might be just the thing needed for this situation.

"If you and Gerard got back together, would you dump him again for no good reason?"

"No! I'd never dump. I love him."

"Why don't you call Gerard and invite him and Candace to The Oak Room two Saturday's from today. No, don't interrupt. Just hear me out." When Ann sucked her teeth and sat back I continued. "You tell him you didn't realize breaking up would mean you would lose him as a friend. Tell him you still want to be friends and this is your way of burying the hatchet."

"Why the fuck would I say that?"

I rolled my eyes. "Your mother ever wash that mouth out with soap?"

"Hell no!"

"Anyway," I said on a sigh, "what we'll do is fix you up on a date with someone that night. Someone good looking. One of Meagan's friends. That way when Gerard gets there and--"

"And he sees me with another man he'll get jealous."

"Bingo. So what do you think?"

She didn't answer right away. I could see her tossing the idea around in her head, thinking of possible scenarios. "I say hell yeah! Let's do it."

I gave her a thumbs up sign. "You call Gerard and I'll call Meagan."

"Oh, this is gonna be good," she said, bounding from the chair and trotting to her desk. A moment later, she had her phone pressed to her lips and was saying, "Hi Gerard. It's me ... Ann. I'm calling because I want to apologize...."

* * * *

4:43 p.m.

As anticipated, "Operation Lure and Deceive" was in full force. Meagan rushed to my place as soon as she got off work. The plan was for us to go over a list of possible men with Ann. The list of Meagan's ex's was long. And she'd brought pictures.

"Gerard wouldn't feel threatened by this guy," Ann said, adding another photo to the reject stack. "Or this guy. But this one is promising. What's his name?"

Meagan smiled. "His name is Sean. He's a veterinarian, has a house in Fells Point, and would do anything for me."

"Anything?"

"You name it."

Getting up for coffee refills, I glanced at the picture. Sean was a good-looking man. "You threw this one away?"

"He was looking to get married," Meagan explained. "I'm not ready for marriage."

Leaving them hovering over the coffee table in the family room, I grabbed their empty mugs and went into the kitchen. I was pouring cream into our mugs when the doorbell clanged.

Katarina was still at work and I didn't remember having any appointments after three today.

"I got it," Ann said, rising from the sofa and setting out for the door. Seconds later, when Ann strolled into the family room, Kool-Aid grin plastered to her face, I knew things were about to get interesting.

And they did.

Walking behind Ann was Dev.

CHAPTER SIXTEEN

Jake's lover was at my house.

Dev was in my kitchen.

I'd only seen Dev twice before. Once at the gym and the last time had been at Hammerjacks. Onstage, dressed in black leather, he'd been magnificent. The leather had hugged every delectable inch of his body. The pants fit like a second skin, molding to his form as he danced across the stage.

The man was a walking, talking billboard for sex.

Now, with Dev standing in my kitchen, his hair falling in loose curls around his shoulders and a cocky grin on his lips, I had to blink a few times to make sure this was real.

He sauntered (yes, sauntered) through my family room and toward the kitchen. This was a man who was positively awe-inspiring. My eyes roved up and down his body of their own accord. I was making a fool of myself, but I couldn't stop. One look simply wasn't enough. He was wearing suede today. Black suede so tight, I wondered how he could breathe. The wool turtleneck was a good touch. The royal blue was a nice contrast to the pants. The shiny, black, knee-boots he had on weren't too bad either.

I opened my mouth to speak, couldn't tell if any sound would actually come out, and shut it.

"Stella," he said.

Dear God, my name sounded amazing on his lips.

I darted a look at Ann, who shrugged. "Dev?"

He rounded the breakfast bar and came to stand beside me at the center island where I'd been stirring cream into our coffee mugs.

"I've been looking forward to seeing you again," he said.

That's when I remembered my most recent get-together with Jake. You know the one. The sex on the desktop, I want to have a ménage a trois with you, get-together.

My cheeks warmed at the memory and I hoped desperately my thoughts weren't written all over my face. "Oh?" I said. Stupidly.

"Oh," he agreed, with a nod.

"Yeah, last time I saw you was at Hammerjacks last month."

His grin broadened. "Your knee to the groin didn't do any lasting damage to Jake, but I guess you already know that."

I swallowed. "Oh! Jake told you about *that*? About--"

"His desk," Dev finished, tucking his thumbs into the waistband of his pants. "Jake tells me everything." He leaned in close and whispered, "Even about the red paddle."

I wanted the floor to open up and suck me in. This could very well be the most embarrassing moment of my life and, considering my history, that was saying a lot. Allowing Jake to paddle me last month had been one incredibly erotic experience. And it was private. Not something Jake should go around telling his friends about. Not even Dev had a right to know. That wasn't the kind of thing people needed to know. "What else did he tell you?"

Dev slid onto a counter and made himself at home. Brushing hair out of his face with one bejeweled hand, he informed, "Jake told me he invited you over on Valentine's Day."

I could hear Ann and Meagan giggling. Clearly something about this exchange was amusing to them. "And what do you think of that?"

"That's why I'm here."

"I didn't know he was seeing anyone," I said quickly, fearing this conversation was about to go south.

But Dev shook his head. "Hush."

I opened my mouth to object but closed it again when he frowned. "Okay, say what you came to say."

He looked toward the family room where Ann and Meagan were hovering. Turning back to me, he suggested, "I think you'd rather have this conversation in private."

Considering the things Jake had told this man, I figured Dev was right. So I asked the girls, "Can you give us a minute, guys?"

Ann looked like she wanted to refuse, but at Meagan's prods, the two exited. I had no doubt they'd gone as far as the outer wall and were listening to every word we said.

"Dev and I are lovers, you know that. And we're both bisexual." He paused. "And we're both very domineering men."

"Okay," I said, wondering where he was going.

"I like to be on top, and Jake likes to be on top. Sometimes sex turns into a wrestling match, if you get my meaning."

I didn't. The idea of wrestling with either man was so alluring I couldn't see a problem. But I was curious and wanted to know more so I told him, "I see."

"Do you? You can't have two domineering people in the bedroom. It doesn't work. Don't get me wrong, Jake and I have a good time, but it could be better. He shifted on the counter, sliding forward until he was poised at the edge. Eyes intent on mine, he said, "That's where you come in."

Having delivered the first part of his speech, Dev rested his weight on one hand and crossed his legs. For any other man, the pose would have seemed effeminate. But Dev wasn't any other man. The muscles in his thighs flexed as he moved, his bicep bulged under the weight of his body. There was nothing effeminate about Dev. Even the way he watched me was indescribably masculine. There was a glimmer in his eyes, a mischievous look hidden just under the surface making me wonder what he was thinking. And there was something primal about his stare. A primordial hunger that said Dev might slide off the counter at any moment and advance on me.

"Where I come, eh. This should be good."

"You don't know me so I assume the idea of spending the night with me is giving you some trepidation, am I right?"

"To put it mildly."

"So I propose you allow me to take you out on Saturday. You can get to know me and I'll get to know you. I want to put you at ease about Valentine's Day."

"You want us to go out on a date?"

He nodded. "But Jake stays home. This would be our time to get better acquainted." When I didn't answer right away, he continued. "And at the end of the date you can decide if you want to see Jake and me on the fourteenth."

Though my heart was racing, I endeavored to appear cool and unmoved. "What did you have in mind?"

"I haven't decided, but we're supposed to have great weather this weekend."

"Why me? I saw you perform. There are any number of females who would gladly give themselves to you and Jake for a night."

"Jake doesn't want any female. He wants *you*. He seems to have become enamored with you, Stella. Did you know that?" He eased off the counter and edged toward me. This made me uncomfortable on many levels. "I don't want anyone else either. Jake says you're submissive as a kitten in bed. Is that true?"

My brilliant response to this was, "Huh?"

"When he told me about your night together, about the things he did to you, I was so jealous and so turned on I tried to persuade him to bring me here immediately."

"He told you everything?"

"He told me how he bound you to the posts of our bed, naked, but for the loops of rope fastening your wrists. He taunted me, saying how fine your skin felt, how soft and welcoming it was. He says you're the type of woman who takes care of herself. Is that true, Stella?" He moved closer.

When I didn't respond, he continued. "Then he told me how you writhed under the paddle." He paused, mere inches from me, a slow smile spreading on his lips. "You know, he'd wanted to do that to you since the first day you showed up for his kickboxing class. The moment he spotted you he'd made up his mind to have you, as did I."

I would've said something had my mind been working properly. As it was, the only thing I seemed capable of doing was mumbling monosyllables. "Huh? What? Me?"

"Tell me, Stella. Is what he said that happened after he paddled you true? That you knelt between his legs and licked his cock like a starving--"

"He told you that?"

"Mmm. And right through his pants."

"I got caught up in the moment." Damn, Jake could sure run his mouth.

"Wanna know what Jake told me when he got home from the gym on Friday?"

I shook my head. I didn't want to know. I could only imagine.

Dev continued he slow advance. I retreated until I felt the edge of a counter digging into my lower back.

"Jake says you're so tight you feel virginal. I love the sound of that." Dev advanced until his body was molded against mine.

I tried to breathe, an exercise that proved futile when he dipped his head low and captured my mouth.

His tongue lashed my skin, forced my lips open then delved within. The suddenness of such intimate contact with Jake's lover sent my hormones into full alert. His tongue felt sleek within the warm confines of my mouth and his taste was sweetly intoxicating. Like berry wine, chocolate and strawberries. I leaned into him, wrapping my arms around his waist and nearly losing myself in his touch.

The feel of his body, hard and unyielding against mine, made me weak in the knees. I was making out with Dev, the man I'd seen onstage at Hammerjacks last month and had been lusting for.

He easily lifted and set me on the edge of the counter. All the while he stroked me with his tongue. He licked my lips, nibbled, then delved deep for another taste.

In my mind's eye I remembered the sight of Dev hooking Jake by the waistband of his pants at Hammerjacks. The moment their tongues touched I knew they were more than lovers. The two had come together with an intensity that left me scorched. They had seemed ravenous. Now, with Dev's hands all over me, his mouth feasting on mine, the thought of Dev with Jake had my cunt tightening.

I wrapped my legs around Dev and pulled him closer, suddenly needing what he was giving me. I couldn't let go.

He trailed his fingers down my spine before finding the moons of my backside, cupping them in his large hands, and dragging me toward him. With a groan of pure male longing, he rotated his hips and ground them against me where my need was the most fevered. The move was forceful, telling me just how much he wanted me at his place on the fourteenth.

"You're hard," I said against his lips.

He raised one hand so his fingers could twist into my hair, then angled my head to deepen the kiss. His tongue danced against mine, teasing, promising.

I flexed my thighs, fought to get closer. I was quite content to let him take me right there, on my kitchen counter. Hell, I wouldn't be content. I'd be thrilled.

"Oh, Stella. The things I could do to you."

"Could do?"

"Say you'll see me on Saturday," he said, pulling away

long enough for me to catch my breath before prodding my lips wide for another taste.

I ran my hands over his back, letting my fingers play over his shoulders. When my hands fell below his waist, I cupped his ass, kneaded it and pulled him closer.

He moaned, then pushed away. "Jake was right. You're like an aphrodisiac," he said, out of breath. "If I didn't think Jake would kill me ... Say you'll come, so we can finish this on Valentine's Day."

"You're stopping? You can't leave me like this."

"Jake would kill me. He refused to give me your address until I promised him I wouldn't seduce you."

His eyes were glazed, his lids heavy with lust. I knew suddenly that stopping our erotic play had pained him as much as it did me. "He's that possessive of you?"

He grinned. "As a matter of fact, he is. But in this particular case, it's not me he's being possessive over. I don't get to have you unless Jake's present. After he went ahead without me it's not particularly fair, but I've agreed. I think this is the best way."

I sat back. "Well that's presumptuous of him. He has no claim over me."

Dev shrugged. "He says different. So what do you say, Stella?"

I wanted to. I'd never wanted to do anything more than I wanted to go to Jake and Dev's on Valentine's Day. But was it right? Would I feel guilty after? Jake was the first and only man I'd ever had casual sex with. All of my previous partners were always boyfriends. I was truly charting new territory here. Not only were Jake and I not seriously involved, but now Jake was bringing a third person into the mix.

"I don't know. I have a date this Saturday. I'm not sure if canceling would be right."

"If you don't come to our place on the fourteenth, you'll regret it for the rest of your life. Come on, Stella. Live a little."

I knew he wasn't being arrogant, but he was simply speaking the truth. I would regret not going to their place. I'd always wonder what I'd missed out on. So, throwing caution to the wind, I said. "Okay. You and me, Saturday."

He kissed me again. Thoroughly.

"We won't tell Jake about that other date," he said, once he'd pulled away. "Jake wouldn't like that."

"It's not like I was gonna have sex with that guy. I don't do that sort of thing ... except that time with Jake, but that was a one-time thing. And not including the desk time. Then, of course there'll be the fourteenth, but that doesn't count since I know Jake already ... I don't know you, but you know Jake and we both slept with him so I'm sure--"

I was relieved when he interrupted me. If he hadn't I would have gone on indefinitely. "So I'll see you Saturday. I'll come by in the morning, say eleven?"

"Okay," I squeaked, in a kind of shock that I was really going through with this.

He gave me one last, lingering kiss. "See you soon," he said against my mouth.

When Dev was gone, Ann and Meagan came skipping into the kitchen, chortling in high-pitched voices and making lewd comments.

Shit! I'd completely forgotten about them. Damn it to hell. "How much did you hear?" I demanded.

"I thought you were gonna do it right there on the counter," Ann laughed. "Amazing, you don't have a rule about that."

"A no sex on the counters rule," Meagan agreed.

"Oh shut up," I said.

"Poor Gerard, he's going to be disappointed when you cancel on him."

Still giddy, Ann asked, "Hey! Why didn't you tell us about the paddle?"

CHAPTER SEVENTEEN

Journal entry 2/12/05, 10:57 a.m.
The moment I opened my front door and found Dev standing in the hallway, dressed in black jeans and boots, I knew I was in trouble. My trepidation rose to a fever pitch when the first words out of his mouth were, "It's so nice out today I thought we could do something a little different."

I glanced down at my sleek dress, colorful scarf, and pumps and decided I would need to change before venturing out today. Good thing too. In my jeans, wool sweater, and boots I was more prepared when he announced his intentions. He didn't do this until I was safely tucked away in the Jag and glancing at him behind the wheel, thinking I was in love.

The love thing lasted about twenty seconds. Once he said, "I've got this friend up in Carroll County--" it sort of petered out.

"Carroll County?"

"Greg's a friend of mine. He has fifty acres up there."

Already, I didn't like the way this conversation was going. "Like a farm?" I asked, terrified by the prospect of what that would mean.

"Not exactly."

"Exactly what, then?"

"He and his wife have a kitchen garden, a vegetable garden, a few animals of the outdoor variety, and a lot of beautiful land."

I stared at him. "I think I should tell you right now that I don't like being outside. I'm more of a fine dining, art gallery, museum, or go out dancing, type of gal." A shudder swept through me at the prospect of spending the day out of doors. It wasn't the weather that had me worried. Dev had been right on that score. At an unseasonably warm temperature of sixty-four degrees, it was gorgeous today. What I was wary of was whatever Dev had planned for us to *do* outside.

Unperturbed, Dev gave me a sexy half-smile. "Relax, Stella. You're in good hands."

"Good hands? What do you mean by that?"

The smile slid off his face, but I could see the edges of his lips tremble as he struggled to maintain his composure. "Relax. You went to a fetish club with Jake, I thought I'd do something a bit more tasteful. Jake is extraordinary looking, but with those looks he's never had to work very hard at attracting the opposite sex...or the same sex, whatever the case may be. Trust me, Stella. You're going to enjoy yourself."

Forty-five minutes later, we were driving up a winding stretch of road Dev said was Greg and Giselle's driveway. We passed under trees so old I guessed they'd seen generations come and go. Weeping willows hung over the road, pines blocked out much of the sun, and barren cherry trees lined the drive. When we came to a clearing, the first thing I saw was a two-story country house sitting at the end of the drive. With its wrap around porch and the porch swing swaying in the breeze a few feet from the front door, the house couldn't have been more country if it tried. Behind the house and off to the right was a group of utility buildings.

Dev pulled to a stop, got out, then walked around to my side of the car and opened my door. He was a sexy lead singer with manners. That worked for me.

I took his hand and allowed him to help me from my seat.

The sun was a golden disc in the sky; its heat was a warm embrace about my body. An enticing aroma of food hung heavy in the air, making my stomach grumble for attention. The sweet smell of the forest around us was a surprisingly welcome change from the gritty city smells of automobile exhaust and smog. Maybe being outside in the country wouldn't be so bad after all.

"Isn't it fantastic here?"

I smiled and let him lead me toward the porch. "It is."

We'd only managed a few steps when a man, whose face could have been chiseled from stone, brought us to a standstill.

"So you made it!" this new person announced.

The man wasn't what I'd call good-looking. Tall and lanky, with a mop of wild brown hair, he sort of reminded me of Shaggy from Scooby-Doo.

"Greg." Dev grinned.

The man eyed his wristwatch. "Thought for sure you'd get lost. You made good time."

"Just show me to the food and the stables. I can talk to you any time."

"Stables?" I repeated. "As in horse stables? You're kidding right?" I would have said more had I not felt eyes boring into me. I paused, mid rant, and realized I was the object of close scrutiny.

Brows furrowed, eyes narrowed, Greg stared at me as though I were a lab specimen. "This is Stella?" he edged closer, eyes scanning me from my booted feet to the top of my head.

"Yeah," Dev said. "Isn't she wonderful." He wrapped an arm around my waist, tugged me close and squeezed.

Greg opened his mouth to say something else, seemed to think better of it, then settled on giving me a smile and offering his hand. The smile transformed his face. It was like seeing George Washington's face on Mount Rushmore suddenly alight with life.

"Stella," he said brightly, "Stella Rice. Welcome to my home. Come on in. Name's Greg. Greg Hendrickson. I suppose Dev told you we went to college together."

He hadn't. Nevertheless I nodded and said, "Nice to meet you."

He gave my hand three enthusiastic pumps, grinning at me the entire time. I felt like I'd gone from being something the cat dragged in to the status of prodigal son in the space of six seconds.

His hand was callused, but his touch wasn't unpleasant. I found that I was grinning back at him. I wouldn't have been surprised if I looked as ridiculously goofy as he.

"Follow me," he said, letting my hand slip from his. "Giselle's inside fixing brunch. Said she refused to let you go wandering on an empty stomach." He paused on the steps, glanced at us over his shoulder, and then did this sort of body shudder thing.

Clearly, *something* was wrong. Whatever ease I'd felt, slid away. My abdomen clenched and a tight ball of dread formed in the pit of my stomach. I got the distinct feeling that the something was *me*.

* * * *

2:22 p.m.
Thank God! I couldn't wait to get out of that house and away from that horrible woman. What the hell was Dev thinking to bring me there in the first place?

When we stepped onto their back deck and proceeded down the stairs into the yard, I couldn't wait to get far enough away from the house so I could give Dev a piece of my mind.

We were walking across the field behind the house and toward the barn, when Dev stopped and turned to face me. "I'm sorry."

"You didn't tell them I'm black, did you?" His quick glance at his boots was all the answer I needed. "How could you bring me here knowing you didn't tell them? Without knowing if they'd have a problem with it or not?"

"I'm sorry. We're barely three hours in and already I've fucked up royally. I honestly didn't think they'd care. Shit, they've been to our place a million times. I just assumed--"

"Assumed it wouldn't matter? Not everyone is enlightened when it comes to race, Dev. And that Giselle...." I couldn't say any more. I was so furious my hands were trembling.

"Stupid. I know. I'm sorry."

I knew racism was alive and well in America, but I'd never come face to face with it as I had today. In the city, if someone held racist beliefs they simply weren't tolerated. Sure, I'd gotten stared at before, followed in a department store once, but never had I experienced the demeaning treatment I had at the Hendrickson's table. So many times I'd heard racism referred to as hatred, but I didn't think hatred was the right word for what I experienced. Distain was better. Contempt, better still. "She didn't even want to shake my hand," I said. "She didn't want me sitting at her table or eating her food."

Dev's throat worked. His eyes were steady on my face, nearly pleading. "She's ignorant," he said, speaking in a slow, measured voice.

I nodded my agreement. "Please, take me home."

Something crushed beneath Dev's boot as he stepped closer to me. "Let me show you the horses? It's why I brought you here. I thought we could ride out to the river and sit and talk a bit. Dinner tonight, then dancing?"

"I'm not in the mood for horses right now, Dev. Or dancing. I just want to go home."

"Five more minutes. After that we'll go. Promise."

Sighing, I let him lead me to the stables.

We walked in silence, side-by-side, close enough to touch but worlds apart. Could he have been so naïve about his friends as to think the prospect of him dating a black woman wouldn't be an issue? I felt like I'd walked blindly into an ambush.

Giselle had alluded to the inferiority of minorities. She wasn't so bold as to come out and say she thought minorities were inferior intellectually and only able to succeed when given handouts by white people, but she might as well have. When asked where I'd gone to school, I told them I studied ancient history at Johns Hopkins, to which Giselle commented how glad she was to see Affirmative Action at work. Responding to such an ignorant statement was unnecessary, and I knew it. Still, I let them know that graduating from the Johns Hopkins Magna Cum Laude was a result of my determined work ethic, and nothing to do with Affirmative Action. I'd graduated high school with a 3.7 GPA, and I didn't need Affirmative Action to get me accepted into college. Not when I had a working brain, two hands, and a determination to succeed.

"You look beautiful today. Don't think I told you."

I stared into Dev's eyes and forced a smile. "You're not too bad either."

"Come on," he said, pulling me into the stable yard. "Let me introduce you to the horses."

When we stepped into the cool confines of a barn, it took my eyes a moment to adjust to the dim interior. Strange smells rose around me--mingled odors of hay, soil and manure. As I gazed around the barn, stared up at the beams high overhead and at the wooden partitions separating the animals, I realized this was the first time I'd ever seen horses up close.

He took me through to the opposite end of the building, naming horses as we progressed. As we passed, they whinnied and snorted. They seemed pleased by our arrival, anxious to be touched and petted. To my vast surprise I wanted to stop and touch the creatures. Even though my day had been pretty terrible, I could appreciate the beauty of these beasts.

"Have you been riding before? My mum kept horses when I was a kid," When we reached the far wall, he turned and led me toward the center of the room.

"No."

"You should do it at least once in your life. I think you'd like it. There's nothing like riding a horse. Not even riding a motorcycle."

That he loved horses was more than evident. It wasn't only the way he spoke of the creatures, but the way he looked at them, the absolute adoration in his eyes as he gazed into the stalls. Seeing Dev onstage dripping leather I never would have figured him for a horse lover, but I supposed that's part of the reason why Dev wanted us to get together today.

We paused in front of a large mare that whinnied and nodded as we moved closer. I was taken by how magnificent she was with her sleek black coat and mane of raven hair hanging over her neck. Her chocolate eyes regarded us with interest.

"Her name's Roxy," Dev said, dragging his hand through his hair. Once we were close enough, he began giving her long, loving strokes. "She loves to be rubbed."

He turned to look at me and at that moment he looked so indescribably gorgeous I nearly said, so do I. Instead, I said, "She's gorgeous."

He let his hand drop and stepped closer to me. I could smell the good clean scent of him when a stray breeze brushed passed us. His hair was a little disheveled, but I didn't mind. Instead of appearing messy, the tousled look of it made him seem sexily mussed as though he'd just rolled out of bed, fresh from a long, hot ride in the sack.

"You look enchanted."

I stiffened. Shit! Was I that obvious?

But I noticed his focus wasn't on me any more, but on Roxy. I nearly sighed my relief. He meant he could see the horse enchanted me. He hadn't been referring to himself.

"I am," I said. "They're all so beautiful."

"Wanna take a ride with me?"

"Are you serious?"

"Tell you what," he said. He walked a few feet away and stuck his hand into a wooden bin. He pulled three wrapped packages from within and tucked two of them into his coat pocket. Coming back he said, "I'll show you how gentle Roxy is."

I smiled despite myself. "I don't know. I don't think Giselle would like it too much if she saw me riding around on one of her horses."

Dev rolled his eyes. "They're not her horses. They belong to Greg. And Greg won't care. Greg likes you. He thinks you're pretty."

He tore into the package he'd kept out and pulled a brownish thing from inside. It wasn't very large, bigger than a dog treat, but clearly it was a sort of horse snack. When he was standing beside me he said, "A horse biscuit. Give me your hand."

I asked why even as I was lifting it.

He placed my hand beneath his own and then set the biscuit on the palm of his hand. "Watch."

When I realized what he was about to do, I snatched my hand away. He offered the biscuit to Roxy and she delicately took it and munched contentedly.

"You try."

"Are you crazy? What if she takes my hand off?"

"Take your hand? She's gentle as a cub."

"She doesn't know me."

"Okay, watch." He stepped behind me and took my left hand in his. A shiver ran through me at the contact. His skin was warm, and the press of him against me was enticing. Something in the lower regions of my body began to uncoil and demand recognition. My vaginal lips quivered and my stomach did a flip-flop. He smelled amazing, though I knew he wasn't wearing any cologne. His musky scent was all-natural and all man. Soap meets Old Spice.

He placed the second biscuit in my palm, and then brought my hand to Roxy's mouth. She deftly removed the proffered item and munched.

"See Stella," he bent low and whispered in my ear. "She's just a baby, couldn't hurt a fly."

Unable to take another moment of this sensual torture, I stepped away from him and began brushing invisible dust from the front of my jacket.

"The river is just a mile or so past the house. Let's go for a ride. We came all the way out here. Might as well enjoy the rest of the day. We don't have to go back to the main house when we leave. Greg'll understand."

"You sure this will be okay with Greg?"

He turned, gave me a smile. "Of course."

"All right then, let's do it."

He led me to the stall next to Roxy's. "This is Max," he said, referring to the horse. "He's smaller than Roxy but just as gentle. I think you can handle him."

I was thunderstruck. I didn't ride. He couldn't expect me to ride. "I don't ride." I backed away from Max. "I can't ride him."

"You can ride with me, then. Actually, I prefer that arrangement."

I loved the idea too, and so hated it even more than the idea of riding alone. Already my hormones were on full alert. I'd promised myself I wouldn't have sex today and I refused to go back on my word. Problem was, I didn't know how successful I'd be if I had to ride a horse with Dev. Just the idea of it had a host of enticing possibilities running through my head. "I'm not sure about that."

"Come on," he insisted. "It'll be fun.

"Maybe we should do this another time."

"You really want to come back here?"

Okay, so he had a point there. Wild horses couldn't drag me to this house a second time. So, for the sake of experiencing all life had to offer, I agreed.

I waited while Dev got Roxy ready for a ride and led her outside. After he called me over, I let Dev place my foot in a stirrup and hoist me into the saddle.

There was one thing I quickly realized. From the ground Roxy had seemed large, however, from atop her she was positively massive. I felt like I was sitting on the edge of a rafter twenty feet off the ground. I would've slid off her back and told Dev I'd changed my mind if he hadn't started talking, distracting me.

"Stella," he said, poised to mount. "You're gonna have to take your feet out the stirrups so I can mount up behind you."

A pleasant thrill ran through me at the thought of Dev mounted behind me, his thighs pressed against me. His crotch against my backside. With a little slick maneuvering our little ride through the woods could become interesting. Damn! If only I'd worn the dress. It wouldn't have taken much to slide the hemline of the dress to my waist, free Dev's cock from his jeans, and lower myself on it till he was buried to my core. That would have been a horseback ride to remember. The gentle rocking of the horse beneath us as we lost ourselves in the delicious thrill of our joined bodies.

I did as I was told, and in seconds, Dev was seated securely behind me. The saddle, however, wasn't made for two people. We had to maneuver around a bit to get a comfortable fit. I had to bite my lip hard to keep from moaning. More and more I was longing for that dress. Hell, maybe if he took us deep enough into the forest I'd forgo the dress fantasy and simply take my pants off...but then again, maybe not. I'd only been with Jake a few days ago.

Stella, I told myself, *get your mind out of the gutter.*

"How's that?" he asked. "Does it feel good?"

Not nearly as good as it could, I thought, then took a deep breath, "Sure, it feels fine."

"Now, rest your feet on mine and hold tight to the pommel."

I gazed down at the object he was fisting and nearly fell off the horse. The pommel was part of the saddle. I knew that. But just then, buried in his clenched fist, it didn't seem so much like an inanimate object as it did a very large, very hard, cock head. Dear God, was the man trying to torture me?

"I feel like I could fall at any second. I don't know about this, Dev."

"Don't worry Stella," he said, reins in hand, "I won't let you fall."

We started out at a trot, then picked up speed. I could feel the muscles in his inner thighs tighten and flex against my backside as we rode. It felt good to be there, within the hollow of his body. It felt safe. I knew if indeed I did slip, he would catch me.

"Relax Stella, you're stiff as a board," he said. His lips brushed gently against my ear, sending a jolt of sensual awareness through me.

"I am relaxed." Saying this, I forced my body to loosen

and rest against him.

He released a satisfied sigh. "Mmm, that's more like it. Now let me show you what Roxy can do."

He emitted a noise that sounded like, "Yah!" and Roxy broke into a gallop.

The house and stables faded behind us, then out of sight completely. We were swallowed up into the mass of trees that surrounded the property. I would've been frightened if I didn't see the clearly marked path below us. This was a trail Roxy had traveled on a regular basis, and as such, she wouldn't accidentally run headlong into a tree.

I lost track of time, reveling in the experience. The wind whipped through my hair, and was cool on my skin. I felt as though I were a bird in flight. Short of sex with Jake, this horse ride was the most exciting thing I'd done this year, so far.

Then, I gave myself a mental kick. Why the hell was I thinking about Jake? What was it about that man that had gotten under my skin and stuck? Bloody hell! Here I was, with a perfectly nice man, a very attractive man, and my mind was on Jake.

"Look Stella." At the sound of Dev's voice in my ear, I started.

Before I saw where he was pointing, the sound of rushing water caught my attention. As the prickly ends of branches brushed against my jacket, and the rich, earthy smells of the forest became faint, I glanced ahead. My two-handed grip on the pommel immediately loosened. Concerns for safety were forgotten as the most magnificent vista I'd ever seen appeared before me.

"The river," I said, awed by the sight. I'd seen rivers before, of course, but none like the one at the end of the dirt lane we'd been traversing.

"Isn't it great? I knew you'd like it."

The path beneath us became jagged with rocks. Large boulders lay scattered to the left and right of us, just beyond the trail. Ahead, the path didn't end so much as it led into the water. There was a small clearing in the trees where Dev brought Roxy to a stop and dismounted.

Smiling up at me, he offered his hand then seemed to think better of it. Clasping me around the waist, he helped ease me off the horse. I slid down the length of his body, feeling every muscle in his chest ripple and flex as he lowered me. He didn't let me go immediately, but kept his hands around my waist, holding me closer than necessary. I didn't complain. I was still too enchanted by the scenery; too charmed he had thought to bring me here. "If this was my backyard I'd never leave home."

He smiled, edging closer. His lips hovered inches above mine, moist and welcoming. I knew he wanted to kiss me. I wanted to kiss him too, but something inside of me rebelled.

"Do you have to tie her up?" I asked, before he could lower his head.

"No. Roxy's a good girl. She won't leave us."

"Oh." I swallowed.

He stared at my lips, blinked, then released me and stepped back. "Let's go sit by the river." As he spoke, he went to Roxy and pulled something free from the saddlebag.

Dev offered me his free hand. "Come on. It gets pretty rocky so watch where you step."

I took his hand, but didn't bother with anything as mundane as watching where I placed my feet. My surroundings were too spectacular to do anything other than gaze around me.

As we neared the end of the path, the vision that had awed me from a distance left me downright stupefied.

Crystalline water rushed by us and carried fallen branches and bits of greenery on its rapids. Larger versions of the rocks dotting the end of the trail peppered the water. Massive, gray stones jutted from the river. Some were jagged with age while others had patches of green fungus marring their surface. To my left--the direction the water flowed from--the waterway descended a series of stony plateaus, making something of a flinty waterfall. It was, in a word, gorgeous. Further up the river, where the forest brushed the water's edge, the reflection of the vegetation--trees, clumps of shrubbery, and yellow wild flowers--shimmered in the water. The very air I breathed was saturated with the fresh scent of the river. The mere act of breathing made me feel pure, cleansed. And the sound. It reminded me of going to the beach as a child when I'd spend hours in the sand digging up the largest seashells I could find so I could put them to my ear and listen to the music they made.

Though the river wasn't very wide, a hundred feet, perhaps a bit more, it was incredibly long. From where I stood I couldn't see where it began or where it ended. However, poised on the water's edge as I was, I could see that the forest continued on the other side of the water. If I stared hard I could make out the faint edges of a path leading away from the water and deep into the darkness of the trees.

"This is amazing," I said. It was like we'd crossed a portal into another time and place, and anything that happened here was for us alone.

"I know. Greg inherited the land from his father after his parents died. Come on, let's sit."

He had a blanket tucked under one arm and led me to a grassy spot. We spread the wooly cover over the browning grass then sat down.

"Comfortable?" he wanted to know once I was settled. "It's not the best blanket, but it was the only one that would fit in the bag."

"The cover's fine. But this isn't." Bending, I lifted my leg and pulled at my boots.

Grinning, Dev crawled around and clasped my foot in his hands. "Let me."

Taking his time about it, Dev slid the boot off. A moment later he had my sock in hand and was tucking it inside the discarded shoe. "Are those fairies?"

I glanced proudly at my toes. I'd just had a pedicure last week. I'd felt whimsical and carefree, and had them paint fairies on my toenails. I nodded. "I think they're cute."

He stroked my instep, applying just enough pressure to bring a sigh of pleasure from me. "I'm a sucker for nice feet."

Things were suddenly moving too fast. He may have been a sucker for nice feet but I was a sucker for a handsome face and talented hands. And the way he was using his hands on my feet had my hormones on full alert. Once he had my other boot off, I thought it prudent to draw my legs beneath me and change the subject. "I can't believe its February. This weather is amazing."

Dev didn't push. Instead, he settled on the blanket beside

me and stared ahead at the water. "Bet you're glad you came now. Enjoy it while it lasts because it's supposed to drop into the thirties tomorrow and snow on Monday."

"Valentine's Day?"

He nodded.

His dark eyes seemed luminescent in the afternoon sun. His smile was slow, almost shy, and I realized suddenly that I was having a nice time.

"I never would've known you had such a love for history," he said after a while. "It surprises me you're not working in that field."

Wiggling my toes, loving the feel of the air against my skin, I shrugged. "Not enough money."

"What era of history is your favorite?"

"My focus was on Biblical history," I began to say.

"But what era is your favorite?"

"I took a class on American history and I fell in love with the Revolution era. Before that, I was something of a historical snob. I was only interested in history if the period in question was at least fifteen hundred years in the past. Anything more recent was never interesting enough ... or old enough."

"So what changed your mind about American history?"

His focus was so intense I had to look away from him. I wasn't quite sure what was going on here, as such an anomaly had never occurred before. But it appeared that Dev was asking me questions about myself. That wasn't all, though. He was asking questions and seemed genuinely *interested* in the answers. So I told him what had drawn me to American history, shared stories about summer digs I took part in at Mount Vernon, George Washington's Potomac home, and told him of Revolution theme trips I'd taken to Philadelphia and Boston.

I had an honest to goodness conversation with this man. We talked until the sun began a languid descent into the horizon. When the air began to chill, we pulled the blanket up around ourselves and cuddled close.

When the kiss came, it was hesitant, unsure. But when I didn't push him away, it became more heated.

His tongue slid easily between my welcoming lips, probing and exploring. My body tingled under his touch, my loins cried out for more.

Eager to feel him atop me, I eased back until I was lying on the ground. Without releasing my mouth, Dev followed me down. He stretched himself over me, arms caging me.

Moaning hungrily into my mouth, he deepened the kiss.

I explored his body, touched every inch of him I could reach. My fingers stroked his back then cupped his ass. He murmured encouragement when I squeezed and urged him closer.

"Stella," he said into my mouth. "This is so good."

The plaintive, fervent sound of his voice had a sensuous effect on me, making me close my eyes in wonder. But I couldn't get too used to this, too addicted. Jake and Dev wanted a woman to play with and share, nothing more. If I didn't keep that fact in the forefront of my mind I was likely to get hurt.

"What's wrong?" he asked, suddenly.

"Wrong? Nothing's wrong. Why do you think something's wrong?"

"You got all stiff on me."

"Did I?"

"You do it almost every time I touch you." Dev rolled away and sat up. "So what's wrong?"

I sat up too. Brushing nonexistent dust from my legs, I told him what was on my mind. "I don't want to forget what this is about. Sex with you and Jake is one thing, but this day has been so nice ... too nice ... too romantic. I don't want to get hurt."

Dev was silent for a long while and I began to fear I'd done the wrong thing by telling him ... and doing it so horribly to boot.

"So you want me to back off a bit?" he said, finally breaking the silence.

"When you say it like that I sound horribly rude."

"No, you're not rude. I guess I can understand." He paused. "I'm not being very fair to you, am I?" Saying this, he began to get to his feet.

"You want me to have fun, nothing wrong with that."

He offered me his hand. "It's getting late anyway. You're probably hungry."

I took his outstretched hand and got to my feet. "Famished. Where are you taking me to eat?"

CHAPTER EIGHTEEN

Journal entry 2/13/05, 8:17 a.m.

"Ann, it was amazing. It's the best date I've ever had," I told her the next morning.

"And all you did was kiss?"

I pulled the phone from my ear, stared at it, then rolled my eyes. "No, Ann," I said into the transmitter. "Haven't you heard a word I've said? We talked, we rode a horse, we ate dinner at a quaint family restaurant in Westminster, then he took me to the Inner Harbor and we walked. We walked and talked. It was amazing. I could talk to him forever. It wasn't like I was talking to a man, but like I was talking to someone who'd known me forever. Like he could see into my soul and--"

"Shit, Stella. It's not even nine yet. Could you please give me a break? It's too early for this. I mean, what the hell did this guy do to you? Are you talking about the same guy we saw onstage at Hammerjacks?"

"Mock if you will, but I had a great time. I knew I should have called Katarina. She'd appreciate this."

It was Sunday morning, well after eight, and I was still in bed and I didn't care. I'd had an amazing time with Dev yesterday and had decided I was due a reward. Today I planned to lavish myself with chocolate treats and hours of *Lifetime*. I'd been so incredibly charming last night. And I hadn't said or done anything stupid.

"Only because Katarina's head is up in la-la-land too," Ann was saying.

"Problem now is that I think I may have had too much fun. I'm not so sure about spending the night at their place tomorrow."

"What! That doesn't make sense. You had such a good time with Dev that you don't want to see him anymore? What the hell? You're turning down a Jake and Dev sandwich? Have you lost your mind?"

"I have to figure out what I want before I go any further with them. If I have sex with Jake and Dev it'll confuse things in my mind. They're both amazing guys, and they're both in a relationship with each other. I don't want to get hurt."

Ann was quiet for a moment. Then admitted, "If you think you're going to get hurt, then no, you shouldn't spend the night with them."

This conversation was getting way too heavy for a Sunday morning chat. I decided to change the subject. "Did Sean agree to pose as your date for Operation Lure and Deceive?"

The thought of making Gerard jealous brightened Ann. "Yep. Everything's set. Gerard said he'd be there at ten-thirty so Sean and I are getting there at ten."

"Good." I was about to say goodbye when Ann started speaking again.

"Hey. Katarina's going out with Jim and Meagan has a date, of course. Wanna go to Club Blue with me tomorrow? They're having an anti-Valentine's Day ball. Everybody comes in black, as usual, and ladies get in free till nine."

I shrugged. Now that I'd decided to turn down Jake and Dev, my night was free. "Okay. Wanna meet here at eight?"

"Cool. Later, babe."

* * * *

12:22 p.m.

"Why?" Jake asked again, despite the fact that I'd been on the phone with him for the last thirty minutes explaining that very thing. If he didn't understand by now, he never would.

"I already told you why, Jake."

"I still don't understand."

"Look. I don't doubt how much fun we'd have if I came over tomorrow night, but I don't think it's a good idea. I'm feeling like I want more than sex."

"What is it you want?"

I shrugged. "I don't know. All I know is playing sex toy to you and Dev isn't it."

He breathed heavily into the phone for a few moments. When he began speaking again, he didn't sound amused. "You're not a sex toy to us."

"I am."

"Are you saying you'd rather spend Valentine's Day alone than with Dev and me?"

"No, I'm spending it with Ann at Club Blue."

"I'm not happy, Stella." Jake said, in a voice that made me feel like I was in his kickboxing class all over again.

"I'm sorry, but this is something I have to do."

"It's not nice to make promises you can't keep."

"Come on, Jake. Don't make a big deal out of this. You have Dev. You guys won't even miss me. I'll bet...." I stopped talking when I realized I was having a conversation with a dial tone. Jake had hung up on me.

"Well isn't that nice," I said to no one, then replaced the phone in its cradle.

CHAPTER NINETEEN

Journal entry 2/14/05, 9:27 p.m.

Club Blue was a mad house. Apparently, there were a lot of people who hated Valentine's Day ... and every one of them were packed on the dance floor. With a strobe light making the room flicker from total darkness to neon white, and the throngs of black-garbed people thrashing around to the techno music thrumming through the club, I felt like I'd stumbled into a Nine Inch Nails concert. I doubted I'd be able to escape any time soon. From the looks of Ann with her MGD raised overhead as she bounced to the beat, she was just getting started. I'd lost much of my fervor two songs ago.

It didn't take me long to remember that dancing at a fetish club was a lot different than dancing at a top forty club. At a fetish club you didn't dance so much as you ducked and swerved out of reach of the flailing fists coming at you from every direction. This wasn't typical dancing. This was power dancing. The odd thing was that everyone seemed to be having such a good time. I'd been bumped, stepped on, and kicked. Basically, I was having the crap beaten out of me. On the positive side, I hadn't exerted enough energy to even work up a sweat, which meant my hair was intact.

Deciding I wanted to see the fantasy complex in the basement," I yelled to Ann, "Come on! Let's have a look around!"

Ann pumped one fist overhead and shook her butt. "One more song!"

"I wanna see the fantasy complex! We can dance again later!"

Ann ducked, spun, then glanced at her watch. "Shit."

I didn't hear her curse, but I could see her lips form the words. "What's wrong?"

"Stepped on!"

"You okay?"

Instead of answering, she grabbed my hand and led the way off the dance floor.

Getting away from the melee had proved far more perilous than remaining. If I managed to leave Club Blue tonight without a bruise somewhere on my body I'd count myself lucky.

"Aren't they doing a spanking scene downstairs at ten?" Ann asked when we'd escaped to the relative quiet of the back stairway leading to the basement where hard rock music was pumping from its depths. "I almost forgot. I want to check that out. We should go down early and find a spot to watch."

Having been spanked, the show didn't hold much interest for me. Still, I wanted to get a look at what else went on down there. Last time I was at the club I'd left with Jake before I had a chance to explore. This time, I planned to see exactly what went on in the fetish area of Club Blue.

"I gotta run to the bathroom," Ann was saying. "Wait here. I'll be right back."

She didn't give me a chance to respond because she'd already spun around and started for the bathroom. I considered going after her, maybe checking my hair in the bathroom mirror, but decided to wait. I loved being away from a crowd too much to venture back into another.

"Stick a fork in me 'cause I'm done," I said to myself.

"You haven't even begun."

I jumped at the sound of the male voice then turned to get a look at the speaker.

The sight that greeted me would have been disturbing if I wasn't in a fetish club. As it was, the leather executioner's mask he wore seemed in keeping with the overall theme of Club Blue. So did the leather vest, leather pants, and leather boots. From head to toe this man was dressed in leather. The only visible parts of his body were his exposed biceps-- very large biceps. He looked intimidating as hell. Not a person I'd like to come across in a dark alley, or anywhere else for that matter.

Thinking I was blocking his way to the stairs, I quickly stepped to the left.

When he didn't descend, I began to feel uneasy.

"We can do this one of two ways," he said. The swatch of leather covering his mouth muffled his voice, but he was near enough to me that I could make out his words. "You can go easy, or you can go hard."

I didn't know if Ann was playing a practical joke on me or if this guy was serious. "Go?" I asked him, honestly curious. "Go where?"

"With me."

"I think you have the wrong person. I don't know you."

"Easy or hard, Stella. You got three seconds."

I stared him up and down and sucked my teeth. "How do you know my name? Oh, who cares! I'm not into the fetish scene; I'm just a visitor here. Sorry, I don't wanna play." I began to turn. My intention was to go to the ladies room, find Ann, and tell her I was ready to go home, fantasy complex be damned. I'd only made it to the head of the steps and already I'd met a freak.

"Hard it is," I heard him say.

Strong hands spun me around and took hold of me. In the space of two seconds the man lifted and cradled me as though I were a baby. Biceps flexing, his arms closed around me, strong and sure.

If I'd been watching this happen to some Hollywood actress on the big screen I would have yelled at her to scream, kick, scratch, claw--fight. To do something other than sit there, mouth hanging open like a weakling. But I wasn't watching it happen to someone in a movie, it was actually happening to *me*. Suddenly, I could understand why those actresses were always wide-eyed, frozen with seeming indecision. It wasn't indecision. It was fear. Blind terror hit me with the force of a speeding truck and I simply froze. I wanted to scream but couldn't. I wanted to fight, but forgot how to move.

The shock of this stranger's boldness barely registered before the next shock hit me. He was moving. He was descending the stairs at a jog with me in his arms!

Knowing this man could very well be a criminal with immoral intentions loosened my tongue. Even though we were the only people on the stairs, I screamed bloody murder.

He didn't seem to care. Instead of my screaming giving him pause, he bounded down the stairs, skipping two or three of them at a time. I thought for sure he'd fall, and I'd be a goner, more than once. When he reached the inter-floor landing I'd had no choice but to loop my arms around his neck and hold on for dear life.

The main hall of the fantasy complex was painted dull black and it was littered with lipstick stained cigarette stubs, sticky bits of chewing gum, and condoms still wet with white strings of semen. A fog of smoke rose in the air and specks of orange darted the corridor where onlookers, high from whatever drug cocktail they had partaken of, watched the scene unfold. They stood--barely--leaning heavily against the wall and looking like dazed zombies.

Music boomed from everywhere. Moans, screams, and other sounds from people in various stages of ecstasy drifted to me from the rooms lining the hall.

With the paralysis I'd initially felt gone, I protested in earnest. I screamed, tried to kick, even tried to punch him now that we were on level ground, but nothing fazed him.

"Let go of me!" I screeched into his ear. In desperation, I leaned into him and bit his throat as hard as I could.

That got his attention. He froze, mid step. Abruptly, his grip loosened enough for me to squirm out of his arms. I landed hard on the floor, my feet moving before I'd made contact.

I ran, mindful of the people watching me as though my dilemma was a performance designed for their enjoyment. Seeing the uselessness of screaming, I stopped and decided it would be better to retain whatever energy I could and use it to get away from this guy. But even as I came to that conclusion, footsteps closed in behind me. I could hear him breathing and feel the heat emanating off of his body as he approached. A second later, I was jerked roughly backward as the fiend got a grip on my hair and entwined one oversized fist in it. He pulled and I lost my footing. I fell to the floor in a mass of hair, legs and flailing arms.

The pain was intense. The sharp stinging in my scalp and the throb in my knees was nearly unbearable as he pulled me forward across the rough cement floor just outside the entrance to some private room where erotic music throbbed from within. A blue strobe flashed, making the room flicker between blackness and dim, baby blue light.

"I don't want to hurt you," the fiend said, belying his words by the grip he maintained on my hair.

He was dragging me toward the back of the club. Toward the bright red exit sign.

Not good.

"Somebody help me!"

He laughed. "You think someone in this place will help you? Look around."

That's when reality hit me. I wasn't being ignored. In the room around me people were getting whipped, beaten, and treated roughly. That's why people went to the fantasy complex. To everyone else it must look like I was just another patron enjoying the pleasures of Club Blue.

On the floor above, where I'd just been minutes ago, the din of computer-generated guitars were muffled under the aggressive stomps of fashionable twenty and thirty-something's releasing their pent-up frustrations of the week. I had to admit that my immediate future didn't look promising.

"Let me go."

In answer, he levered me to my feet, set an arm around my waist and lifted. He ran the remaining distance to the exit. All the while, my legs flailed uselessly in the air. He shoved his body against the exit door. It fell open, letting in a cold gust of winter air. Swirls of white powder drifted in through the open door as he carried me out into the night. The door slammed shut behind him.

"Please," I begged, seeing hope fade as he carried me down the back alley beyond the dumpsters where the reeking stench of rotting food arose from inside.

He chucked me over a shoulder. When my exposed stomach met hard muscle, the wind was knocked out of me with such force it left me gasping for air.

Easily, he carried me past the back of the club and out beyond the reach of the dim orange security lights, and towards a black SUV parked at the end of the alley. The pavement was slick with slush and ice.

As the fiend ran, I could see the SUV moving closer and closer.

The frigid winds whipped around my bare legs and goose bumps rose on my skin. My mind raced through the possibilities of what he would do to me. Rape? Murder? I should have gone to the bathroom with Ann. What would she think when she returned to the stairway and found it empty?

His hand was on my leg, one finger wiggling under the patent leather cuff of my PVC skirt. I squirmed, and when I was finally able to breathe again, I screamed.

"Scream all you want," he said. "Nobody's gonna help you."

He reached the SUV and settled me on the ground near the driver's door. Once he had his keys in hand, he beeped the door unlocked, then pulled it open. "Get in,"

"No." I pushed away from the car, tried to twist away from him, but he was too fast and too strong. The car door was open and I was shoved inside before I could even consider how best to defend myself. He moved in behind me, forcing me into the passenger seat. A moment later I heard him shut the door.

I launched myself at the passenger door and wrestled with the handle. When nothing happened I tried slamming my fists against the glass. Still nothing. I was trapped. Fear coursing through my veins, I glared at my captor over my shoulder.

Nonchalantly, he sat in his seat, pouring some noxious substance onto a cloth. Then he looked up and studied me. It was too dark to see more than the mask, but I saw enough to know he had dark hair, dark eyes, and dark intentions.

"Come here," he said, crooking a finger at me. "I've got something for you."

I screamed.

CHAPTER TWENTY

Later.

I woke to the sound of male voices. One was deep, calm, and I knew it to be the voice of my captor. The other was deep as well, but it was raised in anger. The sound of it was harsh, blunt, and intimidating. "I didn't say to beat her bloody," this second voice was saying.

"What was I supposed to do? You didn't say she'd fight me." Did this guy have an accent? I wondered.

"You're twice her size. You can't handle a woman?"

"She was fighting for her life. At least she thought she was."

"Is it a wonder? You dragged her across the floor by her hair. What the hell were you thinking?"

"She bit me."

"Poor baby. Where'd the little girl hurt you? Want me to kiss it better?"

"You wouldn't be so smug if you'd been the one carrying her out of that club. Soon as I got my hands on her she turned into a she-devil. I thought you said she was docile."

"She is docile. Least she is with a man who knows how to take control of a situation. If I didn't think she'd recognize my voice I would have gone. And I wouldn't have brought her home battered and bloody."

"She's not battered or bloody. She has a few tiny scrapes on her knees. She'll recover."

"You enjoyed yourself, didn't you?"

My kidnapper didn't answer immediately. When he did his voice was soft, as gentle as a purr. "What do you think?"

"I think you're a sadist."

"Maybe if you were a little more submissive I wouldn't get my rocks off..." he seemed to think better of what he was about to say. "She really fought me. She kicked and punched, and it was fucking sexy. Wish I could do it again."

By now I knew who my captors were, and I wasn't happy.

I simply couldn't believe this was happening to me. Why me?

I peeked at them through one half opened eye, just to assure myself that my suspicions were right. Sure enough, Jake sat at the foot of the bed. He was running a hand through the lush waves of his hair and shaking his head. I could hear him breathing. The staccato sound of his harsh exhalations told me more about his mental state than his words to Dev had. Jake was furious. He was shirtless and his shoulders rose and fell in time with his heaving breaths. I couldn't see Jake's face because he was facing Dev, but I wasn't sure if I wanted to when he was in such a state.

In stark contrast to Jake, Dev was sitting in an armchair next to the fireplace taking leisurely sips from a goblet filled with a red substance--probably wine. For a man who'd recently strolled into a nightclub and taken a woman captive, Dev looked pretty damned relaxed. Still dressed in the leather pants and vest I'd seen him in earlier, he sat, legs spread wide before him, as he listened to Jake berate him. He didn't seem overly concerned. He'd discarded the executioner's mask so his curls lay flat against his scalp and hung in limp ringlets around his shoulders. He looked like a fallen angel turned roguish imp. Dear God, Dev was one sexy man.

"I wouldn't mind doing it again," Dev said again. "I don't mind a little fight. I know you don't either. Otherwise, you wouldn't be with me."

I decided it was time for me to officially wake up. This little tête-à-tête was getting on my nerves. Docile? I'd show them docile.

The plan was to appear to wake slowly, stretching tiredly while I faked confusion. Once they came closer I'd kick them both in the balls and make my escape.

However, when I tried to stretch my arms they wouldn't budge.

Rage descended on me in the span of a millisecond and I saw red. "Which one of you did this?" I screeched.

Jake bounced off the bed and into the air like a frightened feline. Dev dropped his glass and leapt to his feet.

"Who tied me up?" I went on, unable to stop myself. "You rotten bastards, which one of you tied me to the bed?"

Slowly, Jake and Dev approached. When both men were

next to the bed, they stopped and stared.

I decided I would like to kick Jake first, since he was the closer of the two, and because kidnapping me was more than likely his idea. I tried to pull my leg back so I could get up enough force to drive it into him. Unfortunately, my leg wouldn't move. They'd bound my legs too. I was trussed like a common criminal, tied down and spread eagle on Jake's four-poster.

I screeched again as another insight hit me. I didn't have any clothes on. I was naked. The bastards had not only kidnapped me and tied me spread eagle to the bed, but they'd also stripped me bare.

Unperturbed, they looked at each other. Dev actually had the audacity to smile. "Docile as a kitten," he said, then went to retrieve his fallen wine glass.

"Where are my clothes?" I managed saying through my clenched teeth.

Jake waved this question off. "You won't need them."

I wanted to shake my fist at him, do some kind of damage to him. But I couldn't. I was helpless as a baby and he knew it. A fresh wave of rage descended on me. "You kidnapped me!"

Jake nodded. "I think that pretty much sums up the situation."

"Bastard! What about Ann? Ann's probably called the cops by now."

"Doubtful. I've taken the liberty of phoning her cell phone to inform her of your whereabouts, leaving out, of course, that you came unwillingly."

"You arrogant son of a bitch."

Head tilted inquisitively, Dev stepped beside Jake again. "She's got a mouth on her. Do you think we should paddle her?"

Jake raised a brow and considered. "Maybe later," he decided.

Standing side-by-side staring at me, they seemed transfixed. Jake's thumbs were hooked in the belt loops of his black jeans, his eyes were frozen on my face, and his lips were parted into a delectable looking O. Again, I was left stunned by his beauty and speechless at the desperation I saw in his level gaze. He made no attempt to hide his desire. He seemed to wear it like a badge of honor. It was evident in the slight turning up of the corner of his mouth and in the thickening bulge between his thighs. It was intoxicating to know how much Jake wanted me. Exhilarating to know the great lengths he'd go to have me. Though I knew it was wrong, I was helpless against the rush of warmth that suffused my body as I looked at him. It had never been difficult for Jake to bend me to his will, and as I lay in his bed, naked but for the ropes binding my wrists and ankles to the posts of his four-poster, erotic need descended on me with the force of a ten-foot wave. Anger was replaced with desire, and resentment at being kidnapped was replaced with bone-deep gratitude. My only saving grace was the fact that my pride remained intact. I wanted to be exactly where I was, but I wasn't about to let Jake and Dev off the hook so easily.

"Untie me," I demanded. I was nearly undone at how wispy my voice sounded.

The two men glanced at each other, then back at me again. "I don't think that's gonna happen," Dev said just as Jake was saying, "No."

"What cowards. Not only did it take the both of you to concoct this stupid plan, but the two of you have to keep me tied up? Aren't the odds in your favor enough without the rope?"

Hands on hips, Dev surveyed me. There was a hungry gleam in his eyes as he ran them the length of my naked body. His tongue glided wetly along his lower lip. Then I noticed something peculiar about the way he was standing, and how stiff his shoulders were. He was statuesque, almost like he stood in military formation and thought moving one inch would mean certain death. His arms were frozen in place, and his legs were rigid as stone. Most curiously, the tips of his fingers where they pressed into his hipbone were blanched white. I suddenly realized Dev was exerting a vast amount of energy on keeping self-control.

But this wasn't precisely right. Dev wanted to advance on me, was seemingly frantic to, and he would have had it been just the two of us in the room. But the stance of both men--Dev slightly behind Jake; Dev glancing at Jake from time to time to seek direction--spoke volumes. I knew at once that the only thing keeping Dev in check was Jake. And once Jake let loose the reins, Dev would be on me in an instant.

The other day at my place, Dev had said both of them were dominant, which I didn't doubt. But it didn't take much observation to know who the alpha was in this pack. Clearly, Jake was in charge, and both Dev and I knew it.

"Please, let me beat her," Dev said plaintively, verifying my silent musings. "I'll be gentle ... sort of." The two stared at each other again, each seeming mesmerized by the other. "Come on, Jake." His tongue slid along his lower lip again and Jake grunted. "You can watch. No rope. No handcuffs. Just me, you, Stella, and my riding crop."

Jake didn't respond immediately. He looked at me instead, his eyes lingering over every bare inch of my skin.

"Remember you told me how gorgeous she was under your paddle." Dev closed his eyes and sighed. "You said her skin glistened with a luminescent sheen. She came alive under the paddle, and even fell in love with it. Remember how you told me that she writhed under every blow, and how she moaned for more? Consider how you enjoyed watching her, taking pleasure as her hips rolled, seeing her ass tense as your paddle struck her skin. You can watch now. You don't have to lift a finger, Jake. Just sit by the fire, I'll bring you a glass of the Merlot, and you can watch."

Jake turned to look at Dev. A smile split his lips. Damn it. Jake was actually considering saying yes. Though I had enjoyed Jake's discipline, I wasn't mentally prepared for another round. And especially not with Sadistic Dev wielding the whip. I had to do something. "Hello! Hate to interrupt, but I'd like you to untie me so I can go home."

Jake stared at Dev a moment longer, longing in his eyes. Then slowly, he returned his gaze to me. "You want us to untie you?"

"Yes."

"What would that accomplish?"

"I don't like feeling helpless," I said, not really telling the truth, but it wasn't a complete lie either.

Jake started toward the head of the bed. Unsure of what he was about to do, I stiffened.

He settled one knee onto the pillow beside my head and bent over me. I nearly couldn't believe what was happening when he started undoing the knots binding me to the posts.

At my ankles, Dev followed suit.

They were untying me. Setting me free. That was what I wanted, right? Okay, so why was I disappointed? Did freeing me from my bonds mean I was free to leave?

Once he undid the last knot, Jake sat up and stared down at me. He didn't look like a man who'd just lost a battle. "So you're loose. Now what? You're no less helpless than you were a minute ago?"

Swallowing, I transferred my gaze from Jake to Dev, who was perched at the foot of the bed ... waiting.

So they called my bluff. Big deal. In actuality the rope had been an unimportant prop.

Well, even if I couldn't actually get away I could do something about my nakedness. I doubted they'd return my clothes, but that didn't mean I couldn't cover myself.

Slowly, careful to not make any sudden movements, I began to lower my arms.

"Look at me, Stella," Jake said, voice smooth as silk.

Damn, I thought, twisting my head around to face him.

Jake didn't seem amused or at all like a man who was about to have a good time. Eyes unreadable, mouth set, and hands fisted on his hips, he looked intimidating as hell. "Did I say you could move your arms?"

Another wave of lust descended upon me even as, without being told what he wanted me to do, I returned my arms to their previous position; untied, but stretched over my head in a wide V.

Jake turned to face Dev. "See, Dev. Docile as a kitten."

At the sound of those words, every fiber in my body longed to stretch out a hand and uppercut Jake to the gut. But I'd taken that route with Jake before and all it had gotten me was a paddle to the ass. I didn't care to have a repeat performance tonight so I bit my tongue and forced myself not to respond.

"I'm impressed," Dev said, coming around the opposite side of the bed. It dipped under his weight when he settled atop it. He sat with his hands balled into tight fists for a moment, then he took in a deep breath. "Can I touch her, Jake?"

There was a rustling of the bed sheets as Jake crouched on his knees. Leaning over me, with one hand propped on the bed to hold his weight, Jake ran the fingers of his free hand over Dev's cheek. There was such love in that simple touch, such feeling that a pang of jealousy lit through me. "She belongs to us both tonight," Jake said. "She's ours. You don't need to ask my permission to touch her or to kiss her. I want you to enjoy her. But remember that she's a woman. She's smaller than we are, more fragile. Making love to her won't be like making love to each other. I want you to be gentle with her. Control yourself, at least until she gets accustomed to us."

Dev leaned into Jake's hand, seemed to revel in the physical contact. "No whipping I suppose," Dev said, sounding sad.

"Not for a while," Jake agreed. "You're too heavy handed."

I should have been annoyed at being the object of such a discussion, but my shock at witnessing the depth of love these men shared left me too stunned to think about myself. Jake and Dev were lovers, in every sense of the word.

When they kissed, each man bending forward to capture the other's lips, a sigh of longing escaped me. I hadn't meant to make a sound, but still, as quiet a sound as it was, it was enough to pull them from their two-person reverie. Dev looped his arm behind the back of Jake's neck, let his tongue slide hungrily over his lips, then released him.

The two settled onto the bed and refocused on me.

"I think someone's feeling left out," Dev said. "Are we excluding you, Stella?"

Though his eyes still simmered with repressed desire, playfulness was there that I hadn't seen a moment before.

I searched my mind for something witty to say, but came up empty. It was difficult to be clever when you were naked and had your arms and legs splayed for the pleasure of your companions.

"Touch her Dev," Jake prodded. "I want to see your hands on her."

"Nothing would thrill me more," Dev said.

My breath caught when Dev ran a finger over my nipple. Desire blazed through me like a streak of lightning, more powerful due the intense feminine longing that had been steadily building within me for the past ten minutes. Still, despite Jake's prodding, it didn't feel right to have Dev's fingers on me, touching me in such an intimate manner. I looked to Jake, hoping to gauge his response. Did his emotions match his words? If I could see what he thought of this, I could better decide how to respond.

"Don't look at him," Dev said. "Look at me."

Jake's face was as expressionless as granite. I didn't have any other choice but to do what Dev said. So I turned to face him.

"That's more like it ... kitten," Dev added, teasing my nipple with the tips of his fingers.

A low moan slid from between my lips before I could stop it.

"You like that?" Dev asked, repeating the movement.

I tried hard to control my response to him but it was near to impossible. The gentle touch of his hand on my skin was incredible. How could something so simple as a touch have me so close to losing control?

"I think she's warming to us," Dev said. He punctuated his statement by giving my nipple a squeeze.

"Oh God!" I cried.

"Is that right?" Jake asked, still not touching me. "You warming to us?"

When I didn't answer quickly enough, Dev gave my nipple another, torturous squeeze.

"Oh, Dev," I whimpered, reaching blindly for him. I wanted to tangle my fingers in the rich honey that was his hair, pull him closer to me and have a taste of him. A longer taste than he had offered before. I wanted to taste and touch until my heart was content, feel his body against me and know the full force of his desire. I wanted him to want me as much as he wanted Jake.

My fingers grazed the collar of his leather vest, but he leaned back and out of my reach before I could get a hold of him and draw him forward. My hands slid down the slick material over his chest and fell into his lap.

Dev's eyes glimmered with mischief ... and pleasure. "Look at her, Jake. She wants this bad. Don't you, kitten?"

Since my hands were already in his lap, I sought the hardening mass of flesh I could see straining at the crotch of his pants. I was so near to touching it, inches from clasping his zipper and drawing it down when Jake moved forward on the bed. He clasped my wrists in one hand and levered them over my head with a quick ease that left me dazed.

"Did I say you could move your arms?" he wanted to know. He pressed my wrists to the mattress, pinning me there. "Move them again and I let Dev get his riding crop."

I glanced up at Dev who blew me a kiss. Getting to his knees, Dev splayed his hands on either side of my head and gazed at me. "Stella," he said in a low, teasing voice. "I want you to touch me. I want to feel your hands all over me."

To accent how serious he was, he stood and slipped his arms from the leather vest. He let the vest drop to the floor, forgotten, then set his knees atop the bed and leaned over me again.

"You're as gorgeous as Jake," I said, before I even considered what such a statement would sound like. But really, what woman in my position could've stopped herself? Though he was nowhere near as muscular as Jake, his body was lithe and every muscle well-defined. He could've been sculpted from marble. Fine brown hair circled pink nipples. There was a trail of curly brown hair descending from his stomach into the waistband of his pants. Suddenly, I wanted him out of those pants. Was desperate to follow that enticing path and see where it led me.

"Touch me then, kitten," he said again. "Touching is the most underrated part of lovemaking. There's so much pleasure in a simple stroke of the finger." To demonstrate what he meant, he ran his finger down the valley between my breasts, sending a riot of delicious sensations through me. "So much satisfaction in the feel of your lover, in the silk of their skin." He found my nipple again and his finger glided over it. "Touch me, kitten."

Though Jake held my wrists pinioned to the bed, I didn't doubt he'd release me if I struggled against him. Unsure of what to do since Jake's whipping warning remained fresh in my mind, I chanced a look at Jake.

Jake stared back. "Who's in control here, tonight?"

I didn't have the faintest idea anymore. Could be either of them. There was one thing I knew for sure. "Not me," I offered.

He gave my wrists a squeeze; I supposed it was to remind me just how little control I had.

"You?" I asked.

"You asking or telling?"

I stared, unsure if this was a trick question. "Telling," I decided, as the word left my lips.

Jake nodded. "And Dev. What do you think will happen if I let you go and you move your arms?"

I stared up and into Dev's brown eyes. Their predatory gleam spoke volumes. "He'll whip me," I said.

"And love doing it," Dev agreed. "And I think you'd love it. You're so turned on right now I wouldn't be surprised if the next time I touch you that you come."

Jake studied me. "She'd better not. You hear me, Stella. You don't climax until I give you permission."

"But--" I tried, realizing that not only had I lost control of the decision on when to move, but I'd just lost control over when I could have an orgasm.

"If you come before I say, I'll bend you over that chair myself and hold you down while Dev beats you. Got it? Tell me you understand."

"I understand," I said, no less aroused. In fact, I found as I gave up control to Jake and Dev, my need for sexual release grew to inhuman proportions. I was weak with my arousal, and so turned on I was willing to do nearly anything if it meant one of them would mount me, slide their cock inside, and ride me hard.

"She is a docile little thing, isn't she?" Dev observed. "Kitten, I can't wait to fuck you. I'm gonna make you feel so good you'll never want to leave us," Dev promised, letting his fingers dance over my stomach. "Would you like that?"

I'd love that. I wanted that. Had been desperate for that from the first moment I saw him strut into the equipment room last month.

Jake sprawled, lengthwise, beside me. He threw one jean-clad thigh over mine, pinning my hips to the bed beneath him. With Dev crouching over me and my wrists held tight in Jake's hand, he kept me splayed beneath him with the press of one leg. I felt stretched, laid bare, and wonderfully helpless.

Jake cupped my other breast and the warmth of his hand radiated through my entire body. When he began to knead and stroke my nipple, my insides turned to mush.

It was a slow torture, this erotic play. Both men touched, just enough to stimulate, stroked, only to tease. I was desperate to be filled, so in need of an orgasm I couldn't think straight.

Dev squeezed the pebbly bud of my erect nipple again, this time punctuating the squeeze with a flick over the sensitive nub with his thumb. "Would you like that?" he asked again, reveling in his slow torture. His eyes were fixed on my face, intense and knowing. "Would you like me to take off my pants, impale that luscious pussy of yours, and fuck you hard?"

I opened my mouth, licked my lips because they felt parched, then Jake was there. His mouth closed over mine with such force it took my breath away. His tongue was hot on mine, demanding, but his lips were soft. His skin was smooth and silky, and he was indescribably delicious. I met his kiss, offered myself to him. As our mouths melded, demanded more of the other, Dev's lips locked onto my nipple.

I arched as soon as the slick wetness of Dev's mouth heated my skin. His tongue lashed the hot bud in long, wet licks. When he began flicking his tongue over the sensitized flesh I thought I'd go mad.

I sighed into Jake's mouth and he deepened the kiss, swallowing my whimpers. Suddenly all of this was too much. There was too much sensation, too much stimulation. Every touch drove me to a higher level of need; every stroke left me more desperate for release.

"I want her first," Dev whispered around my skin. He released my nipple with a wet, *pop.* Eyes trained on mine, he told Jake, "I want to feel that tight pussy you've been telling me about."

Before Jake could answer, Dev parted my thighs with his knee and eased himself into place. Even through the leather pants I could feel his erection. It was enormous and solid as a rock."

"Yes!" I begged. My pride had gone out the window some time ago. I writhed on the bed beneath Dev; too desperate for his cock to behave with any decorum, and too terrified this was merely another tease to truly believe Dev was finally going to take me.

I nearly screamed in protest when he retreated. The only

thing that held me together was the fact that he didn't go far. He crouched between my thighs, hands on his zipper. His chocolate eyes simmered as he gazed at me. The only sound in the room was the soft flicker of the fire, our breathing, and the sound of metal gliding over metal as Dev undid his pants and slid them low on his hips. As soon as I saw the tufts of hair between his legs and the thick erection jetting up from the curls, I let out a soft moan.

Dear God, the man was huge!

Licking his lips, Dev lowered himself even as Jake slid his thigh away to make room.

"You want this bad, don't you, baby," Jake said.

"Oh yeah," I said.

Dev settled on me. Already, his pale skin was slick with sweat. He was hot and indescribably perfect. His muscled chest was hard and unyielding against my breasts. The curled edges of his hair fanned out across his wide shoulders. It struck me again how angelic he looked. But he was no angel.

Dev closed his eyes for a moment, seeming to struggle for control.

"She's tight," Jake reminded him. "Don't hurt her."

"Hurt me," I begged. I was a little surprised to hear myself give voice to the sentiment, but I cared for about a millisecond. "I don't care what you do as long as you do it right now."

Dev's lips quirked into a grin, but he said nothing.

"What a dirty little girl you've become," Jake observed. Still clasping my wrists, he released my breast, slid his arm between Dev and me, and eased it between my thighs. "You are soaking," he informed me, unnecessarily since I could feel the moisture seeping out even as I lay there.

Jake's fingers trailed over my quim, brushed against the skin of my labia, before he found my nub and gave me a slow, languorous stroke.

"Oh God, help me," I begged. "Please Dev."

Closing finger and thumb around my clitoris, Jake stroked, teased, and prodded me to a higher plain of desire. I squirmed beneath this exquisite torture, rolled my head back and forth.

"Please Dev," I said again. "I'm begging."

Jake fell on me. When his lips closed over mine, when I

felt his tongue against my lips, nudging them open, my world stopped. He kissed me with an aggressive eagerness that made my blood boil. I welcomed the taste of him, I breathed in the intoxicating scent of him, cried out for more.

With Jake focused on my mouth and my clit, Dev rotated his hips and positioned himself. "Want me to fuck you now, kitten?" Dev wanted to know.

"Please," I panted against Jake's lips, so excited I could scarce think a coherent thought.

Jake used his thumb on my clit, making tiny circles and driving me to the brink of madness.

"Ask me nicely, then," Dev was saying.

Dear God, he wanted me to ask nicely? "Fuck me," I said, trying desperately to sound sweet. I knew, though, that I sounded more out of breath and needy than anything else.

He shifted his cock, eased it closer, nearer the entrance. "Say, please."

"Please! Please fuck me, Dev. Please, fuck me now."

Dev drove into me fast and hard. The unexpected movement sent shockwaves of pleasure racing through my body. I reeled and bucked beneath both men, twisted uncontrollably when Dev eased his erection back then slid into me a second time.

"Oh God!" I cried, beyond any self-control.

Jake leaned onto an elbow and surveyed the proceedings with obvious pleasure. As though we were his students and this joining was our final exam.

"Oh, Dev," I managed, as he found a rhythm and rode me as hard as he had promised. Our skin smacked, the sound sex seemed to echo off the walls.

Dev bent to me, pressed his lips to mine and kissed me. His tongue moved leisurely over mine as he took his time tasting. Still, his kisses were hungry, like those of a ravenous man. I thought he would have swallowed me whole had he been able.

I would have wrapped my arms around him and pulled him close had Jake not been holding my arms pinned to the bed over my head. I was forced to lay docile beneath Dev, completely at his mercy. All I could do was meet him thrust for thrust as he rode me into a state of complete, all-encompassing rapture.

Beside me, Jake moved. He tangled his fingers in Dev's hair and gave him a tug. I tried to suck Dev's tongue into my mouth, was desperate to keep him where he was, but Jake was insistent and would not be denied. Even as Dev's mouth slid away from mine, Jake edged closer. Their tongues met in the air, parried, then Jake pulled Dev closer still and deepened the kiss.

Even as Dev moved within me, his tongue danced in Jake's mouth. I could hear Jake panting as his arousal increased, see his fingers tighten in his lover's hair as he angled for more access.

When the two parted, both men turned to look at me.

Lost in the thrill of Dev moving inside of me, I didn't realize what they intended until they descended on me.

Jake's lips touched mine first, then Dev was there, intermittently licking my lower lip and sucking the tender skin into his mouth, then doing the same to Jake. All of our tongues met, tasted, and explored. I'd never been kissed by two men before, least of all at the same time. With Dev inside of me, Jake teasing my clit, and both men within my mouth, I did all I could not to scream.

Dev rode me hard, withdrawing till he was nearly free of my body, then thrusting forward. My body had become nothing more than a sensor of pleasure. Dev worked me until I didn't think I could take any more, and then he drove me further. It was better than anything I'd ever experienced in thirty years of life.

Before today I didn't think I'd take to having to submit to both men at the same time, but now I was glad they'd taken matters into their own hands and brought me here despite my refusal to join them.

Lying with Jake and Dev was pure ecstasy.

Abruptly, Jake withdrew from our joined kissed. I felt the pressure on my wrists ease. Suddenly, they were freed. I found I could lift them if I wanted to. I figured I wouldn't press my luck. Chances were that although Jake had released my hands, he wanted them to remain where they were.

Next to go was the tickling sensation on my clitoris.

Before I could protest, Dev sprawled atop me and took over the kiss. He drove his cock into me hard, rotated his hips, and pulsed inside of me. I shuddered under the luscious sensations. Even as I screamed his name I could feel my insides wanting to spasm, feel them drawing an orgasm up and out of me.

I barely noticed when Jake eased off the bed and disappeared from sight. I only saw him, a moment later, when he reappeared behind Dev because the bed dipped when he crawled back on it.

"Does my dick feel good, baby?" Dev demanded.

"Feels amazing," I managed. I was too lost in the feel of Dev to wonder what Jake was up to. I was too close to my own release to consider anyone else but me. "Oh God Dev, I'm gonna come."

Abruptly, Dev stilled. At the same time, Jake reasserted his presence with a dictate. "No you don't," he said. "We haven't given you permission."

I wanted to cry out my frustration, clasp Dev's buttocks and make him move within me again. It took every bit of strength I had to remain still on the bed and wait. They weren't looking for a she-devil--as Dev had called me--but someone more acquiescent. They wanted me pliant and submissive, not stiff and demanding.

"You don't come...." Dev was saying and then trailed off.

Jake's fingers closed over Dev's hips and Jake eased closer to him, making Dev twist his head around. Glancing over his shoulder, he began to say something to Jake. The words, however, never came. Dev swung around to face me and his eyes rolled up in his head. A low moan of pure ecstasy slid from between his lips and he collapsed on top of me.

"Oh, fuck," he muttered. "Stop Jake. I can't concentrate if you do that. Oh!"

Jake didn't stop, however. He thrust again, driving Dev forward so deliberately this time that Dev's cock slid within me, setting off shockwaves in my body. I moaned and Dev went positively mad.

Drawing himself up onto his elbows, Dev opened his eyes and gave me an evil grin. "Now you've done it," he said, finishing on a groan as Jake eased out then plunged again. "Oh, fuck! That feels good."

I cried out, heady with the thought of release, as Dev was forced deeper into me again.

Jake fell against Dev. He splayed his hands on both sides

of my head and rested his entire body weight on Dev. I was grateful Dev had had the foresight to hold his own weight on his elbows. If not, I would have been crushed. Together, I knew they had to weigh a good four hundred pounds. Maybe more.

"Fuck Stella," Jake ordered when Dev seemed completely unable to move under his own steam. He drove into Dev so hard his arms nearly went out from under him. Jake didn't withdraw this time. He pressed his lips to Dev's ear, ran his tongue along the outer edge then began to whisper into it. "Don't torment her, Dev. She wants this bad. Just like you want it bad." Saying this, Jake drew back and sank into Dev again, bringing a plaintive moan from Dev's lips. "Look at her, Dev."

Both men stared at me. Jake's expression was soft, rapturous even as Dev's was dazed with sensation overload. Dev's eyes began to clear though, and a moment later he eased back, his cock setting off tremors in me. When he thrust, it was deliciously hard. I cried out even as he was pulling back. He withdrew, nearly to the point of slipping free, then set his teeth and drove deep into me.

I screamed again, as pleasure descended with a force that staggered me. I bucked beneath Dev, met him thrust for thrust. I was so desperate for release, so in need to climax I thought I'd lose my mind if I had to wait much longer.

Dev's hips moved with piston like precision and strength. Every thrust sent lusciously erotic vibrations churning through my stomach, tingling up my spine, and settling between my legs. I lost all control. Every possession had me crying out for more, every withdrawal had me sucking in a breath in preparation for the next. This was pleasure unparalleled.

The tingle in my quim quickly increased, became more demanding. I knew an orgasm was dancing on the periphery, swirling just out of reach.

"Did I say you could come?" Jake demanded, riding Dev as hard as Dev was riding me.

"Please," I begged.

"No."

Dev groaned, as if the "no" had not been for me, but for him. That's when I realized that there wasn't a state of existence that could adequately describe what Dev was feeling. Even as Dev slid into me, Jake was easing out of him. As Dev withdrew, Jake was slamming himself home. I knew that what I was feeling was as close to euphoria as I figured I'd ever get. I also knew by the rapturous look on Jake's face that he was feeling damn good, as well. But one look at Dev and I would have given my right arm to experience the sensations roiling through his body. No matter what he did, no matter how he moved, two people were pleasuring him. Even as I stared up at him, Dev grunted and groaned, seemed to struggle for focus.

"Too much!" Dev cried out. "I can't hold it."

Mercifully, Jake gave the command I'd been desperate to hear.

"Come," he said.

As if his voice had been the trigger I needed, the orgasm spilled over me like hot milk. I bucked beneath both men, twisted and screamed as I climaxed. Above me, Dev thrust in deep and pulsed. Then he froze and let out a groan, I knew he was ejaculating into me and Jake into him.

When it was over, the three of us collapsed onto the bed in a heap.

I don't remember much after that.

Exhausted and satiated, I fell fast asleep.

* * * *

Journal entry 2/15/05, 4:00 a.m.

I woke with a start, then covered my ears against the obnoxiously loud whining of an alarm clock. I didn't use an alarm clock so I had no idea where this one had come from.

All around me was darkness--at first. Then, as my eyes adjusted to the dimness, I saw the dying embers of what had once been a blazing fire. And that was when I remembered where I was.

"Go back to sleep," a man advised. He fumbled with the clock for a moment, then the horrible sound was gone.

"Jake?" I whispered.

A low chuckle sounded from beside me. "Sorry about that," Jake said. "Dev sleeps right through the alarm so I didn't think to turn it down last night."

I was lying on my side, facing him, with something very hot, and very large curled behind me. Dev, I realized.

I reached blindly in front of me until I found Jake's arm. "What's going on?" I asked.

I felt him stretch, listened in the darkness as he yawned. "Work," he said.

"Do you have to go? It's not like anyone can fire you."

"Do you ever blow off work?"

Sighing, I released him. "No. Sorry." I hated it when people assumed that because I work for myself I could arbitrarily take off days whenever I pleased. Working for yourself didn't mean you could be lax. Quite the contrary, it meant you had to be ten times more devoted and put ten times more of your energy and strength into your work.

Jake sat up, then eased out of bed. Immediately, I felt his absence. I wanted to reach for him and pull him back to me, but I fought the impulse.

"When will you be back?" I asked his retreating form.

"I'll be home around one-thirty." He stepped into the bathroom, flicked on the light, and turned to face me. "Will you wait for me to come home?"

I considered, but only for a moment. "Can't. Have too much work to do at home."

Nodding, he disappeared into the bathroom and shut the door. I heard the shower come on a moment later.

I was debating the merits of getting up myself and heading home when I felt Dev move behind me. With an unintelligible murmur, he slid his arms around my waist and pulled me close. The warmth that had escaped when Jake left the bed was replaced with Dev's body heat.

"You're not going anywhere, kitten. Not yet," he said, as if he could read my mind.

Then he was there, the taut length of him stroking gently between my cheeks, prodding me to open my legs for him. At his touch, my body began to waken, to rouse with languid desire. Even as I leaned into him in welcome, he rocked his hips against me. He eased between my thighs, not entering me, but slowly lubricating himself with the moisture seeping from between my folds. His movements were slow, unhurried.

When I thought I couldn't take anymore of this delicious torture, he slid into me.

I would've cried out if he hadn't covered my mouth with one large hand.

"Not too loud," he advised. "Don't want Jake to hear?"

I wanted to know why, but my body and mind had

descended into a sexual haze. Nothing mattered but the delicious sensations sweeping through me as Dev moved inside.

He cupped my breasts with his free hand, teased my nipples until I was gasping for air. The combination of the slow rocking of his hips and the gentle touch of his fingers felt too good.

He traced a path over my stomach, then between my legs. Gently, almost playfully, he tickled my clitoris.

"God, Dev," I hissed against his palm. I wanted to scream his name, to cry out how good this felt.

He seemed to want to draw the pleasure out, to slowly ride me until I was mad with my need for release. But my body was too sensitive to his touch for a leisurely coring. I whimpered against his hand, rode his thrusts, pushing back until the full length of him impaled me.

"Yes," he whispered into my ear.

He seemed to sense my need, to know I couldn't hold on much longer. He quickened the pace, driving into me, possessing me totally, then retreating. Each penetration felt better than the last, each withdrawal left me closer to climax.

As Jake turned off the shower in the bathroom, I crested hard. The orgasm rolled over me, making me moan even as Dev spilled into me for the second time in mere hours.

When we were done, we both lay still, panting.

Jake's soft footfalls as he moved around the bathroom were the only sounds I heard as Dev drew me onto my back and rolled onto me. The kiss that followed was slow and deep.

* * * *

7:58 a.m.

"Wake up."

I rolled over and shoved my face into the pillow. "Go away Ann."

"This isn't Ann." A warm hand pushed under the comforter and a finger slid down my spine. Leisurely it moved over my skin until it came to the juncture of my lower back and buttocks. "It's Dev."

I shifted my head to the side, opened one eye and peeked. Bright sunlight streamed into the bedroom through two huge picture windows. Dev was on the opposite side of the bed so I couldn't see him, but I could see a few tangled snarls of black hair on the pillow beside me. Unfortunately the black snarls belonged to me.

That's when it hit me.

Dear God above, what had I been thinking? Bed Head! I had Bed Head. I had bed head and Dev was in the room. Dev, the lead singer of Maverick was going to see me with bed head. Dev the rock god! And the room was alight with morning sunshine. Last time I'd stayed over I'd had sense enough to shower and dress when the room was still shadowy and dark.

He'd take one look at me and never want to see me again. *Argh!*

"I made breakfast. Don't want it to get cold." The lone finger glided over my right butt cheek and paused. "Belgian waffles."

The covers were piled high around me, a fact I was grateful for. For a second I was tempted to pull them over my head and hide until he left the room. "I'll be down in a minute."

The finger made tiny little figure eights on my rear, tickling my flesh and awakening a part of my anatomy best left to slumber. "I'll walk you."

A delicious shiver moved over me and I had to swallow down the sigh of pleasure this contact produced. For about a millisecond I considered rolling onto my back and pulling Dev on top of me and then common sense kicked back into place. Women with bed head didn't do the sexy vixen thing. Women with bed head never rolled onto their back in bright sunlight. Women with bed head hid under the covers until the coast was clear lest their lover take one look at them and run for the hills.

Desperate for Dev to leave, I announced, "I have to pee."

The finger paused again. A moment later the hand slid away and Dev rose from the bed. "All right, kitten. I'll be downstairs."

* * * *

8:22 a.m.

The day was sunny, but the temperature had dropped considerably. Dev had left me on the chilly terrace while he went to the kitchen and gathered our reheated breakfast. The idea was to eat under the crystalline February sun with the city skyline visible across the harbor. Problem was it was far too cold to enjoy the view, the sun, or even the company. I was settled on a fat cushioned deck chair, drowning in one of Dev's jogging suits, and shivering so badly I doubted I'd be able to eat. Though I'd only been outside for about five seconds, the wind cut into me like shards of ice. The morning air was chill. I could see white puffs of breath hover over my mouth when I breathed.

"Want me to light a fire?"

I turned in time to see Dev step from the French doors with a glossy silver tray piled with dishes, mugs, coffee, and a syrup decanter, balanced in his arms. The wonderful aroma of Belgian waffles, strawberry syrup, and French vanilla coffee filled my nostrils. For a moment I forgot about the cold. But an icy breeze off the harbor remedied that. "Isn't it illegal to use a grill in Maryland if you don't live on the ground floor?"

Dev settled the tray on the glass top table before me and waved my words off. "From this high up nobody will see the smoke."

"Your neighbors?"

"They do it all the time too." Dev walked to a far corner of the terrace giving me an opportunity to stare at his butt.

He was wearing loose, black jogging pants, a sweat jacket, and was trolling around the cold floor barefoot. Damned if he didn't look good. For some reason the sight of his naked feet left me wanting to see the rest of him naked. Again. I had a sudden vision of Dev returning to me, lifting me onto the table and spreading my thighs, then plunging inside me. The memory of his body on mine as he rode me to my climax was still very vivid. Jake hadn't been kidding when he said Dev was good in bed.

"Looks like you're in fantasy land."

My face grew hot. Was I that obvious?

Dev dragged a large object close to the table, then pulled a plastic cover off of it. Beneath the cover was a copper fire bowl. It was relatively large, and set in a wrought iron stand with an iron screen grill cover. Dev crouched, lifted the screen, then began poking at three charred logs inside the bowl. The remnants didn't look promising. "I'll be right back." Saying this, he rose and went back inside.

Okay Stella, I told myself, *it's time you got your mind out of the gutter. Stop thinking about sex.* But it was hopeless. Every other second I'd catch myself thinking about Jake and Dev's kisses and a fresh shiver would light through my body as though they were there, kissing me. Or I'd close my eyes and remember the lush sensation of having Dev fill me.

I had to get out of there and back home. If I stayed much longer there was no doubt I'd say something to make a fool of myself.

Dev returned while I was alternately berating myself and fantasizing. Within minutes he had a fire blazing in the copper bowl. Heat rose from the bowl, warming my legs, hands, and face. It felt wonderful.

Dev rose and came to the table. He rubbed his palms over his thighs to dislodge any loose dust stuck to his hands. Just watching him made me heady with desire. "So what are you thinking about, kitten?"

"Just wondering what size you wear." I lifted an arm to display the loose sleeve of his jogging shirt.

Hands clean of dust, he bent over the table and forked two waffles onto my plate. He was laughing to himself and shaking his head. "You look like a little girl playing dress up. You're positively swimming in my clothes."

"I'd have worn my own if you'd given me a chance to grab my coat last night."

"Yeah? How would that have worked?"

I shrugged. "I don't know. I might have gone with you if you'd just asked."

He settled across from me and poured sweet strawberry syrup over his waffles. "My way was more fun. You really put up a fight. That was so sexy. I nearly creamed my pants before I'd even gotten you out of there." He paused, glanced at me. "Admit it, you enjoyed yourself."

"I could have hurt you, you know."

He snorted. "In your dreams."

"I could have kneed you in the balls, or poked your eyes out, or scratched your face, or...." I ran out of possibilities.

"Kitten, from go I had total control of the situation and you know it."

"Says you."

"That's right. Says me."

I didn't know what to say to that kind of logic so I didn't

say anything at all.

I forked food into my mouth then was unfortunate enough to catch my reflection in the silver. I didn't have any of my hair products with me this morning and hadn't even thought to twist my hair before I'd gone to sleep. I'd managed to get my hair into some semblance of order. It was loose, brushed straight, and it hung with about as much life as hay. I'd had to apply extra eyeliner and lip-gloss to make up for the hair.

"Rest assured, you're beautiful as ever, kitten."

Sheepishly, I set the fork down and smiled across the expanse of the table at him. His hair fell around his head in loose curls and his lips were curved into a sensual smile. This was a man who oozed sex. It didn't matter that it was just after eight in the morning, the man looked primed and ready for carnal play … and I was just as ready. "Thanks. And breakfast is good. Did I say that already?"

"Nope. Did I tell you how much Jake and I enjoyed ourselves?"

My face went hot with embarrassment, so I changed the subject. "Does Maverick have any CD's out?"

He stared at me for a beat then arched a brow. "Change of subject, eh. Don't want to talk about sex? No, don't answer. I can see by that wide eyed, deer caught in headlights look you're giving me that you don't." He tilted his head to the side and fingered his lower lip. "Maverick, right? You asked me about my band. Well, as a matter of fact we do have a CD out. Two in fact. We were picked up by an independent label a while back." He shrugged. "We've been on 98 Rock a few times but that's about the extent of our radio career. We sell most of our CD's at shows."

"I thought you guys were great at Hammerjacks. You have amazing stage presence…and a wonderful voice … it's all dreamy and sexy." *Shut up, Stella. Shut up, now!* "Seeing you onstage was like watching a rock god." *Did I just say that?* "It's not like you're an upper case G kind of god, not like you're God or anything, but a lower case G kind of god. I just mean you're…great…in a lower case G kind of way." Before the words were out I gave myself a mental slap. Could I have possibly said anything stupider? I doubt it. But what did I care? The chances Jake and Dev would want to see me again were slim to nil.

Dev merely smiled. "Rock god, eh. I like that."

I fixed my eyes on my plate and endeavored to keep my mouth shut.

"I want to do this again."

I slowly raised my head. "Huh?"

"Jake and I always talked about sharing a woman, but I don't think either of us anticipated how enjoyable it would be."

Had I heard him correctly or were my ears playing tricks on me?

In the manner of a half-wit, I smiled inanely. "Yeah?"

"Yeah."

Both Dev and I looked up at the sound of this new voice.

Jake closed the doors behind him and stepped out onto the terrace. "I left work early. Couldn't concentrate knowing you were here, Stella."

Dressed in a black track suit with a white stripe running the length of both legs, Jake looked amazing. His hair was pulled into a ponytail that looked slightly damp, so I figured he'd showered before coming home. He was big, and sexy, and apparently had come home for sex ... with me ... and Dev.

Dear God, what should I do? "I'll be going home soon."

Jake crossed to the table and loomed over me. He smelled spicy and delicious. The luscious scent of his body filled me. "I think you should stay, Stella."

"I've got work to do at home."

"I've been thinking about the fact that you left the gym and probably haven't had a good work out in weeks."

"Huh?"

Casually, he brushed a few strands of hair from his face, then proceeded to inform me that, "Stella, I think it's time we put together a new fitness program for you."

CHAPTER TWENTY-ONE

I shoved my plate away and glared at Jake. "Do what?"

"You left my class, which I understand, but I think it's time you start thinking about a workout routine, don't you. You're not getting any younger, and it's obvious you've no intention of rejoining my class."

I was speechless. What could I say to such an announcement? And delivered with such stone-faced determination. I gathered my thoughts and uttered the only coherent word I could think of. "Exercise?"

Jake looked me over, then nodded. "You're weak, Stella. I thought we discussed this already."

"Yeah, but then we had sex. Didn't sex cancel out the exercise thing? I thought it did."

"Don't concern yourself, I won't work you too hard. And you don't have to rejoin the gym so don't worry about paying a membership fee. We have everything you need right here."

Won't work me too hard? Rejoin the gym? Membership fee? What in the hell was Jake talking about? Had he lost his friggin' mind? If he thought I was going to spend my day being stretched out and overworked by him he had another thing coming.

Too stunned to take part in this discussion anymore, I turned to Dev for support, which proved an act in futility.

"Don't look at me, kitten," Dev said with a shrug. "Fitness is Jake's department."

"Okay then." Jake offered me his hand. "Come on, Stella."

"What?" I'd been bamboozled. "What about breakfast. I'm not finished yet."

Across from me, Dev was on his feet. As Jake waited for me to rise, Dev lifted my nearly empty plate from the table. The bastard. One look at him and I knew I'd been duped. He moved around the table, collecting our glasses with quick efficiency, making no effort to hide his smile.

"Stella," Jake said, easily slipping into kickboxing

instructor mode. "I'm waiting."
Shit!
Shit! Shit! Shit!
He was serious. Jake wanted to work me out...and not in the way I'd been fantasizing about half the morning. Back in January when Katarina and I made the mistake of taking Jake's kickboxing class, I'd regretted it from day one. It hadn't taken long to realize Jake Santos took fitness way too seriously. One hour in his class was enough for me to know Jake wasn't teaching a kickboxing class; he was conducting boot camp. I'd never experienced more pain than I had for the two weeks I'd been a prisoner in Jake's class. There was no way in the world I was going to subject myself to the horror of Crazy Jake the Fitness Nazi, again. In a class of thirty-four--including me--Jake was an absolute menace. I couldn't imagine what he'd be like giving one-on-one instruction. "I don't think this is such a good idea, Jake."

Jake stared down at me, expression bland. "You don't trust me?"

Quite frankly, I didn't. "Trust is such an overused word."

"Either you do or you don't."

Dev, who'd left the terrace with our glasses stacked in a neat tower seconds earlier, returned holding a floral print gift box. "Don't badger her, Jake. If she doesn't want to, she doesn't have to." He slid a glance at me. "But I think you'll want to, kitten, if you know what I mean."

"Private lessons, Stella. I've always told you that's what you need," Jake added.

"We took the liberty of making this purchase for you," Dev added. Dev brought the box to me and placed it in my hands. "Surprise."

Suspicious of this turn of events, I studied the box. It seemed harmless enough. Pretty pink and lavender flowers printed across the surfaces, it even smelled faintly of "Poison". This was disturbing. Clearly Jake and Dev were up to something. Exactly what that something was, remained to be seen. "A present for me? Why?"

Jake's expression had gone from bland to glassy eyed and dreamy. "Why not?" He palmed his crotch and gave it a gentle squeeze.

My hungry body roused and the desire I'd been trying to

control all morning nearly crushed me. I watched Jake massage his cock, stared on as it lengthened in his pants and grew hard.

"Kitten." I pulled my gaze away from Jake and looked at Dev who was sliding his tongue over his lower lip. When he spoke his voice was little more than a hoarse whisper. "Go to the bathroom on the second floor and put your present on. We'll be waiting for you in the bedroom down the hall from ours."

I watched Dev a beat longer, then refocused on Jake. Gnawing on my lower lip, I pulled the top of the box off and stared inside. Buried in piles of pink tissue paper was something red.

"You don't like it?" In his loose jogging suit Dev looked disarmingly boyish. A wave of guilt washed over me as I took in his look of disappointment.

"No," I said quickly, putting the top back on the box. "I love it."

"Good," Jake said. "Go try it on."

A good ten minutes later I stood in the upstairs bathroom, staring at myself in the mirror in stunned silence.

They'd brought me a two-piece, workout uniform ... in red spandex of all things. The top barely covered my breasts, and the bottoms were so tight as to be obscene. Designed to look fashionable, as though the wearer would be exercising in a nightclub, the two-piece get up sported a low-cut neckline, a hip hugging waist ... oh, and no crotch. Okay, so maybe I was exaggerating. There was a crotch, but I didn't see the purpose of it since there was a wide slit where it would have counted. I didn't know whether they wanted me to work out or pose for a camera.

I supposed I was to go sans panties while wearing it.

I did love the white and red matching Sketchers they'd purchased. They were cute and made my size seven and a half feet look dainty and at least one size smaller than they were.

Still, I wasn't sure what Jake and Dev were up to. Did they want to exercise or did they want to have sex? Though I was wearing a spandex workout suit, it was crotchless. Clearly the exposed crotch meant they wanted sex.

As I thought about this, the idea held more appeal. Jake,

fitness guru that he was, wouldn't seriously expect me to exercise in something that was missing a crotch. So that meant it wasn't exercise they had on their mind, but sex.

Deciding to go with the flow, I unlocked the bathroom door and stepped into the hall. Dev said they'd be in the bedroom at the end of the hall. Feeling more confident than I had since Jake brought up the subject of exercise, I sauntered into the bedroom, and froze, aghast.

Bedroom my ass! This wasn't a bedroom, it was a medieval torture chamber! There were no beds to be seen, no armoires or dressers, nothing of that sort. Instead, oversized fitness machines filled the room. In the far corner I spied two treadmills, beside them, two stair masters. There were punching bags, free weights, jump ropes, barbells, and all manner of horrid exercise things. But the crème de la crème was the oversized, inhuman torture device that Jake was standing beside. It was one of those monstrous pieces of exercise machinery crazy people with too much time on their hands purchased. There was a place to do leg curls, leg presses, chest presses, crunches, rowing, and my personal favorite, the dreaded butterfly. Ugh!

I looked at the pain inducing apparatus, then at Jake and glared. "I'm not exercising."

Undaunted, and sporting a hard-on I was finding it very difficult to keep my eyes off of, Jake motioned me forward. "Trust me."

Under normal circumstances, I would have found his outfit very appealing. Wearing nothing but sinfully tight black spandex, Jake looked good enough to eat. He didn't have to flex to make the muscles stand out on his body. They were there no matter what he did.

Pushing off from the horror machine, he came forward a step then halted. "Come here, Stella."

I didn't know if I could, or if I should. My knees were weak and my head was too clogged with lust for any sort of movement to come easily to me. "What's going on?"

Jake did something that never failed to make me weary. He smiled. "Exercise. I thought I explained that already."

"I knew red was your color," Dev added, stepping into the room behind me. "Looks wonderful on you."

I turned to face Dev, and let out a cry of surprise. Dev had on loose gray jogging shorts that rode delectably low on his hips. A more disturbing aspect of his clothes, though was the leather tool belt he had hooked around his waist. Hanging from the tool belt was a loop of rope.

I swallowed. Hard. But didn't move.

Dev pushed the door shut behind him, an unnecessary act since there was only the three of us inside the condo. The lock slid into place a moment later and my heart kicked into overtime.

"I don't want to exercise?" I said. "And these pants are...." I sought to find an appropriate word. "They don't have a … crotch. I thought that you guys wanted to--"

Jake pointed to the butterfly machine. "Come sit, Stella."

I opened my mouth to protest, then thought better of it. Jake didn't seem in the mood for questions. Though my legs were weak as ever, I managed to walk to the machine without help. "If you'd tell me what was going on I'd feel more at ease."

"You wanna know what's going on?"

Dev crossed the room and moved to stand beside me. "I think we should tell her. It's only fair."

Jake settled his hands on my hips and steered me into the seat. Gently, but firmly, he lifted my arms and set them on the pads at either side of my head. "I'm gonna fuck you, that's what's going on."

I whimpered and then tried to remember how to breathe. The tension I'd felt in the pit of my belly deepened.

Jake went on. "How does that sound to you?" Jake glanced at Dev over my head and grinned. "Spread your legs, Stella."

I gazed at Jake and hoped he couldn't hear my heart thundering in my chest. Slowly, I did as told. The mere act of spreading my thighs wide, of setting my legs in place so my sex was exposed for them had my insides clenching with feverish need.

I heard Dev move behind me, heard the rustle of him dislodging the rope from his belt and looping it around the cold metal at either side of my head. "Hold your arms still, kitten."

The moment I felt the rough sprigs of rope touch my wrist I began to tremble. Lust was descending on me in waves, threatening to completely engulf me if I wasn't sated soon.

Dev tied me tightly to the machine then gave the rope a

tug. "How's that?"

Jake, who'd been watching us with rapt interest, nodded his approval. "Perfect."

"Should I do her thighs?"

Jake rolled his shorts down to his ankles and stepped out of them. I caught a brief look at his thick cock before he stepped into the V of my legs. The heat of his skin seared me, but I didn't hesitate to draw my legs around his waist and lock my ankles over his buttocks.

Jake squeezed my hips and pulled me closer to him. "No need."

Dev's hands came up around me. He cupped my breasts, plucked at my nipples, pulling low sighs from me. I was near desperate for release, so hungry for both men I could scarcely think straight.

I groaned when Jake edged closer. His lips hovered scant inches above my own. "Do you want me, Stella?"

"I need you."

With a hoarse groan he fell on me. His lips sought mine and ravished. Hungrily he sucked my tongue into his mouth and devoured me. A taut cord of sensation tickled my nipples where Dev continued his gentle teasing, and ran the length of my body to the juncture of my thighs where my need of Jake made me hot and moist.

"Now Jake. Take me now."

Jake leaned back and gazed, glassy eyed, at me. His breathing was hard and fast and I knew that despite his attempt to look calm and unmoved, he was as aroused as I was. "I thought we'd take our time. Slowly torment you--"

I locked my ankles tighter around him and clenched my thighs. I met his eyes and shook my head. "I can't wait."

I'd scarcely had the words out when he gave my ass a squeeze then eased his swollen erection inside of me. "Neither can I."

I moaned. In reflex I flexed my arms, but tied to the metal bars as they were, they remained in place. Hot pleasure oozed through my body like something alive. I writhed on the leather seat, desperate for my climax.

Dev glided his hands over my belly. I could feel his lips on my throat and smell the sweet strawberry syrup we'd had at breakfast. He licked me like a starving kitten and I reveled in his touch.

Jake eased back, then sank in again. The pleasure of this, the sheer rapture of being taken again by them was nearly too much. My body was on fire for them, sensitive to their every touch and ministration. I was too aroused to be slowly tormented, too turned on to hold off my climax. Already, release danced just out of my reach. So close I could taste it.

Jake set a rhythm I was only too happy to meet. His hips moved decadently as he thrust into my depths, sending pleasure rocketing through me like white lightening. I was dizzy with it, overwhelmed by it, and so lost in it that I didn't feel Dev's fingers moving lower until he'd stroked my clit and lit an inferno in me.

"Like that, kitten?"

In answer I bucked, thrusting into Jake even as my binds held me in place. I was mad with need, insatiable, and ravenous. The tension mounted inside of me, rose fast and hot. I clenched around Jake and I panted into his open mouth.

Dev pressed his lips to my ear and licked. "I think this one's gonna be a quickie." When neither of us responded, he chuckled. "For you both."

Jake melded his lips to mine, a low grumble rose from deep in the back of his throat. "So good."

Frantic for him, I nodded.

Jake's fingers dug into my hips and he thrust deeper. It felt so good I thought I'd explode. I could feel my passion near to bursting, sense my climax on the periphery.

"Can't hold back," Jake murmured into my mouth. "Have to come."

With Dev tickling my clit and Jake filling me so thoroughly, I couldn't hold on anymore either.

Jake drove into me like a piston, his thrusts hard and sure enough to drive me backward along the seat. The lush thrill of it mounted. The pleasure rolled over me, pushing me to a higher level of sensation until Jake's head fell against my shoulder and he groaned. Hot spunk filled my quim even as the climax I'd been staving off finally descended.

I came hard. Wave after wave of pleasure engulfed me, wrapped around me until I was little more than sensation. My hips bucked in time with Jake's slowing rhythm. My engorged clit spasmed as Dev slowed his erotic teasing.

When at last I returned to earth I realized Jake and I were saturated with sweat and completely spent. For long moments we panted, each of us needing a few minutes to catch our breaths.

"Well then," Dev said from behind me. "That was fun."

Jake and I ignored him.

CHAPTER TWENTY-TWO

2:32 p.m.
"What do you mean you're not surprised?" I demanded.
We were both at our desks in the office, supposedly getting work done. The only things that had been working for the last twenty minutes were our mouths.
Ann swiveled away from her desk and faced me. "Look," she said. "Jake called Monday morning while you were meeting with Mr. Peters. I may have mentioned something about us going to Club Blue for Valentine's Day."
"And," I prodded.
"And, he got off the phone after that." She shrugged. "I didn't know he'd use what I told him to *kidnap* you of all things. Who the hell kidnaps a woman anyway? Jake has some serious control issues. And anyway, didn't you tell me that you told him on Sunday where we were going on Valentine's Day?"
So what if I had.
"Are you mad?"
"If it hadn't turned out so well I might have been."
"I thought Jake sounded sort of odd when he called me last night. All smug and satisfied." She stared past me at the wall for a beat. "You gonna see them again."
I shrugged. "I don't know. Dev mentioned something but I guess I'll have to wait to see what happens."

* * * *

Journal entry 2/17/05, 3:03 p.m.
I still don't know what to do about the Jake and Dev situation. I've spoken with them today. They want me to come over but I'm hesitant. I really like them, but…I still don't know what they want from me.
Argh! I don't know what to do.
I spoke to Chester again. I agreed to see him on tomorrow night. We're meeting at my place, then we're heading to The Oak Room. We'll see how that goes.

CHAPTER TWENTY-THREE

Journal entry 2/18/05, 10:05 p.m.
The night started out fine. Perfect even. For about ten seconds. Then everything went to hell.

Chester and I arrived a little after ten. Katarina and Jim, Meagan and Peter, and Ann with her prop date, Sean, were already in residence. Everyone had been briefed as to the situation, and Operation Lure and Deceive was in progress.

The first sign of trouble was the state of near pandemonium reigning in The Oak Room. Waiters and waitresses scurried about with trays of food, drinks, and desserts balanced precariously over their heads. Sebastian, the owner, who usually greeted me with questions and conversation whenever he saw me, gave me a quick air kiss.

"It's busy tonight," he said, hardly able to stop smiling.

Unable to hide my dismay, I frowned. "I noticed."

Completely oblivious, Sebastian rattled on, "Isn't it great. Hired a PR firm last week. Expensive as hell." Head tilted to one side, Sebastian surveyed his domain. I could almost see him counting all the money he'd make tonight. "Isn't life fucking awesome!"

"Yep. And thanks for hooking us up tonight. We really appreciate it."

"Promise me you'll spend lots of money."

I raised my right hand. "Scouts honor."

"Oh, and tell Katarina that I can reserve The Tower for you girls every Saturday night for five hundred dollars. Ciao!"

I gaped at Sebastian's retreating form. When had the girls decided they wanted to rent The Tower every Saturday night? Five hundred dollars a month to reserve one friggin' table? They must have lost their damned minds. I wasn't kicking in. What's one fourth of five hundred dollars ... a hundred and twenty-five dollars for a table? I didn't care if it was The Tower.

And why had Sebastian hired a PR firm? Okay, so I knew

why, but I didn't like it. The Oak Room had been a cozy hangout for locals. Now it seemed The Oak Room was *the* place to be. Seeing the hordes of beautiful people crowded at the bar, on sofas in the lounge, and in the dinning area made me long for the good old days of last week when The Oak Room was a secret getaway for me and my friends. There was never a crowd to elbow past and never so much noisy chatter that a person had to yell to be heard.

This was a horrible turn of events. A disaster. My Shangri La, my Utopia was being overtaken by obnoxious twenty-something's.

"Hey beautiful."

Forcing the unfolding disaster of The Oak Room to the back of my mind, I smiled and turned to face Chester. "Hey yourself."

Chester did look pretty amazing tonight. The thick, cream-colored sweater made his blue eyes even more luminescent than usual. There wasn't anything outstanding about his black pants, except the way they hugged every inch of him. This was a man who looked good in everything. Suits, casual clothes. Under normal circumstances, I wouldn't have been able to keep my eyes off of him. Hell, I would've fought to keep my hands to myself, but just now, my life was anything but normal. I feared Chester could've appeared for our date in nothing but a G-string and a smile, and I would've still been spending more time than necessary thinking about Jake and Dev.

He held me at arms length and looked me over. "You get more gorgeous every time I see you. I'm glad you called yesterday. I was disappointed when you cancelled last week."

An hour ago, when I was slipping into the sleek, zebra print dress with its sparkly bodice, low neckline, and non-existent back, I'd worried that I was over doing it. Now, faced with a room full of women ten years my junior, I was glad I had. My black, strappy sandals added a final sexy touch to my outfit. They looked killer and made my legs look long and sleek, however it had been hell getting from the car to the club without stepping in snow. But then Chester carried me--actually carried me--over the bad spots.

"You look great too." Grinning at Chester, I took his hand

and began to wind through the labyrinth of sofas, bodies, waitresses, and anything else that happened to cross our path.

Walking close behind me, Chester gave my hand a squeeze. "This place is packed, Stella. I don't think there's anyplace to sit."

"Don't worry. My friends reserved a table."

"You don't see places like this in Virginia," he confided.

I looked at him over my shoulder, smiled at the sight of his eyes darting around the room, taking it all in. "Don't usually see places like this in Baltimore, either, but this is a city on the rise."

"We're going up there?" Chester asked a moment later, when we reached the stairway to The Tower.

"Yep."

Named for its placement at the top of a lush, red velvet stairway, The Tower was located in a loft that overlooked The Oak Room's lounge.

We ascended the stairs, then I paused at the top to push aside the sheer gold, purple, and red curtains. As soon as Chester saw the room within, he murmured appreciation.

The Tower boasted a Mediterranean décor. It was extravagant dining at its most opulent. Instead of an ordinary eating space, it had a knee-high, oval shaped table surrounded by fat red, gold, and purple pillows. Each pillow was large enough to serve as a seat. Sheer draperies hung on the walls, the glimmering material reflecting the soft light of numerous candles positioned around the room. A mammoth fireplace was the crowning glory. It was so large, I worried that if things didn't go as planned, Ann would get drunk again and fall in.

When we entered, everyone looked up.

"Stella!" Katarina announced, as though she hadn't seen me in centuries. "You made it."

Nodding, I found two over-stuffed pillows and settled in.

After introductions were made, Katarina depressed a hidden button on the underside of the table, notifying our waitress that we needed her. Though, I had no idea why. Already they'd ordered Buffalo wings, chicken quesadilla's, lobster and artichoke dip, fried calamari, mussels, a fruit and cheese platter, and a platter of coconut shrimp. There was so much food on the table already I wondered if ordering an entrée would be necessary. The smell of all this delectable food was intoxicating. I wasn't hungry when I arrived, but the more I smelled the delicious aromas wafting up from the table, the hungrier I became.

"Why so many appetizers?" I asked.

Jim leaned forward and gave me a wink. "Nobody's eaten dinner yet. And we couldn't agree on anything, so we ordered all the appetizers on the menu."

Not only had they ordered every appetizer available, but they'd also ordered two bottles of French wine and a pitcher of beer. They also had several half empty margaritas on the table.

Jim looped an arm around Katarina and proceeded to start a discussion sure to get every man at the table fired up. "So, what do you all think of the Ravens' chances of making it to the Super Bowl next year?"

Not realizing how rabid Baltimoreans can be about the Ravens, Chester grimaced. "What chances?"

And they were off.

Why men cared so much about football, I'll never know. But I took this opportunity to get Katarina's attention. "What's this about a monthly rental? I think our usual table is fine."

Looking more at ease with her faux date than I thought necessary, Ann leaned into him and shook her head. "We don't have to shout up here. I'd pay a hundred and twenty-five a month for that alone."

I eyed Meagan. "You agree?"

Shrugging, she gave me a half-hearted nod.

"Look," Katarina began. "Did you see the lounge when you came in? It's like a madhouse down there. And according to Sebastian, this is just the beginning. I figured we should reserve The Tower while it was still affordable."

"Five hundred dollars a month on a table is affordable? Why can't we find someplace else to hang out?"

From the melodramatic gasps and throat clutching, you would've thought I proposed we take off our clothes and walk butt-ass, naked through the streets.

"Have you no loyalty?" Katarina demanded. "Sebastian would die if we went someplace else, he'd absolutely die. He's like family now."

"I don't know about your family, Katarina, but mine

doesn't charge me five hundred bucks to sit at the table."

"It's hardly the same thing," Meagan advised. "Sebastian has a business to run, and we like coming here. Personally, I prefer to socialize without being propositioned by twenty-one-year-old boys. How about you?"

Damn it to hell. Even as I sat with three pairs of eyes on me and three matching looks of determination pointed in my direction, I knew I was fighting a losing battle. In a last ditch effort I focused on Ann. Since I'd made her a co-owner of AIR, she didn't work for me anymore, she worked for the company. Still, I knew how much money she brought home. "You can afford this?" I asked her.

"It's an investment."

I stared up at the ceiling. Clearly I wouldn't win Ann's support. Katarina had already convinced her. Katarina was big on "investing," just not on financial investments for the future. She invested money in a gym to find a husband, she invested money on a maid, to save time, and now she was ready to invest money on The Tower to have ... I wasn't sure. I didn't think she was so enamored of quiet that she'd think five hundred a month was a reasonable expense. No, it probably had more to do with the image of having a VIP table reserved just for us, one always available on a Saturday night whenever we wanted.

"All right, fine," I said. "I'll put in too. But I don't like it."

Katarina beamed. "You won't regret it."

"I already do."

I was about to ask Ann to remind me what time Gerard said he'd show up when I heard the unmistakable sound of footfalls on the stairs.

Ann's back went ramrod straight. Katarina's eyes widened, Meagan bit her lower lip, and my arms broke out in gooseflesh. As one, the four of us turned to stare at the doorway.

"You rang?" our waitress asked.

"Shit!" Ann said, deflated.

"Can we have a bottle of Dogfish Head," Katarina looked at me for guidance.

"Whatever brew you have is fine," I told the waitress.

"Stella hates mixed drinks, is particular about wine, and--"

"Thank you," I interrupted, wondering why Katarina

thought she had to give the waitress an explanation of why I was ordering a beer. Then I remembered the copious amount of alcohol already on the table and understood. Katarina didn't want the waitress to think we were drunks.

The waitress left, promising to return with my beer shortly.

"What time is it?" Ann wanted to know.

Meagan raised her wrist and squinted at her watch. "Ten thirty-seven."

Slumping slightly in her seat, Ann gazed at her nearly empty margarita and declared forlornly, "He's not coming. He said he'd be here at ten thirty."

"He's only seven minutes late," I said. "He'll be here."

Sean slipped his arm around Ann and pulled her close. "I'm sure he's coming."

Beside me, Chester laughed. "So Stella wasn't kidding. You guys have really set up Ann's ex to come here and see the two of you together," he pointed to Ann and Sean, "and get jealous?"

"Let me tell you something about Gerard," Meagan said. "For two years, for as long as I've known Ann, I've known Gerard. And Gerard has always been in love with Ann. The only reason he's dating Candace is to get Ann jealous."

Chester grimaced. "Sounds confusing if you ask me."

I shrugged, still annoyed that I'd been roped into renting a VIP table.

"You've never been in love?" Meagan asked.

Chester rested his elbows on the table, opened his mouth, but didn't get a chance to speak. Another set of footsteps sounded on the stairway.

"Can't be the waitress this fast," Meagan said, when she saw Ann's back stiffen a second time. "It must be Gerard."

The purple, gold, and red panels slid apart and a familiar figure stepped from the opening.

Sporting a wide grin, Gerard crossed the threshold into The Tower.

My mouth fell open and I did a double take. At first glance I'd assumed it was Gerard, but maybe this was some kind of Gerard-clone or something. Never in two years had I seen Gerard dressed as he was tonight.

He wore a very chic pinstripe suit, and a power tie that said, *I have money and I know how to spend it.* A brand new Rolex--I'd never seen it before--gleamed from his wrist, making me wonder when Gerard had acquired taste. His blond hair was combed neatly away from his face, and it shimmered with platinum highlights. I'd be a monkey's uncle if Gerard hadn't been to the beauty salon in the last few days.

However, despite Gerard's GQ appearance, the most noticeable thing about his arrival was that he'd come alone.

NO CANDACE!

I had no idea what Gerard was up to, but whatever it was he had the full attention of everyone.

Ann blinked. "Son of a bitch!"

I think I may have said or did something to indicate my surprise, but I don't remember.

Beside me, Chester didn't seem to know who to look at. I caught a glimpse of him from my peripheral vision, and it was enough for me to see his head bobbing back and forth between Ann and Gerard.

Casually, as though he had no inkling of the shock he'd caused all of us, Gerard made his way around the table to Ann. His focus was so intent on her, I wondered if he was aware of anyone else in the room.

He gave Sean a cursory glance, then crouched before Ann.

She panted, stunned silent for the first time in her life ... and probably the last.

Gerard smiled, nodded, then leaned close and pressed his lips to her forehead. "Did you miss me?"

Having obviously forgotten about Sean, Ann stared into Gerard's eyes and nodded back.

She actually looked contrite. I could just kick myself for not bringing my camera. I doubted I'd ever see such a look on Ann's face again.

Ann raised a hand to stroke Gerard's cheek, paused when she realized her fingers were trembling, then cupped his face in her palm. "I'm sorry for everything, Gerard. I know I'm not the easiest person to be in a relationship with."

Someone muttered, "Amen to that." I suspect it was Katarina.

Neither Gerard nor Ann seemed to hear. They were in their own world now.

"Hush, Ann. That's behind us." He fumbled in an inner pocket of his suit, showing signs of nerves for the first time since his appearance. Finding his quarry, he fisted it and took a deep breath. "There's something I want to say ... that I want to ask."

Ann gazed at his closed hand for a few seconds, then into Gerard's eyes. His gaze was intense, reflecting a desperate longing that I supposed had always been there, but it was never quite as obvious as it was tonight.

"Oh shit," Ann muttered.

"I love you Ann, and I know you love me." Gerard paused to take a deep breath. "And I wanted to know...." Big breath. "... if you would do me the honor...." He twisted his fist until the object in his grasp was visible, then opened his hand. Resting neatly on his palm was a purple and cream-colored velvet box.

It was just large enough to hold a ring.

"Oh shit, Gerard," Ann said, breathlessly.

"If you would do me the honor of being my wife?"

For a moment, Ann continued gaping at him, then at the open box in his hand. The table went quiet.

One fat tear slid down Ann's face. Despite this, her lips turned up in a smile. "Of course I will." And she glided off her pillow and into Gerard's arms.

CHAPTER TWENTY-FOUR

Journal entry 2/19/05, 2:07 a.m.
I stared at the ceiling of my bedroom, unable to fall asleep.
Ann is getting married.
Ann is getting married.
One of my best friends is getting married.
I figured if I said it enough, it would sink in.
Obviously this was a time of joy, a time to celebrate. But no matter how much I tried to be happy for Ann, I couldn't muster anything better than resignation. This didn't have anything to do with some adolescent fear that once Ann said *I do* I'd lose her to Gerard. He had always been a fixture at Ann's side. They were always a couple, nothing would change.
What was changing, however, was me. I couldn't say how or why, but somehow, when Gerard had crouched before Ann, jeweler's box in hand, my no-man vacation suddenly seemed ridiculous. It *was* possible for a man and woman to truly love each other ... happily-ever-after *was* a possibility. The thing that scared me, though, was the thought that maybe it wasn't a possibility for me. What was more upsetting was I knew if I kept seeing Jake and Dev, I'd never fall in love. How could I while I was involved in a perverted sex triangle with two bisexual men? I couldn't! And I refused to delude myself into believing I could have anything meaningful with Jake and Dev. They were in love with each other, not me. I was a sort of sex toy for them. I went to their condo, we enjoyed a few hours of great sex, and I returned home afterward. It was sex they wanted from me and I knew it. And I had to live with knowing it. Unfortunately, regardless of the emotions involved, or not involved, I didn't want to end things with Jake and Dev. They'd sucked me into their world, seduced me, and now I was addicted.
A sudden wave of rage descended on me. It was all well and good for them to amuse themselves with me because in

the end they'd always have each other. Who did I have?

"That son of a bitch!"

I sat up in bed, fumbled on my bedside table for the telephone. It took me a few seconds to punch in the number, but once I did, I listened to the ringing on the other end of the line, stewing in anger.

"What the fuck?" Jake said groggily into the phone.

"What do you want from me?" I sounded slightly hysterical, but I didn't care. My future was on the line here. "Do you hear me Jake? What do you want from me?"

"Stella?"

"Answer me, Jake."

"What the hell is wrong with you? It's close to two-thirty in the morning."

"You wanna know what happened to me tonight? I found out that my best friend is getting married. Married! Gerard broke up with his girlfriend because he realized Ann is the only person in the entire universe that he wants to spend the rest of his life with."

Mutters and moans greeted this speech. In the background I could hear Dev asking Jake who was on the phone.

Finally, Jake asked, "Is everything all right, Stella?"

Argh! Had the man heard a word I'd said? "Hell no! Everything is not all right. I want to know what you want from me. If it's just sex, tell me now and I'll move on with my life. God knows I enjoy sex with you and Dev, but I'm thirty friggin' years old. I need more than sex."

Jake sighed. "I suppose you're going to tell me what it is you think you need."

"Damn straight. What I want, Jake, what I need is to be with a man who wants *me*. Someone who cares about who I am, as a person, not how tight I am or how good I feel."

Jake cleared his throat. "You're serious, aren't you?"

"Yes! Do you think I'd call you at two-thirty in the morning if I wasn't?"

"Good point." Jake put his hand over the phone so he could have a conversation with Dev. I couldn't make out anything that was said, but figured I could put it together when Jake returned and said, "We're on our way."

Oh shit! I hadn't expected that. I was in my pajamas for crying out loud, and I didn't have on any makeup. *Argh!* And my hair was in a frumpy bun. "No!" I said into the phone, but it was too late. Jake had disconnected.

I flew out of bed and ran around my bedroom in a panic. Hair, face, clothes, I didn't know what to attend to first. Sliding across the floor to my door on stocking feet, I found the light switch and flicked it on. Then I screamed. My room was a wreck. Unfortunately, I couldn't worry about that. There wasn't enough time.

I threw myself down in front of the vanity and undid my bun. My hair tumbled free to the middle of my back. I thanked God above when I saw it had maintained most of the curl I'd put into it before going out tonight. Next on the list was my face. The best I could do with mere minutes to work with was drag flesh-colored lip-gloss across my lips and line my eyes with liner.

In the next five minutes I changed out of my flannel nightgown and into a slinky, ankle-length Victoria's Secret gown. It was a delicious shade of cream with intricate lace work along the bodice and hemline. It was sexy, yet not so sexy that it would seem unlikely I'd wear it when I slept alone.

I'd begun shoving shoeboxes and articles of clothing under the bed when my doorbell rang.

They were here.

* * * *

2:37 a.m.

I stared at the ceiling of my bedroom, unable to fall asleep. Dev was curled beside me, arms wrapped tight around my stomach. Though his T-shirt was soft, the texture of it, the feel of it against me was nothing like lying with him and feeling the warmth of his naked skin. Still, I couldn't complain. Dev being with me in bed and fully clothed was a clear sign that maybe I was more to these two men than a sex toy.

Jake lay on his side facing me, caressing my face. "Did you ever think that maybe we want more than sex too?" he asked quietly.

"You and Dev?" I whispered back.

He gave my cheek a paternal pat then eased closer. His breath on my face was gentle. The scent of toothpaste and mouthwash was strong on him--I wasn't the only one to clean up before this unexpected meeting.

He'd come wearing a jogging suit, which he still wore

when he got in bed beside me. He'd combed his hair and wore it loose just the way I like it. He looked as wonderful as ever and smelled intoxicatingly good. Especially his hair. It always smelled like apples.

"Dev and me," he agreed.

"But you're already in a relationship. With each other."

Beside me, Dev shrugged. "Give us a chance."

Jake nodded. "You'll never know until you try."

"I suppose," I said. "But what will people say? What will they think? This isn't a normal relationship?"

"Normal according to who?" Jake asked. "I don't care what anyone thinks of us. You shouldn't either."

"I know I shouldn't. But I've never done anything like this before."

"Trust us Stella. Just give us a chance. Can you do that?"

I didn't answer immediately. Instead, I thought of all the stares we were likely to receive whenever we were in public, all the comments that would be casually thrown our way from people who couldn't understand us. And I realized something. I didn't care either. Why on earth should I let my happiness depend on what others deemed permissible? The majority of these faceless threats were strangers. I wouldn't live my life to please people I didn't even know. Anyone I cared about, anyone who cared about me would try to understand.

So I met Jake's gaze, smiled, and said, "I can do that."

Dev burrowed closer. "Good. Can we get some sleep now?"

And for the first time since I'd known Jake and Dev, we spent the night together without having sex. We slept side by side as lovers.

Printed in the United States
49411LVS00002B/148-1008